Spiritual Vengeance

Spiritual Vengeance

BOOK THREE IN THE MORAL VAMPIRE SERIES

ROSEMARIE E. BISHOP

Library of Congress Number:		2001117499
ISBN #:	Hardcover	1-4010-1599-9
	Softcover	1-4010-1600-6

This is a work of fiction. Names, characters, places and incidents either are the product of the author's imagination or are used fictitiously, and any resemblance to any actual persons, living or dead, events, or locales is entirely coincidental.

This book was printed in the United States of America.

To order additional copies of this book, contact:
Xlibris Corporation
1-888-7-XLIBRIS
www.Xlibris.com
Orders@Xlibris.com

For Christopher, my husband.
Without his love my foundation would crumble.

5-BISH

Acknowledgements

THE author photo on the back cover was taken by Jim Rhoads Photographer in Fort McCoy, FL. I would like to thank both him and his wife, Viki, who has shared all her beautiful poetry with us, for their friendship which happened so quickly and has continued to grow. Look for Viki's poetry written under her captivating pen name, Sonserra V. Hayden. I would also like to thank both Kathryn Williamson, author of "Secret In the Rose Room" and "Painted Spider", and Barbara O'Neill, author of "Second Chance" and "Luck of the Toss", for their advice and inspiration, their shared experiences, and their shared knowledge of the industry. They have both had a profound impact on my life as an author.

My thanks also go out to Denise & Frank Laratonda and Karen & Larry Wood: thank you for the friendship, laughter, and new experiences you have brought into our lives. Between the animal antics provided by Denise through her animal control experiences and Karen's incredible cooking that is frequently shared with us, our lives are both humorously and physically. . . . stuffed!

I would like to thank Father Florent Bilodeau

for reinforcing my vision of the perfect priest just by being himself. He has been both an inspiration and an uplifting guide, not to mention a wonderful friend.

I need to take this opportunity to thank the people who have always been in my life, have always been friends, and have always been a part of my life's support structure. Two of them, in particular, are Anne Marie Meyers, Canadian author of "Mama Means Milk", and as always, Michelle Grucela who was, and still is, my inspiriation for Chelle Gambert. Congratulations to Michelle and her husband, Ron, on the birth of their first child, Evan Miklen. The stability of true friendship is one of the greatest gifts the Universe has given me.

A special acknowledgement is also sent out to my godmother, Loretta Katra, who has always held, and still holds, a very special place in my heart. She has been everything a godmother should be and more.

I need to extend a special thanks to my parents, Elaine and Steve Mandy, for the doors they opened, for all the lessons they allowed me to learn on my own while they stood back and held their breath, and for the person they let me become. There is no greater love than that.

And, of course, for Christopher, my husband. Without him, none of the wonderful dreams I've been able to see for real would ever have happened or been allowed to grow. He is the rock that holds open the door to my artistic vision.

"ALL THAT IS GIVEN IS NOT LOST."

CHRISTOPHER A. BISHOP

Prologue

JESSE awoke with a start. He sat up, looked around, then wondered what had pulled him from his usual, sound sleep. A loud noise, maybe? He briefly shook his head, knowing it couldn't be that. There was nothing in this remote area of Nantucket that would produce a noise loud enough to wake anyone. He took a deep breath, then shrugged. Maybe something in one of his dreams startled him awake. He thought about it, but couldn't remember what the dreams had been about. Still, an uncomfortable feeling had begun to develop in his psyche and he needed to understand what was causing such a distraction.

He shook off his concern as best he could and surveyed the room once more for anything that might be out of place. He saw no signs of an intruder, then laughed to himself as he realized how human and paranoid that suspicion was. No one would venture this far just to break into his old house. He looked straight ahead and noticed how dark it was except for the moonlight shimmering across the area carpet that lay on the hardwood floor. He frowned. What was it that woke him? He stood up and stretched, then sat by the window that overlooked the Atlantic Ocean. He tried to take his mind off his inner disturbance by watching the still, black ocean water. The stars reflected off its smooth surface, reminding him of the peaceful stillness he knew back home, but the beauty there could never be matched by anything he'd seen here.

Jesse watched a small animal weave its way among the brush that grew in the sand between his house and the water's edge, but it quickly disappeared in the clump of trees far to the left of the property. He yawned and realized he still needed more rest. His human form was cumbersome in so many ways, yet one would think that after all this time he'd be use to it. But he wasn't. Instead, he was simply tired. Typically, humanly tired. He stretched once more, then laid back down on the sofa to try to go back to sleep, deciding it must have been a dream that awoke him in the first place.

He closed his eyes, then heard it, again.

"Jesse," a soft woman's voice nearly whispered.

Jesse opened his eyes for the second time and saw her floating inches above the floor. She was as beautiful as he remembered with her waist length, blonde hair gently suspended around her as if it were the physical manifestation of her aura. "Serella," he said. "Is that you?"

She smiled as her eyes closed a bit, seemingly content. "Yes, Jesse. It's me."

He pushed himself up on one elbow to see her better, then stared for a moment, astonished. "It's been centuries," he said, taking in her presence. Her rose-and-crimson-colored dress flowed as if a gentle breeze moved through the room, but that was not the case. No windows or doors were open. "You haven't changed."

She smiled, but her eyes held a worried look. "I never will," she said.

Jesse sat up further and studied her, but he wasn't sure what to think of this most unexpected visit. "Why haven't you come to me before now?" he asked her.

She looked at him for a moment before she spoke. "You know the rules, Jesse," she said. "I can't cross over without permission."

Jesse looked at his hands, then at his legs. He nodded, then turned his attention back to her. "Like me."

She smiled at him, then nodded as she began to float closer to where he sat. The look on her face became a mask of hidden concern. "I came to warn you, Jesse."

"Warn me of what?"

Serella looked at the window, then floated toward it. "There's a strong evil on its way."

"To me?" he asked.

"Not directly," she said, turning to face him. "But you will be involved."

Jesse sighed. It wouldn't be the first time. "Who is causing it?" he asked her.

Serella moved closer to him. Her long blonde hair flowed around her shoulders like a cloud. "I don't know," she said. "All I can tell you is that those who you think are gone still exist on this side."

"Where you are?" Jesse asked her.

Serella shook her head and smiled. "Not where I am. You know there are many levels here, Jesse. I don't know where the evil is coming from."

Jesse leaned forward, placing his arms on his knees. How was it possible she didn't know who was causing the approach of evil when she existed in that realm where there were no secrets?

"I was only given permission to warn you," she said. "I wasn't given details. I'm not allowed. But I asked to come here because you saved me when I was mortal, and I've always been grateful. Now it's my turn to help you."

"Serella," Jesse said. "I'm not mortal."

Serella looked at him, her body floating to the side, closer toward Jesse. "Neither was I," she said. "But I didn't know it back then. None of us are mortal." She looked away with an expression on her face that appeared almost sad. "We go on forever."

Jesse looked at her and smiled, his heart moving toward her, feeling her despair. "Will you be there when this evil arrives? Did you come to warn me so I'd know to call you?"

"No," Serella said. "I'm here now. This is all I'm able to do."

Jesse stood up and watched her move closer until she floated just inches from him. Her aura mingled with his until it felt as if she were part of him.

"I was in love with you," she said.

He searched her eyes for any indication that this might all be a trick, but only saw truth. "I know, Serella." He reached for her, but his arm passed through her form as if she weren't really there at all. "Love is good."

Her gaze bore through him, down to his very essence. "God's love is good," she said. "But what I felt for you was too human. That's why I've never been allowed to come here." The sad look on her face grew serious. "I would only cause distractions in the work you're here to do." She looked deep into his eyes and reached one hand toward his face. "But you can come home whenever you choose."

Jesse let his arm drop to his side as he took a step back. "I know the door is always open to me, but I can't leave here."

Serella tilted her head to one side and frowned. "Do you like being in the physical?"

Jesse sat down and looked across the darkened room. How was he supposed to answer that question? "It has its drawbacks," he said. "But it's where I have to be." He turned to her. "I'm needed here."

Serella nodded. "You're needed more than ever."

Jesse stared at her. "I thought you didn't know the details."

Serella smiled as her form began to fade. "I lied," she said. "I'm not you."

PART I

Life is mostly froth and bubble;
Two things stand like stone:
Kindness in another's trouble;
Courage in our own.
—Adam Lindsey Gordon

Chapter 1

March 3 6:00PM

RONI sat in the doctor's office with Christian and waited for Dr. Reno to enter with her MRI test results from three days earlier. Plants in the room created a welcome atmosphere, but the solid mahogany furnishings that surrounded her were like a mirror image of the heaviness she'd been experiencing in her right leg for over two weeks. After the usual blood and urine tests, an electrocardiogram, and a myriad of tests she couldn't even pronounce, Dr. Reno still hadn't given her any indication what might be causing her discomfort. Not knowing only added to the tension already building inside her from the worry over the possible conditions she might be suffering from. Cancer in her muscles? In her bones? What?

She felt Christian squeeze her hand and she turned to look at him. His black eyes glistened with love and concern. "It'll be all right," he said, smiling, but the fear in his eyes gave him away.

She nodded. "I know." But the truth was, she didn't know anything at that moment. And the voices she heard on the other side of the door only made her nerves jump before it even opened.

Dr. Reno entered carrying a manila file folder that he appeared to be reading as he walked to his desk. He rubbed his short, salt and pepper hair, set the file down without making a sound, and stood looking at Roni for a moment before he sat in the big, leather chair across from her. "How are you today, Ms. March?" he asked Roni, his Pakistani accent coming through quite thick. "Has there been any change?" He smiled, but his smile seemed rehearsed, almost forced, yet sincere in a strange kind of way.

Again, Christian squeezed her hand to give her support and reassurance. She was thankful for the small gesture that did, in fact, boost her confidence and give her the strength to move forward with the purpose of this visit. "No," she said. "Nothing's really changed. Not worse, but not better, either." She nervously crossed her legs, placing the stronger left one over the pained right leg, then adjusted her blue, rayon skirt to let it gently hang about her ankles. She looked up to face the doctor and waited for him to continue.

Dr. Reno nodded once, then opened the file, creating a subtle movement of air that made the leaves on the dragon tree sitting at the right corner of his desk gently quiver. He put his glasses back on and scanned the pages in the file as if to be sure what he was about to tell her was accurate. "Well," he said, then let out a huge breath. "There is one more test we could do." He peered at her over the rims of his glasses without moving his head. "A spinal tap."

Roni felt herself inhale deeply, but the mere mention of such a test frightened her enough to cause her to hold her breath as if to brace herself.

"But I've conferred with a few of my colleagues and we are in agreement." Dr. Reno removed his glasses and gave Roni a look that was almost sympathetic. "You have multiple sclerosis."

Roni felt the tension in her fly away only to be replaced with a dreaded fear like she had never known. "What does that mean?" She looked at Christian, but he was now watching Dr. Reno as if he had to understand every word that was about to be said. "Will it get worse? What is it, exactly?"

Dr. Reno leaned back in his chair and rubbed his forehead. "Multiple sclerosis is a condition where the protective casing around the nerves in your brain are not being replaced as they should be in the normal wear and tear process of your body's function." He looked at her, using his hands to display a wrapping effect. "Depending on what part of the brain is effected seems to determine how the disease manifests itself." He leaned forward and placed his elbows on his desk, then folded his hands in front of him. "We don't know what causes it. Normally, its earliest symptoms occur with vision troubles in the form of optic neuritis." He placed an index finger to his right temple and held it there. "That's a swelling of the nerve behind the eye." He lowered his right hand and paused, looking at each of them before he continued. "But sometimes, we see it start in the extremities as in your case."

Christian had not released Roni's hand, but was now holding tighter. She knew he was as frightened as she was, only in a much different way.

"Then what is the cure?" Christian asked Dr. Reno. "What I can do to help? Just tell me." He turned to her and she saw the moistness in his eyes that made them look full of crude oil. He was doing his best to hide it, but she was sure the doctor had seen it, too by the way he stared at Christian with pain and sorrow on his own face.

"There is no known cure," Dr. Reno said. "Only treatments that will help lessen the symptoms as they progress." He hesitated. "If they progress." Suddenly he looked at them both in alarm and held up his hands, brushing the leaves of the dragon tree in the process. "Don't get me wrong," he said. "There's no guarantee the symptoms will progress at all. I don't want you to be alarmed unnecessarily. I do, however, want you to be aware of the possibilities just in case."

Christian released some of his firm hold on Roni's hand and leaned back in his chair as if the life had just been drained from his body. "Such as?"

Dr. Reno briefly glanced down at the file in front of him, then looked up, again. "The worst case could be that you might eventually lose the use of your legs altogether. Or you might experience an overall weakness in all the extremities as well as many of your bodily functions."

"Death?" Roni blurted out.

Dr. Reno appeared surprised, but only for a moment. "Not on its own," he said. "But the end results of it could turn out that way. You see, we cannot predict what course this disease is going to take. It effects everyone differently."

All three of them were suddenly silent. Roni's worst fears were now a distinct probability for her future and she found it impossible to control the pounding in her chest. She felt like a balloon that had just burst. She shook her head and felt Christian let go of her hand and put his arm around her shoulders instead.

"It'll be all right," he said. "We'll make sure it's all right."

The tears were beginning to well up in Roni's eyes and she knew she wouldn't be able to hold it in much longer. How could such a thing happen to her? What had she done? She looked up at Dr. Reno. "How long will it take before . . . you know. . . . before all that . . ."

Dr. Reno held up his right hand and shook his head. "There's no way of knowing," he said. "None of that might ever happen. And then again, some of it might. The problem with this disease is that it is unpredictable, so we have no way of knowing. All we can do is monitor you and your progress and act according to what we see transpire as time goes on. For now, you only have the one symptom, your leg." He smiled at her as if he were talking to his daughter. "As far as that goes, you're very fortunate. It's at an extremely mild stage and there's really no treatment at this point. The heaviness and cramps may go away on their own and you might not feel it ever again. As I said, Roni, we have to watch and see what happens."

Without warning, Christian stood up and began to pace back and forth across the front of Dr. Reno's desk brushing the branches of the ficus tree that stood to the left of it. He ran the fingers of one hand through his nearly black hair, then turned to face Dr. Reno. But Roni caught the flash of red that clearly shown from his eyes. "What is the use of all the years of training in medical school if the best you can do is tell us you don't know and you'll have to wait to see what happens?" His voice was firm, but the anger was evident. "What good are you? All you have is a title that gives you the right to earn huge amounts of money, but you have no obligation to give anything in return for such a healthy income." He leaned on the desk, a challenging scowl spread across his face. "So what kind of phoney are you? Tell me, what are you going to do about this?"

Dr. Reno shook his head and stared at Christian, a mask of fear spread across his face. Roni knew what he saw. She'd seen it herself many times. She looked at Christian's profile and saw the veins that ran through the whites of his eyes shimmer as if through glass. Christian turned to her, but she said nothing. He closed his eyes, took a deep breath, then turned back to face the doctor.

Dr. Reno shook his head and blinked, then looked at his desk. He sighed as if he suddenly felt deflated. "I wish there was something I could do." He looked at Christian. "But this is one of the many diseases that we are so limited in knowing how to handle. It is by no means the only one."

Christian threw his arms up and spun around. He continued to pace all over the office this time.

"Christian," Roni said. "Please sit down. You're only making this worse."

But Christian said nothing.

"We're only human," Dr. Reno said. "We're not miracle workers, though we all wish we were. We go to medical school to learn in the hope that someday we'll each be the one to develop the cure for at least one of the many illnesses in this world that take so many of us before we've reached our full potential." Dr. Reno stood up and walked around to the front of his desk where he sat at the edge and looked at Roni as if to apologize.

Roni smiled. "I understand, Doctor."

"Well, I don't," Christian said firmly from behind her.

Dr. Reno raised his head and breathed a sigh. "I'm as human as you are, Mr. Desmonde. Neither of us could do anything for this situation until a cure or cause is found."

Roni felt it coming before Dr. Reno had finished his last sentence. She could feel Christian's anger as if she were him.

"No, Doctor," Christian said as he walked toward them. "I am not as human as you are and don't even try to presume that I am." Christian leaned on the back of the chair he'd been sitting in and gave Dr. Reno a smile that was almost evil. "In all honesty, Doc, it's times like this in particular that I'm glad to be exactly what I am." He turned to Roni and placed a hand on her shoulder. "If you're ready, I think we should go home and give ourselves a little time to digest all of this."

Dr. Reno gave Christian a puzzled look that Roni had long been familiar with, but she knew he would not comment on the personal aspect of Christian's reaction. No one ever did. "I agree," he said. "This is obviously not the sort of thing you can accept on a moment's notice. Please keep in mind that I am here for you to answer any questions and advise you in any way I can." He smiled at Roni. "I'm only a phone call away. I will be with you through all of this."

Christian pressed into Roni's shoulder as Dr. Reno spoke. "No," he said when Dr. Reno was finished. "I will be with her through all of this. Where you might be is doubtful at this moment."

Dr. Reno nodded as he walked around to the other side of his desk, obviously choosing to ignore

Christian's angry comment. "I understand your frustration and concern," he said. "Nevertheless, I will be here for both of you."

Christian removed his hand from Roni's shoulder and walked beside her. "Are you ready?"

She looked from him to Dr. Reno, then nodded her head as she stood up and gently hung her purse over her left shoulder. She reached out to shake Dr. Reno's hand. "Thank you," she said. "I understand the predicament you must be in every time something like this comes up with one of your patients. And I appreciate all you've done. I know we'll be in touch quite often." She peered through the corner of her eye at Christian for only a moment.

"We will," Dr. Reno said. "On your way out, please make an appointment to see me in six months so we can review how you're doing at that time. I really don't expect there to be any change by then. It would be too soon, but I'd still like to keep on top of this."

Roni smiled. "I will." She turned around and headed for the door with Christian beside her, his hand on the small of her back. When she reached the door she turned around. "Thanks again, Dr. Reno."

He nodded and took a deep breath just as she left his office.

Out in the brighter reception area decorated in pastels, Roni made an appointment for the end of August while Christian stood by the glass door that led outside and waited. She tucked the appointment card in her purse, but hit something hard that bent the card and cracked a nail. She looked in the pocket where she kept miscellaneous items and saw the amethyst crystal her friend, Chelle, had given her a few years ago when she was closing on her house.

She made a mental note to return it, made a second attempt to tuck the appointment card in her purse, then went to where Christian stood waiting. "What was all that about?" she asked him. "I know you're upset about the news, but it's my health we're talking about, Christian."

He opened the door and motioned for her to walk out into the early evening. As she did so, she looked at him and wondered what he was feeling. Normally, Christian was calm and in control. That was his strength and it was also hers when she was stressed from her job or her life in general. Right now, she needed his strength, but he seemed to be walking a very thin edge that might cause him to snap at any moment. And it was her fault, or rather, her illness's fault.

They walked across the parking lot to the car without either of them saying another word. But once they were on their way home, Christian finally spoke up. "You don't have to go through this, Roni." He turned his head sideways and gave her a brief, but decisive look. "We can stop this right now."

Roni felt herself being pushed against the seat by her own feelings of surprise. "Please, Christian. Let's not talk about this. You know it's not an option."

Christian stepped hard on the brakes and pulled in to the little parking lot by the convenience store to their right. He slammed the gear shift into the park position, shut the engine off, and turned around to face her. "It is an option, Roni." His voice was firm as if he had already made the decision for her. "It's right there for you to take advantage of. My blood will stop it. You will be healed. You won't have to go through the pain or discomfort." He ran his right hand through his hair and shook his head. "What's the matter with you?"

Roni sat up and faced him squarely. "I'm Roman Catholic, Christian. You have always known that. Don't act like it's news to you. If this is what God has chosen for me, then so be it."

"Roni, it doesn't have to be this way," he said. "You have a choice. It's no coincidence that I'm in your life and so much in love with you. We've been through this before."

"I know. But nothing has changed." Roni turned and sat back in her seat, staring out the side window. The sun was setting fast, making the world around them take on an eerie, late winter glow. What kind of spring and summer was she facing if this new complication in her life became worse? "Did you think a little bit of bad news was suddenly going to change my mind? Well, it hasn't." She looked at him and placed her hand over one of his. "I love you, Christian. But I can't put you before my faith. It's just the way I am. God and vampirism don't mix well." As soon as the words were out, Roni realized what she'd said, but it was too late.

Christian looked up and glared at her. "But up until now, God and I mixed just fine as far as you said. You gave me faith in Him. You taught me not to fear Him, but to go to Him. Have I been dreaming, or am I still a vampire?"

Roni stared at him, but said nothing. She knew he was right. There were no double standards where God was concerned, but she had accidently turned it around to be exactly that.

"What did I miss?" Christian said, his voice dripping with sarcasm.

Roni shook her had and felt the tears start to build in her eyes as the sadness grew in her heart. “Nothing,” she said. “Nothing.”

Christian looked at her for a few seconds more, then started the engine and pulled out of the parking lot back on to the road. “Then I’m confused,” he said and sighed. “Again.”

“Don’t be,” Roni said. “I’m upset, but I didn’t mean to take it out on you.” She fiddled with her hands for a few seconds before she continued. “I’m sorry, Christian. You know I didn’t mean anything by it. I’m just. . . . just scared, I guess.”

“As I said, Roni. We can put a stop to this whole thing right now.”

Roni felt the anger in her begin to rise. How many times did they have to have this same discussion before he got the idea that she didn’t want to discuss such a thing. “No we can’t and I don’t want to talk about it, anymore.”

“And I don’t understand how you can be so stubborn about this. Your life may be at stake here and you’re closing the door to the only option that will put a stop to the possibility.”

“That’s just it,” Roni said. “It’s only a possibility right now. Why don’t we worry about it when and if things start to get worse?”

“And why do you even want to take that chance?”

Christian was begining to yell, but Roni refused to back down from this argument. “Because it’s my life and I have the free will to make that decision for myself.” She knew it was lame, but she wasn’t happy right now and she didn’t care how she sounded. She wanted to win at something, even if this silly argument was all she had to succeed at right now.

Christian didn't say anything for a few seconds, then he reached over and took her hand in his. "I don't want to argue, Roni. We're both upset about this and we're just taking it out on each other. I'm sorry. I do know how you feel about making the change and I swore I'd never force you." He slowed the car slightly and looked over at her. "I just don't want to face losing you this soon." He squeezed her hand. "I don't want to lose you ever."

Roni felt the tears well up in her eyes. "And I'm not ready to go anywhere, so let's just take it one day at a time." She wiped the first tear that had finally begun to fall from her cheek. "OK?"

Christian nodded. "OK."

Chapter 2

March 3 7:00PM

THE early evening air wrapped its unseasonably warm comfort around Chelle Gambert as she sat on the railing of the gazebo watching the geese and ducks swim by in the still pond below. She could still taste the veal marsala she'd had for dinner and the incredible slice of pumpkin pie she'd chosen for desert at the Swan Song where she and Joe Gardner had just eaten. Dinner had been wonderful and the relaxing stroll around the water helped her digest the five course meal. . . She turned to look at Joe, studied his profile, his brown hair that was longer in back, and his brown eyes that reflected the setting sun. She saw the old friend in him from years ago mixed with the new romantic interest he had become and marveled at the twists and turns her life had taken in recent years.

She remembered the moment she and Joe bumped into each other at the mall and she knew her old feelings for him were still very much alive. Throughout the weeks and months they spent afterward getting reaquainted she kept wondering why they hadn't gotten together sooner. Maybe it was because she always believed she was the only one of them who felt the way she did. She never had any idea that Joe had feelings for her as well. Or maybe she was afraid to lose the friendship they shared back in high school if things were to get serious. Right now, however, it didn't matter. She was in love. For the first time in her twenty six years, she was really in love. The very thought tied her stomach in knots.

"You're deep in thought, tonight," Joe said, gently taking her hand in his. "Do you want to tell me why?"

Chelle looked up into his face and studied his brown eyes. She saw his feelings for her as clearly as she felt her own for him. Running her fingers through the strands of medium brown hair that lay flat along his back somehow made her feel more connected to him. It didn't matter why and she didn't try to analyze it. She simply smiled at the comfort she felt with him. "I was just thinking how we've known each other so long and wasted so much time that we could have spent together." She turned her head in time to see two ducks swim by within a few feet of where they sat. "This should have happened sooner."

Joe's hand covered hers with its strong warmth. "It happened now because it was time," he said. "Life is just funny that way."

Chelle turned back to look at him. She admired his easy smile and the accepting look in his eyes. There were no questions there. Everything was always so simple to him. "I suppose."

He caressed her hand and wrist. "And I think our relationship will grow along its natural course like all things do when they're left alone," he said.

Chelle felt a nervousness in the pit of her stomach. What did that mean? Breaking up already? Maybe she hadn't really seen his love for her in his eyes as she thought. That would figure. "Let's not talk about it," she said. "This has been a wonderful evening and I'd really like to just enjoy right now the way it is. I'd rather not talk about the natural course of things."

Joe smiled. "And why not?" He touched her chin and moved her head to look directly up at him. "What are you afraid of, Chelle?"

She turned away and stood up. "Just life, I guess. It's too unpredictable." She walked to the opposite side of the gazebo and pulled her grey, wool jacket tighter around herself while she looked out over the pond. The sun had already begun to set and a chill was moving in. Even with the changing temperature, she didn't want the night to end.

"Cold?" Joe asked.

Chelle shook her head, but remained silent for fear of saying something that would cause the inevitable to occur sooner than she'd like. None of her relationships lasted. Her heart had been broken in so many ways that she had finally put walls up around her feelings and developed a sarcastic edge designed to turn most men away before they ever really got close. But she'd known Joe almost her entire life and such things just didn't stand once they had met up again after so many years. Still, as much as she loved Joe, past experience had taught her not to expect this one to be any different and so she braced herself the best she could.

She heard Joe walk up behind her and felt him put his hands on her shoulders. "I love you," he said so soft it was almost a whisper. "I think I always have."

She did not look at him. She couldn't. "But will you always?" she asked, afraid to hear the simple, rational answer she now expected from him.

Joe did not answer immediately which only told Chelle that she was on the right track in what she feared most. So she'd be hurt. It wouldn't be the first time and it certainly wouldn't be the last time, either. She always managed to get herself back in this same position.

"I believe I will," he said.

Chelle was suddenly confused. How was she supposed to interpret that? Wasn't he sure how he felt? Was he afraid to tell her the truth? She took a deep breath and braced herself. "I guess time will tell."

Joe moved to stand beside her and leaned on the rail, his shoulder touching hers. He looked at her and smiled. "It always does."

Chelle sighed, then felt a shiver run through her. So simple, again. "We should probably get going. It's getting cold out."

Joe rubbed her back, then pulled her close to him. The lights that decorated the pond's borders had just come on to illuminate the water around them. It was beautiful with the sun still setting, and the multi-colored reflections shimmering on the water. "We'll leave in a minute or two." He took his arm from around her and stepped back, slowly. "There's something else we need to discuss." He reached in his pocket, then lowered himself on to one knee, taking her left hand in his at the same time.

Chelle didn't want to believe what she saw coming next was for real. Had she simply been misinterpreting everything he'd said in the past half hour? Was it possible that he had never intended to break up? It would be too good to be true after all the relationships she'd suffered through, and especially after all the strange doubts that had just passed through her mind even about Joe. Had life made her so paranoid that she couldn't even enjoy the chance to finally see just one dream come true?

"Chelle," he said. "I love you. And I would like you to be my wife." He produced a diamond ring as if from thin air and placed it over the tip of her finger. "Will you marry me?"

Chelle was stunned. She had never expected this, though it had been in the back of her mind hoping it might happen one day. But this was too soon. Or was it? They hadn't been dating that long. But they'd known each other for many years. She looked at him and saw the memories of the special things they'd done together go through her mind like a movie. Scenes from the day they'd first met when she was in second grade and he was in fourth, kickball during gym class at school, varsity football games in high school and all the times she'd thought about him as the rest of her life progressed. She felt the knots that had been in her stomach move up into her throat. She smiled as he pushed the gold ring that held a single, sparkling, marquis stone further on to her finger and felt the cool air around her disappear as the moment warmed her soul. There was never a doubt in her heart and in a single instant she knew it. "Yes," she said. "I will marry you, Joe."

He stood and took her in his arms, holding her off the ground while he kissed her. Chelle began to cry as the truth of the moment sunk in and she felt Joe's contentedness mixed with her own joy for what they had just decided to do. Chelle experienced a moment's last question, then briefly disregarded it. She loved Joe, was in love with him, and she knew that was not going to change. But life had caused her to be cautious and to question everything. Don't believe in anything because it would only cause disappointment. But this was different. This was Joe Gardner, the boy she had a crush on all through grade school, then high school. The boy who had been her pre-school playmate, according to her parents, and later a friend to ride the bus with, before the responsibilities of high school reputations took over. Then college separated them. Chelle was going to nursing school, but Joe had plans to go to New York to study architecture. And so they parted. Through it all she watched him with other girlfriends and figured he'd marry one of them, but when he moved away not one of them followed him. And Chelle went on with her intended career until she graduated and landed a job at Massachusetts General Hospital. After a number of transfers and normal attrition as it goes in Boston, she became head nurse during a particularly trying time of day, the nine to five shift. And now their paths crossed again, as it was obviously meant to be. But this time, it would be forever.

Joe was different. This relationship was different. Her feelings were even different. Somehow she just knew this was going to last. "We'll have a lot to plan, now," she said to him. "Do you have any ideas about the kind of wedding you want? Or where you'd like to have it? St. Joseph's maybe?"

Joe held her at arms length and smiled. Behind him the sun had finished setting and they now stood in almost pitch dark except for the lights around the pond. "St. Joseph's is fine," he said. "But as for the rest of it, I guess something simple would be nice. We'll handle it as it goes."

Chelle smiled. Typical Joe. "OK. You're right," she said, rubbing his upper arm in a gentle, loving manner. "We have all the time in the world for that, don't we?" She held her arm out in front of her and took another look at her ring in the moonlight.

Joe nodded. "Yes, we do. There's no hurry, but it won't be that long." He smiled and raised his eyebrows in a playful manner. "I don't know how long I can wait."

Chelle nudged him, then briefly shivered. "Wait for what?" She gave him a teasing look. "What haven't we done?"

Joe's face took on a serious expression that caused Chelle to feel slightly unsettled. "I haven't awaken in the morning next to my wife," he said. "I haven't experienced the feeling of Father's Day. Should I keep going?" He definitely had a way with words.

Chelle felt as if her spirit was huge, even as she shivered, once again. "And what about a family?"

Joe just smiled. "It will all happen when it's meant to happen. You already said, 'Yes' , to me. That's all I want to enjoy right now."

Chelle didn't think her heart could hold any more love, but she was wrong. "Joe, I don't think I've ever felt this way about anyone in my life."

"You don't think?" He chuckled almost to himself.

She playfully tapped him on the shoulder. "You know what I mean."

"Yes, I do," he said, pulling her close to him.

"I do know one thing already, though," Chelle said.

"And that is?"

"I need Roni to be my maid-of-honor when the time comes."

"Need?" Joe asked, surprised. "Or want?"

"Both," Chelle said. "It wouldn't be right any other way. She's my best friend. And we've been through so much together already. This will just be the icing on the cake, so to speak. She's been like a sister to me."

"How's she been feeling, anyway?" Joe asked, turning to look out across the pond. "You mentioned that she was having a problem with her leg. Has that changed? She really should see a doctor, if she hasn't already."

"No," Chelle said. "She's still limping and it's been so obvious. In fact, she went to the doctor with Christian this evening to find out about a bunch of tests they had to run on her last week. I'll have to get ahold of her to find out what he had to say. I only hope the news was good enough that she can finally relax. It's really been eating away at her." Chelle shook her head and sighed. "I think she's just been working too hard, Joe. The business is all hers and she's only had the house a few years. She's really got her hands full."

"She's a strong woman, Chelle. She just needs to learn how to treat herself to life's smaller joys, once in awhile." He smiled. "I like her. She and Christian actually make quite a unique, but wonderful pair. I'm looking forward to getting to know them better. Especially Christian." Joe shook his head as he looked at the sky. "There's something so wise about him, but I can't put my finger on it. It's as if he knows everything."

"Sometimes he thinks he does," Chelle said, laughing inside herself.

"I don't mean it that way," Joe said. "Not like a Mister Know-It-All. I mean for real. He really seems to have an authentic air of antiquity about him. Is he from another country?"

Chelle nodded, trying hard not to laugh. She hadn't told Joe the truth about Christian, yet, and she didn't think she'd be doing so any time soon. She might even leave that up to Christian to handle for himself. She'd have to wait to see how things turned out. "Actually, he's originally from somewhere in France," she said. "His family grew grapes for wine in one of the provinces there. I don't know the whole story. When you finally have a chance to get to know him better, why don't you just ask him?"

"I think I will," Joe said. "It will at least give us something to talk about instead of that terrible silence that happens sometimes in conservations. Everyone likes to talk about themselves, though, so that would be a great opener for us."

Chelle shrugged slightly. "Sometimes he does, and sometimes he doesn't. It depends on what part of his life you're trying to talk to him about."

"Well, tell me. What *doesn't* he like to talk about?"

"It would be easier to tell you what he *does* like to talk about," Chelle said, hoping she was right. Almost everything was taboo with him since it was difficult to keep his vampirism out of the conversation, sometimes. She was just going to have to leave that up to him, too. "He likes to talk about his family and two of his friends, Samuel and Jesse. They're his closest friends. And he loves to talk about Roni."

"Typical guy things," Joe said. "We'll get along just fine."

"I hope so," Chelle said, smiling, but inside she was truly praying that they might be friends. Christian was not easy to get along with and it would probably be best for him and Joe not to get too close, but that was entirely up to them. For right now, Chelle just wanted to enjoy her own moment, her own happiness, and be certain her best friend could share it with her. "My biggest concern is Roni and how she's been feeling. She's always doing too much and I'm always having to tell her so"

"That could be," Joe said. "Well, maybe if you tell her about her upcoming role in your life she will feel better."

"I hope so," Chelle said. "I haven't seen her as much as I used to because of all the time I'd rather spend with you, but I can't imagine getting married without her by my side."

Joe kissed her forehead, then placed a hand on the side of her head. "Then that's the way it will be," he said. "Now, you just have to tell her."

Chelle smiled. "When it's time."

Joe nodded. "When it's time." He pulled her closer to his chest and laughed. "As if you can really wait until we make a firm decision about the date."

"As if," Chelle said, laughing. "I'll probably end up calling her tomorrow. I want to find out about her doctor's appointment, anyway so it'll kill two birds and all that. And I can find out what she thinks about wearing purple or lavendar or some other shade of violet or . . . . ."

Joe laughed and held her close to his chest. "Sounds like a good excuse to me."

"I'm glad you understand that already. It's a pretty good start for us."

Joe smiled. "That it is." He motioned toward the parking lot. "Come on. I'm going to get you home."

Chelle began to shiver repeatedly as an evening breeze kicked up around them. "Home?" she asked. "I hate for this evening to end." She held her hand out in front of her as they walked beneath one of the lights that shown along the sidewalk. "I'm going to be your wife." She almost couldn't believe it was real. She turned to him and softly placed her hand on his cheek. "I love you, Joe." They stopped walking and stood beneath the starry sky that was only slightly washed out by the artificial lights below. Chelle felt his arms encircle her waste, felt him pull her closer, felt his breath on her neck. Neither of them were shivering now.

Chapter 3

March 3 10:00PM

AUDRA Trivette stood among the flames of her own creation and worked on the next part of her plan. The burning heat surrounded her limbs like a garment, but it was a garment of torture; a feeling she was all too familiar with both in her physical existence and now here, on the other side. Roni's illness was not created by her, but it did fit neatly into her long planned scheme. Now that it was in place she could use it to her advantage. All she needed was the help of the one who had caused the disease to manifest itself in Roni's body in the first place. That one was Gaetano Minotti, the most evil mass of negative energy that ever existed. He had more power than any other entity she knew and Audra craved the presence of that power. She wanted to be able to call on it at will as she carried out the method by which she planned to take revenge on Christian for his part in removing her from the earthly realm. And she would not forget his friend, Samuel, who was by his side through the entire ordeal.

She missed her body, missed the power she wielded on earth. She missed her fangs and the taste of blood. She missed the terror she was able to incite in those around her. Now, all she had left was this world she brought with her when her soul left the rest of her behind. This world, born of her own anger and hatred, filled with the flames of envy, malice, and greed. The heat seared her soul and burned the depths of her emotions. Feeling her body go up in flames would have given her less pain than what she experienced here. Who ever said there was no hell?

Still, in time Audra had grown somewhat accustomed to her existence in this place. It suited her in many ways and had ~~its~~ advantages ~~which~~ she'd been unable to enjoy in the physical. There were no do-gooders to deal with like there had been on earth. Everyone here was of the same mind as she was; nasty and vengeful; angry and vile. And traveling about was already second nature. It only took a mere thought to transport herself anywhere within the heated confines or to spy on those left behind on earth. There was no doubt she'd find Minotti, eventually. And she had no doubt of her ability to convince him to join her just as she had convinced Christian to give her immortality on that night in 1784 when he'd finally given in to her repeated pleas. It was the night she'd finally won. The night she was granted an eternity of power.

But that was over now and a new chapter had begun. The very thing Christian gave her, was also taken away by him. It was time for vengeance and she would not rest until it was hers.

Audra was certain the Minotti entity was close. She could feel him. That kind of evil couldn't be anywhere else but here, burning in the heat of its anguish, finally defeated after centuries on earth. Her two hundred years were nothing compared to what he had been able to see. The existence that began long before Jesus was ever born must have given him an insight into the powers of evil that no other man could ever dream was possible. If she had known of him when she was on earth, she would have left Christian without a second thought. But her attention was drawn to him after she'd already become a new resident in this inferno. She watched from her fiery perch and cheered for him to bring misery to everyone she wanted to repay. But Minotti had destroyed himself by his overconfidence. Only a male entity would do battle within the walls of a church where he was so terribly outnumbered, and still expect to win. That was Minotti's trouble. His pride had finally caught up with him the way Audra's greed had caught up with her. Still, she had to find him. No matter what his shortcomings might be, he had the power.

* * *

"She still won't do it," Christian said to Samuel. "Even with this new development in her life she won't do it." He breathed in the aroma of pine scent at night and listened as they walked through the woods to the next street. "I don't want to be alone again, Samuel. The very thought of such a life sickens me."

Samuel looked at him through the pitch black and shook his head. "You could change her when she's sleeping," he said. "It would be for her own good, anyway."

Christian stopped walking and pulled Samuel's arm to make him turn around. "That's not what I'm talking about," Christian said, frowning. "I only want to give her some of my blood to see if it will heal her." He let go of Samuel's arm and glared at him. "I can't believe you would even suggest such a thing."

Samuel chuckled, his head tilting back, as he slapped a hand on Christian's shoulder. "Mon ami. You cannot fool me." He turned and continued walking the last hundred yards through the woods to the street on the other side with Christian next to him. "I know how you feel about her and I know you've wished for her to ask for the change. You told me that yourself."

Christian placed a hand in his pants pocket and stared at the ground, but he didn't say a word. Samuel was right. He couldn't fool a vampire's telepathy, not to mention a friend's familiarity.

"I'm surprised she didn't want you to stay home with her after receiving such terrible news today," Samuel said. "How is she taking it? Really?"

Christian ran the fingers of his free hand through his black hair and took a deep breath. "That's why I'm glad Diana is with her while we're gone. On the surface she's being very brave. She says she's accepting it as God's will."

Samuel scowled. "Him, again?"

Christian gave him an angry look. "I was raised with the same beliefs. I don't want to hear your sarcasm."

Samuel held up both hands. "Sorry. It will not happen, again."

"Yes, it will," Christian said. "I know you better than that. Just don't ever make such comments in front of Roni."

They reached the street and began to walk along the wide gravel shoulder that bordered the trees. Christian scanned the midnight, country atmosphere for signs of life and did his best to keep his feelings under control, but it was nearly impossible to do with a vampire as old and strong as Samuel right beside him. "All right. So, I wish Roni would want to join our immortality. There's nothing wrong with wanting that." He looked around, certain to have heard voices, but they stopped. "You and Diana have that gift and your life together has been wonderful."

Samuel gave Christian a sympathetic look and exhaled deeply. "That was entirely her choice, Christian. Your sister has always been a decisive woman. She's not Roni."

Christian looked at him, then nodded. "Yes, I know she's not. But maybe she could talk to her."

Samuel smiled. "She already has."

"Well, she should try again. She's at the house with Roni right now. Why don't you send her a message and suggest it?"

Samuel stopped walking and turned to Christian. "No," he said. "You should accept what is happening. Accept who Roni is and deal with everything you experience with her in truth. You love each other, but you're both very different people. You have more adjustments to make than Diana and I did simply because of those differences, but your feelings are the same and they are very strong." He put his hands on Christian's shoulders and stared into his eyes. "Cherish what you have, Christian. Don't push it. Don't try to change things unless you and Roni are in agreement. Otherwise, you will reach the day when you're alone again, and regretting the energy you wasted trying to make things the way you wanted them to be instead of enjoying what they already were."

Christian saw the intensity in Samuel's hazel eyes and knew his friend was sincere and determined to make sure Christian understood every word he said. "For a sarcastic prankster you're making far too much sense. A few minutes ago you were telling me to change her in her sleep. Now you're telling me not to do anything unless she and I are in agreement. Don't disturb my sanity like that."

Samuel let go of him and laughed. "All right, then. Let's go get dinner."

Christian gave him a look of disgust, then shook his head. "I really hate when you put it that way."

* * *

Audra watched Christian and Samuel as they made their way through the woods. She hated them more and more every time she saw them; every time she heard their voices. Such good friends who teamed up against her, destroyed her. She almost had Christian under her control. Almost, until Samuel came along and helped him take her from the physical, forcing her to move on. They would never get away with it. Not now that she had heard of Minotti and saw the chance for power that would help her obtain the vengeance she craved.

Audra suddenly felt a presence nearby. She looked around and saw an entity among the flames. She moved toward it in the hope that it might be Minotti. She wasn't sure what Minotti looked like, but she had a vision of him in her mind and she was sure she'd recognize the energy as she got closer to him. This, however, was definitely not him.

The energy from this entity was, indeed, male, but he did not seem to notice her. She moved closer and pushed the flames from him so he would see her. It worked. "Minotti?" she asked.

He shook his head and moved his mouth to say, "No," but no sound came out.

"Do you know where I can find him?"

He slowly raised his left arm and pointed behind her, but still was unable to make a sound.

She turned to look where he indicated, but all she saw was fire. "There's nothing there," she said, her anger rising with the flames that burned around her. "What are you telling me?"

He still held his arm out, but made stronger gestures, repeatedly pointing as if to force her to pay attention to whatever might be behind her.

She looked at him and frowned. "Are you telling me to go in that direction?"

The man lowered his arm and nodded.

"Hhmm." Audra turned around and did as she felt she'd been told.

* * *

"Wonderful," Samuel said, brushing back his thick, blonde hair with his hand. "Do you hear them?"

Christian listened with an attentive ear. He heard chains, bottles, and boisterous voices approaching from behind. "How many of them do you think there are?"

Samuel appeared thoughtful for a moment. "Six."

"You're sure?"

Samuel nodded. "And they're feeling quite jovial. Do you smell it?"

"Yes. Hundred proof."

Samuel smiled. "Jim Beam to be exact."

Christian turned his head slowly to look at his friend who never stopped surprising him. "I didn't know you were such a whisky connoisseur."

"It's necessary," Samuel said. "The less alcohol we have to sift out through ingestion, the better." He appeared to smell the air before he continued. "Tonight, however, it looks as though we have no choice." He shrugged. "No matter. Blood is blood."

Christian shook his head, then turned to wait for the men to appear. "Well then, how do you want to do this?" he asked. "We don't need that much blood between us." Samuel smiled a mischievous smile that made Christian nervous. "OK. What's the plan? What are you dreaming up this time?"

"Well," Samuel began. "We only need two of them and it will have to be the two with the least amount of alcohol in their blood." He turned to Christian. "Unless, you're not that picky."

Christian shook his head and shrugged his shoulders.

"The other four will have to be immobilized. How would you like to do that?"

Christian pointed at his own chest and raised his eyebrows in question. "Me?" he said. "You're asking me? Why, you're the king of the compromising positions. You're the inventive one who's always creating new ways to knock out, hypnotize, or whatever else you can think of. You tell me. And think fast because they're close enough now to see us."

"Ah, well. No time," Samuel said. "Simple hypnosis will have to do."

They turned to face the six men who had traveled up behind them so quickly. Even in the dark they could see the lack of balance each of them had. "Good evening, gentlemen," Christian said, waving a hand. "How are you tonight?"

One of the young men who was wearing a pair of black chinos with rips down one side, held up a can of beer as if he were toasting to Christian. "None of your fucking business," he said, slurring his words. "In fact, I think you're in our way." He made a move as if to shove Christian, but ended up falling to the blacktop instead.

Samuel stood back and placed a finger against his nose. "I think this is going to be less work than we expected. He's only drinking beer. Much easier to ingest." He leaned forward over the man on the ground, then stood straight and looked at Christian. "Do you think he's unconscious, yet?"

Christian laughed and placed a hand on Samuel's back. "I don't know, buddy. What do you think?"

One of the other men took a step toward them, but nearly tripped on the untied laces of his sneakers. He righted himself, then stopped and stood as if prepared for an attack. "You think he's funny?"

"No," Samuel said. "I think you're all funny." He turned to Christian and shook his head. *Whisky. He has to go,* he thought to him so the others wouldn't know their next move.

The man lunged at Samuel, but Samuel caught him around the waist and held the man up in front of him. He stared into the other man's eyes, willed him to fall asleep, then gently lowered him to the ground. "Two down, four to go," he said, keeping his eyes on the rest of the men.

"Hey, what did you do to him?" the man with dirty blonde hair asked. His angry voice barely hid his fear. "That's my brother. If you killed him, I'll have to kill you."

Samuel held up one hand and stopped the man where he stood before he could even make a move. He turned to Christian. "His brother. Whisky, again." Then he looked at the two men in leather coats who stood beside the blonde brother. "You two gentlemen had better be ready to catch him," he said to them. He quickly willed the man to sleep while the other men grabbed his arms at the last minute. While they helped their friend to the ground, Samuel felt the stare of the last man in the group who stood watching what was happening around him as if he were in awe. Samuel looked at the men in leather who had just straightened up. "One more," he said to them. They looked at Samuel, then to their friend who waved an empty bottle just in time to catch him when he fell asleep.

"Beer drinkers?" Christian asked.

Samuel nodded as he and Christian approached the two men left standing who had been so helpful. Neither of them would remember the rest of the night. In seconds, Christian and Samuel were behind them, cutting off the flow of blood to their brains just long enough to knock them out. They carried all six men into the woods, laying them on the ground among a thick grouping of trees and brush. Then they fed.

* * *

Audra was at the edge of the flames and unable to go any further. In her search for Minotti she couldn't help but see what Christian and Samuel were up to. She had made it a point to keep track of them until she was ready to make her move, but what she saw disgusted her. They wouldn't kill anyone. Knock them out, drink a little blood, let them sleep it off. It made her sick. She would've destroyed all six of those mortals and drained every last drop of blood that flowed through their skinny veins. But Christian and Samuel were sissies.

She closed her mind to them and continued to look for Minotti. She concentrated on the evil essence she felt growing stronger as she continued her search. She felt a tug on her mind, and looked up and straight out before her. In the distance she saw the form of a man with very long, black hair and eyes like pitch. She knew it was him, but why was he over there, floating in the middle of nowhere? Away from all the flames. Was it better there? From the peaceful look on his face she guessed that it probably was, but how could she get to him? She waved at him and sent thoughts in his direction, but he didn't seem to see or hear her. Why wasn't this working? It was supposed to be easy, yet she wasn't exactly surprised to find so many obstacles in hell. She thought for a moment, looked around, toward him, again, and that's when it hit her. He was in Limbo. She had no idea how she knew it or why he would be there, of all places, but that was exactly what she was seeing; exactly what she felt. Now she had to find out how to get to him. Or how to get him out of there. She moved back into the flames and began to search for other souls who might have the answers she needed. She had to find someone who could tell her what Minotti was doing in the middle of space. And it had better be someone who would actually talk to her this time.

* * *

"How would you like to leave them?" Samuel asked. He stood with his hands on his hips surveying the sleeping drunks who lay in a mess on the ground.

"You're on a roll," Christian said, shrugging as he finished wiping the last of the blood from his lips. "Keep going."

Samuel stroked his chin with his fingers apparently thinking what to do. "They were quite belligerent, weren't they?"

"Cocky."

"Yes. With egos the size of Mount Everest."

"Not all of them." They looked at each other and laughed. "A little too physical, wouldn't you agree?" Christian asked. "It's really a good thing for them that they were as drunk as they were. It made it all much easier on us. But the whole beer muscle thing has really got to go."

"My thoughts exactly." Samuel reached down and lifted one of the men in leather as if he were a doll. He positioned him sitting on the ground beneath an oak tree that stood only five feet from the gravel that trimmed the road. Christian carried the second leather man and sat him next to the first. He laid the man's head on his friend's shoulder and placed his arm around the man's waist. Samuel carried the blonde brothers, one under each arm, and laid one on the ground with his head on the first man's lap and both arms wrapped around one of his legs. The other blonde brother was placed in a similar position, but beside the second man Christian had carried to the scene. Samuel looked up. "Where are the other two?" he asked.

"Over there," Christian said, motioning behind them where he had just finished propping up the last two men in their own situation beside a tree that stood a few feet away. The one with the torn chinos was sitting against the tree's trunk while the other sat in his lap, the untied shoe laces dangling to the ground.

Christian and Samuel stood back and admired their work. "We did it, again," Christian said, shaking his head.

Samuel nodded toward the group of four men. "Now, which brother is it that was going to kill me?"

"That one," Christian said, pointing to the blonde brother whose arms were wrapped around the other man's leg. "I'm almost positive he was the one."

Samuel crouched down and studied the man. "I believe you're right." He moved the man's head just enough to make it look as if he were kissing the first man's leg. "That'll teach him." He stood and looked at Christian. "Ready to go back and see what the women are up to?"

Christian nodded. The mention of home made him think of Roni and he felt the concern for her surface, again.

"Relax, old man," Samuel said, beginning to walk back into the silent, dark woods. "Why don't you go see Jesse and ask for his help? There might be something he can do for Roni."

Christian nodded, but said nothing.

"I'll even go with you just to say hello."

"That might be a good idea," Christian said. "I don't know if Roni would want me to go to Jesse, so I'd rather she didn't know."

"Why wouldn't she want you to go see Jesse?" Samuel asked. "Doesn't she like him?"

"She likes him in a polite sort of way, but beyond that I think she isn't sure just what the full scope of her feelings about him should be," Christian said. "Think about it. Roni's mortal, while you, me, and Diana are immortal. Then there's Jesse who's an angel in fully human form. What would you think?"

Samuel laughed, placing his hand across his stomach as if to control himself. "I can't tell you, mon ami. It's been so long since I was mortal I don't remember what a mortal would think of the situation Roni is in. It is most unusual from her point of view, I'm sure. But I'll go with you and make it look like us guys are out for awhile. When do you want to go?"

"Let's give it a day or so," Christian said. "Roni knows you and I don't feed often. If we go out two nights in a row, she'll wonder what's going on. I don't want to arouse her suspicions."

"Good idea. In a day or two it is, then." Samuel looked at him. "Don't worry. This will all work out for the best."

Christian nodded, but was silent as they headed home.

* * *

Audra had run into different entities in this blazing place, but only one was willing to give her any information about Minotti's current position. It was a female form that seemed to sympathize with her quest, though why, Audra didn't have a clue. What she learned only made things appear worse. Minotti was in Limbo because that was the only choice for someone like him who had to be removed from all parts of existence until the evil energy had enough time to settle down. The female explained to her that energy cannot be destroyed, only converted, reformed. She said that it is the energy that makes up all things that is truly immortal. From what Audra understood of their conversation, it seemed that until Minotti loses most of his evil power, he would remain right where she found him. That could be for centuries or for eternity. Apparently, it was one of the laws of nature, but already Audra was formulating plans to break that law.

Chapter 4

March 3 11:00PM

RONI carried two glasses of port wine into the living room that was being warmed by the fire Christian had built before he and Samuel went out for the evening. "Here you go," she said, handing Diana her wine.

"Thank you." Diana smiled and leaned back on the sofa, curling her feet beneath her. She took a sip, then lowered the base of the glass onto her free hand, tracing the bottom with her finger.

Roni nodded, then walked to the fireplace and opened the black, metal screen that shielded the room from flying sparks. She placed a large, white birch log on the fire to keep the flames alive while her male, tabby cat brushed against her back. When the log was in place she closed the screen and went back to sit on the opposite end of the sofa from Diana. They sat in silent discomfort while a few seconds elapsed before either of them spoke.

"I'm sorry to hear about the news from your doctor," Diana softly said. "If there's anything I can do, please let me know."

Roni knew Diana's concern was genuine, but it made her feel uncomfortable nonetheless. A wave of embarassment went through her and her emotions were mixed. How was she supposed to react to this type of comment? She didn't want pity. She didn't want anyone wasting their concern on her, but she knew it was inevitable, human nature. "Don't worry about it," she said, waving a hand as if to push the thought away. "I'm fine. It's just one symptom. Not a big deal." She took a large sip of her wine, then placed the glass on the coffee table, pushing the dried flower arrangement aside as she did so. "But I do appreciate your concern."

Diana looked at her as if she were trying to think of what she wanted to say next, then took another sip of her wine, instead. But her eyes glanced over the edge of her glass while it was still at her lips. "Did the doctor say what they're going to do next?"

Roni saw her gaze shift to the side as she placed the glass back onto her other hand. She took a deep breath, wishing the topic of her health had no place in her home. But it did and she would just have to learn to deal with it in as diplomatic a way as possible. "Nothing," she said. "They have to wait and see how it develops."

Diana's eyebrows raised slightly, but the expression lasted only a few seconds. She nodded, but said nothing.

"What?" Roni asked.

Diana shook her head. "Nothing, Roni."

But Roni already knew. They'd had the discussion before. "Don't even say it," she told Diana. "It's not going to happen."

Diana shrugged her shoulders as if she didn't care, but smiled. "It's up to you," she said. "I don't understand why you wouldn't even consider it, though. It might save your life."

"And it might cost me my life," Roni said.

"You won't know until you try."

"Well, as I've said before, I'm not willing to take the chance."

"I don't understand why not."

Roni felt her defenses go up inside her as she watched the fresh birch log catch in the fireplace, giving birth to new flames. She did her best to control her response in spite of the emotional intrusion she felt inside. "Because there's nothing really wrong with me, yet," she said as she stroked the white, female cat who lay across the back of the sofa. "Why would I jump to conclusions and make a rash decision that might not even be necessary?"

Diana took another sip of wine, put her glass on the table this time, then leaned forward with her arms bent in front of her as if pleading with Roni to understand. "Don't wait until it's too late, Roni. Don't put this off because you're afraid to make the decision. Please."

Roni felt her anger rise up inside her. She did not want to be preached to. If Diana wasn't Christian's sister, she would have lost her temper completely by now, but the brother-sister bond between them was strong and she did not want to cause a strain in that relationship. "Diana, please don't lecture me. I'm old enough to make my own decisions. I know you're just trying to help and I know you're also looking out for your brother, but it's still my life. My conscience and my beliefs would never allow me to become a vampire just to avoid dealing with a natural, human condition. It wouldn't be right."

There was a mix of anger and disappointment in Diana's eyes. "Is it right to suffer?" she asked. "What's natural about that when most of the health problems today are the result of mankind's abuse of everything on the planet? It's the chemicals and pollution and all the junk floating around in the air and in the ground that's causing so many of these illnesses. These things didn't even exist a few hundred years ago. I know. I was there. Some of them just started within the past hundred years. But human beings have been here a lot longer. It wasn't natural then, so why is it natural now?"

Roni stared at her in silence, searching for an honest response, but the truth was, she didn't know. She didn't have an answer for Diana. All she knew was that she was raised a certain way, by very specific principles and she still believed in those principles even though most of society seemed not to agree anymore. "I can't answer that," she said. "But I can't lie to you, either. The truth is that I'm just not ready for that kind of change."

"Why not?" Diana still sat, poised physically to show her intent on getting through to Roni. "You live with a vampire. You're in love with him. You and I are becoming friends and I'm a vampire. So is Samuel. You don't have a problem with us, but yet you refuse to become one of us. Tell me, Roni. What's wrong with us? Really. And don't try to save my feelings just because you're worried about Christian and my relationship. We're blood in the familial sense of the term. And that truly is thicker."

That was a subtle but strong slap and Roni felt its sharp sting, but she also knew that her own defensiveness caused it. She took another large sip of her wine and thought about it. What *was* wrong with them? All three of them were wonderful people and had been a huge source of support for her and for each other. They were as human as any human she knew and much more pleasant than most of them. In fact, they seemed happier than anyone else. The only thing that bothered her was the blood they drank to survive. And that alone was enough to turn her away from such an existence. Now, how was she going to explain that to Diana?

"You don't have to," Diana said. "Sometimes you forget how telepathic we are because Christian will not intrude on your thoughts. But I don't see things the way my brother does. If it's going to help someone, then I'm going to intrude."

Roni felt her face grow hot as her cheeks turned red from embarassment. "I'm sorry," she said. "Are you angry?"

Diana let out a light giggle that caught Roni off guard. "No," she said. "How can I be angry when the answer is an honest one. It's the truth. But we get used to it."

"And it doesn't bother you to drink from people you pass on the streets or in the stores?" Roni shook her head. "How is it possible that you don't feel bad about that? I couldn't life with myself if that was the only way to survive. Living the way you do would put me in my own hell on earth."

Diana picked up her wine again and sat back comfortably. She twisted a strand of her long, brown hair around her index finger and stared into her glass as she seemed to mull the answer over in her mind. Then she looked up at Roni and smiled. "We get used to it, Roni. It really doesn't take long. None of us have ever killed a mortal because we do have a sense of scruples as far as they can apply in our situation. What other way is there for us when we need the blood to survive? Look what happened to Christian when that monster, Audra, was alive and deprived him of it. I know I wasn't there like you were, but Samuel told me how horrible it was."

Roni felt herself shudder at the mention of her encounter with Audra. "I was there," she said. "I saw him shortly after Samuel had already fed him as much of his own blood as he could. Even then Christian looked terrible."

"But you gave him your own blood to help him fully recover," Diana said.

"I did it because I love him that much."

"But your very life was at stake."

"I know it was. I knew it then, too."

"But you did it, anyway."

Roni nodded. "I couldn't bear to see him suffer the way he was."

"That's what would happen to any one of us if we tried to stop. We wouldn't die, but we'd be stuck in a place somewhere between death and here." Diana finished the rest of her wine in one big gulp. "Thank heaven for port wine." She giggled. "So what choice is there?"

"None," Roni said. "And that's why I don't want to live that way. I'd miss my vegetables and fruits." She smiled. "I'd miss cereal in the morning and hot cocoa on a cold winter day."

Diana turned visibly ill at the mention of food.

"I'm sorry," Roni said. "Christian doesn't seem to be bothered by it. In fact, he sits with me most times when I eat."

Diana swallowed hard, touching her throat with her hand, and looked away disdainfully. "He's used to it, I suppose."

Roni nodded, smiling. "Let's talk about something else. I don't want either of us to be upsetting each other. What time do you think the guys will be back?"

Diana shook her head and held up her empty glass. "May I get myself another?"

Roni laughed, knowing the guys would be back when they were finished dining in their own way. Christian always kept that part of himself away from her. "It's in the fridge, Di. Help yourself."

* * *

At the mention of her name, Audra was transported to the source of her summons. Diana, Christian's sister and Samuel's little girlfriend. How sweet. Sitting in Roni and Christian's living room, of all places. And talking about how Audra had almost killed Christian. What a joke that was. Christian was never going to die because it wasn't possible. Not the way Audra had things set up for him. She had him in a coma, under control for the first time in their two hundred year relationship. She was so close to getting all the secrets about what a vampire was really capable of, but Samuel came to Christian's rescue and revived him. Audra had almost forgotten about Roni's part in the whole ordeal, but now that her memory was refreshed she had even more reason to use Roni as the means to get back at Christian for what he'd done. Roni was the one who had finished bringing Christian to his senses, and she had protected him when she pushed Audra away and halted her last, fatal blow that was intended to take Christian out of the existence he knew.

Audra's growing anger brought the flames closer. The heat was so intense, her soul burned with hatred.

She quickly grew determined that Roni had to pay a larger price for what she'd done and it had to start now.

Audra concentrated all her anger and vengeance into one solid stream of energy and directed it straight at Roni. She saw Roni flinch, then fall over doubled in pain, holding her leg just as she was about to stand up. Audra laughed a raucous insane laugh, she was so pleased with herself. Let her suffer with that symptom for awhile. In the meantime, Audra had to find a way to free Minotti from Limbo so she could exercise the main part of her plan.

* * *

Roni heard Diana come running from the kitchen as soon as she fell, pushing the contents of the coffee table aside. Now what? This wasn't supposed to be happening. She felt Diana's hands on her back, then felt herself being lifted and placed gently on the sofa.

"What is it?" Diana asked. "What happened?"

Shaking her head, Roni propped herself up on the sofa and stared in disbelief at the area of her leg where the pain had unexpectedly begun. "All of a sudden I felt an awful pain go through my leg," Roni said, trying to hide her fear. "Then I fell. I didn't even feel it coming, this time. It just. . . . just happened."

Diana looked at her leg, then at Roni's face. "How does it feel, now?"

Roni was still shaking her head as she began to rub her right thigh with both hands. "Numb," she said. "It's just all numb."

At that moment Christian and Samuel came in through the sliding door in the kitchen. Roni saw the look of alarm on Christian's face when he noticed her rubbing her leg and saw Diana attending to her. In a moment he was by her side, holding her gently against his shoulder. "Are you alright, Roni?" He looked from her to Diana and saw the look on Diana's face that clearly told all of them that she was not alright.

"I'll be fine," Roni said. "It's just the same symptom. I suppose it's going to do this every once in awhile. It'll be fine."

Diana stood and turned to Samuel. "Would you get me a glass of water for her?"

Samuel nodded, but Roni stopped him. "I'm fine," she said. "I have my glass of wine right here." She smiled in a sheepish manner. "At least that didn't get knocked over."

Samuel sat in the burnished, rose colored chair across from Roni and Christian, while Diana sat on the arm next to him, but neither of them seemed to know what to do next.

"Go get yourself something to drink," Roni said, still smiling. "Stop worrying about me."

Christian ran his hand along Roni's arm and kissed her hair. "I think you should get some rest. Why don't you lie down for a bit?"

Roni pushed him away and sat up straight. Her smile was gone and anger had taken its place. "Stop that, Christian. I'm not a child and I'm not an invalid. Let it go. I'm fine, I told you. The pain is gone." But it wasn't. The pain was still very real and Roni wasn't sure how she was going to be able to hide it from three highly telephathic beings. She looked from Christian to Samuel, then moved forward as if to get up. "I'll get you both a glass of wine."

But Diana stood and put a hand in front of Roni to stop her. "I was getting one for myself," she said.

"I'll get theirs, too. You just sit there with Christian and relax." She gave Roni a look of understanding that told her Diana was fully aware of her pain and her desire to hide it, even if Christian wasn't.

Roni smiled, felt the warmth of embarassment rush to her cheeks, and sat back down, relieved. "Thanks."

* * *

Audra laughed hysterically as she watched Roni suffer while trying to be strong. Everything was working out too perfect. Christian had entered the scene at just the right time. Seeing the pain and worry on his face gave Audra a surge of satisfaction that renewed her sense of power in finding a way to free Minotti. Christian was already beginning to panic over Roni. Every little thing Audra could do to him now would only make the pain in his heart grow until it tore him to pieces. She laughed a terrible, raucous laugh as she turned to search the flames for an answer and felt the strength of her own evil grow. Combined with Minotti there was nothing they couldn't accomplish. Oh, she was so anxious to find him just to let him know of her plan and how much of it she had already managed to accomplish without his help. He would have to be very impressed with her efforts. Impressed enough to want to add his own strengths to her little project. He had just as much reason to want vengeance on all four of them, Diana included, but Audra would have to devise a plan to release him from his current prison. And she would, there was no doubt.

Chapter 5

March 4 8:00PM

RONI stood in the kitchen making a pot of tea, while both cats continuously wound themselves around her ankles. When the telephone rang they both ran into the living room as usual, leaving her in peace. She picked up the cordless phone that was only a few feet away on the counter top. The pain in her leg had continued to ebb and flow like the tides and she was thankful she did not have to run across the room to get the telephone that was mounted on the wall. "Hello," she said, squeezing the tea bags and discarding them.

"Hi, Roni."

"Chelle," she said, excited to hear her best friend's voice. "What have you been up to? We've been playing phone tag for weeks, except for that one short conversation a few days ago. I hope you have time to talk today. I was starting to worry, except I knew that Joe was probably taking up all your time. You never did tell me what was happening with the two of you." She opened the cupboard and removed a few treats for the felines who had already made their way back to her, then grabbed a mug from the bottom shelf for her tea.

"I'm sorry." Chelle let out a soft chuckle. "I was in such a hurry that day with all the running around I had to do. But you were right. Joe and I have been spending a lot of time together. It's been wonderful."

"So, things are going well with him, then?" Roni asked. She wanted so much for Chelle to finally find the one man who would make her happy the way Roni had found such happiness with Christian. "Tell me about it."

"Things are going too well," Chelle said. "Wonderful, actually."

"You said that already," Roni teased her. She was thrilled to hear it, but concerned about the slice of doubt she was sure she'd sensed in Chelle's voice. "So, why don't I feel convinced that your relationship has really hit it off? What's going on that you're not saying? Have you two finally had that first fight?"

Chelle hesitated on the other end of the line. "What do you mean?"

Roni squeezed a bit of lemon juice into the teapot and wondered if Joe had done something to upset her friend. "I hear your words, Chelle, but your tone of voice is telling me something a little different." Roni hoped this wasn't another man who was going to take Chelle's heart and smash it to pieces. She knew Joe mainly by reputation only, but everything she'd heard about him was very positive. "What's going on with the two of you?"

Chelle cleared her throat and took a deep breath. "Are you sitting down?"

Roni laughed and sat down at the table. "I am now. Tell me what's wrong." She heard Chelle breathe deep again as if she found courage in the act.

"He asked me to marry him."

"That's wonderful," Roni said, ecstatic. "I hope you said, 'Yes.'"

"I did."

"Them why don't you sound as happy as I would've thought you'd be? He's a terrific guy."

"I know he is," Chelle said. "And believe it or not, I'm thrilled. I love him, Roni. I mean, I really love him like I've never felt before."

Roni laughed again and went to pour herself a mug of the tea she'd been brewing. "Then what is the problem?"

"What if it doesn't last?" Chelle asked. "What if something happens and I end up disappointed, again? Or what if it really ends up being too good to be true? Then what do I do?"

Roni listened to her friend, then took the first chance she got to jump in. "Chelle," she said. "Calm down and think about this. Love relationships always start out on a cloud and end up settling on the ground. But by the time your cloud had evaporated, and your feet are firmly planted back on God's green earth, the love should have evolved, matured, and grown into a solid bond. Only time can determine how that will work out. But if you don't take that chance, you're never going to know."

"That's what I'm afraid of," Chelle said. "What if our love doesn't grow the way it should?"

A smile slowly grew on Roni's face. She fully understood Chelle's fear, but her friend had never been as far into a relationship as she was right now. This was all so new to her. "But what if it does?" Roni asked.

"Don't answer my questions with a question, Roni. Tell me. What then?"

Roni took a sip of her tea and put her feet up on the chair on the opposite side of the table. Her right leg had started to throb and she thought that elevating it might help to quell the discomfort a bit. "Already you have a great start just because you've never felt this way before. And because you've known him for so many years. You didn't just meet him yesterday. It's no coincidence that the one guy you've had in the back of your mind all these years has come back into your life. From where I sit, I'd say this is meant to be. But if you talk yourself out of it and never find out for sure, you can bet you're going to have a ton of regrets over it for the rest of your life. And I can guarantee you that no one wants to live with those kind of questions hanging over them for the rest of their life."

Chelle sighed. "Great. So, I'm damned if I do and damned if I don't."

Roni couldn't help but laugh. "No," she said. "You're not listening to me. What I'm saying is to trust in your feelings, trust in him, and take the chance. That's all it is, Chelle. There's no sure thing in life. None. And everything changes, as it will with the two of you. But if the love is strong, which I think it is, then you will go through it all together and come out stronger. All of that is the best life can give you."

Chelle chuckled, then took a deep breath. "OK. I know what you're saying and you're right. But you know I'm going to worry, anyway. I don't know why, but I just can't help myself."

"You always do," Roni said. "But don't worry yourself out of a good thing. That's all I'm saying to you."

"And I get it," Chelle said. "So I'll just enjoy my engagement and let myself float around on that cloud for awhile. I hate it when you make so much sense."

"That's why you always come to me with these things," Roni teased. "Because you hate it so much."

"Something like that," Chelle said, but Roni heard the smile in her voice. "So tell me. What have you and Christian been doing? What did the doctor say about your leg? You did have that appointment last night, right?"

Roni cleared her throat, then sipped her tea before she answered. "We went yesterday for the test results." She wasn't eager to start telling anyone about the diagnosis, but Chelle was her best friend and there was a different level of comfort in their relationship. "In the past few weeks I've been going through all kinds of things, but we finally got the results."

"And?"

Roni hesitated, sipped her tea, then looked out the sliding glass door as she spoke. "The doctor says I'm in the early stages of multiple sclerosis," Roni said, choking on the name of the disease. "And there's no cure. Only treatments for the symptoms as they progress; if they progress." A rabbit hopped by the base of the bird bath outside in the dormant garden and stopped, then turned to look in at her as if in sympathetic understanding. "Encouraging, isn't it?" Roni knew she'd let her sarcasm show, but it slipped out on its own before she could stop it. Heck, she was entitled to it, right now.

"Oh my God," Chelle said, sounding frightened. "Now what? How did Christian take it? He didn't start pushing you to change over, did he?"

Roni sighed, still watching the rabbit who seemed intent on staying close by. "Well, first of all there's nothing to do now except wait and see what happens." Roni took another sip of tea to moisten her mouth which had started to feel dry. "As for Christian, he's upset, obviously. And yes, we did have words, but it wasn't so much because he wanted me to change as it was that he wants to see if his blood will heal the disease, somehow. But the change is always the main topic of conversation because he also doesn't know if just a little bit of his blood would make it happen or not. That would be a chance that I'm not willing to take."

"But Roni, you know how much I hate to agree with Christian on any subject," Chelle said. "But what if you'd be giving up the only chance you have at a cure for this thing?"

"Yes, and what if I end up living off other people's blood for the rest of eternity?"

"Roni, you're my best friend and I love you as if you were my sister, so I feel I can say what I need to say." Chelle cleared her throat before she continued. "I know how you feel about Christian. And aside from the fact that he and I didn't hit it off in the beginning, I think he's been good for you. He loves you like nothing I've ever seen. So, I couldn't blame you one bit for making the decision to spend eternity with him. And really, when you think about it, how could God find fault in that? Your kind of love is a great thing. You'd actually be doing God a great honor by preserving your love for such a long time."

Roni laughed at Chelle's reference to the Almighty. "Since when are you preaching about God? You don't even go to church. I've tried for years to get you to go with me. Father Larry has asked you repeatedly to come to his masses. So when did God become part of your repertoire?"

"Since Joe took me to church with him two weeks ago," Chelle said, her voice giving away the smile she wore. "And I actually got something out of it. We went to St. Joseph's, too. That's where we want to get married."

"Oh, so that's it," Roni said, watching the rabbit nibble on something edible it had found. "And you never even told me. Joe was able to get you to go to church, but your best friend couldn't. Now I know how I rank."

"Don't be silly, Roni. You know what you mean to me. Now let's get back to your diagnosis. I want to hear everything Dr. Reno told you. What did he advise you to do next? Anything? Did he prescribe something for your leg?"

Roni closed her eyes and sighed.

"I'm a nurse," Chelle said. "I know what multiple sclerosis is. I know what it can do and I know there's no cure." Chelle was silent for a moment. "But I also know that many people with M.S. go through their whole lives with nothing more than what you're experiencing right now."

"Yes," Roni said, trying to ignore the pain in her leg. "And others end up as total invalids. Dr. Reno told me all the possibilities."

"Well, don't plan for the worst."

Chelle sounded a bit frustrated, so Roni made a mental note to curb her sarcasm and keep her own attitude positive. "I'm not planning for the worst," Roni said. "I'm not planning for anything yet except your wedding. When is it?"

Chelle sighed. "Alright. I give in. We won't talk about it. But you and I will be having this discussion, again."

"I'm sure we will," Roni said. "So tell me. What plans have you made so far?"

"Well, we haven't set a date or started planning anything big. You know the way Joe is. He's Mister Simplicity. I imagine we'll end up having a nice, small affair. But we did discuss having it at St. Joseph's, like I told you, and I wanted to get your opinion on dress colors. I'm thinking some shade of purple for the girls in the wedding and that includes you, but you're the ones who will have to wear it, not me. I'll be in white, of course."

"Are you sure?" Roni teased her.

"Yes, I'm sure. So, tell me. What color would you like to wear?"

"You know my favorite color is blue," Roni said. "But it's your wedding, Chelle. You have to make that decision. What does Joe think?"

"He just laughed and said to have something simple."

"Until your mother finds out you're engaged and plans a wedding for three hundred people," Roni said, laughing.

"Honestly, I think we'll deal with that when it's time," Chelle said. "For right now, I'm going to take your advice and float on that cloud for as long as it will hold me up. But I'd like you to think about some of what I said, too."

One of the things Roni loved about her friend was her subtle way of getting back to her point. "I will. Don't worry. I'll think about it."

"Look at it this way," Chelle said, sounding a little mischievous. "I'm a nurse and the head nurse at that. If you had to survive on blood for all of eternity I have access to an entire hospital with storage banks full of blood on every floor. You'd have a supply for as long as I'm alive, at least."

"Oh, Chelle, that's disgusting. Thoughtful, but still disgusting." Roni shook her head and winced at the very thought. "Keep me posted on your plans."

"I will," Chelle said. "One thing I know for sure right now, though."

"What's that?"

"I want you to be my maid-of-honor."

Suddenly Roni had tears in her eyes and her emotions welled up inside of her. "Thank you, Chelle. I'd be so honored. You have no idea."

"Oh, don't cry about it," Chelle teased her. "I know how you feel. We've been close for some time. Believe me, I know. Now settle down and I'll call you in a few days. In the meantime, think about the colors."

"I will. Who else will be standing up for you two?"

"I don't know," Chelle said. "We didn't even get that far. I imagine his sister will have to, but aside from that I couldn't tell you right now. Just think about it like it was your wedding. OK? And we'll talk in a few days."

Roni swallowed hard to get her emotions under control. "That sounds good to me. I'll be home for the next few days."

"Doctor's order?" Chelle asked.

"No," Roni said. "I just need a sanity break."

"Well, just remember. I'm here if you need me. Don't be too proud to ask."

Roni smiled through her blurry eyes and watched the rabbit take one last look into her kitchen before it turned and headed back to the woods. "I know. I'll call you if I need you."

"Good. We'll talk later."

"Alright. Bye."

Roni hung up the phone, then turned back to look out the window at the little paw prints her furry neighbor had left in the last few traces of snow that were still on the ground. Spring seemed to be arriving early this year which meant she'd be able to get outside sooner than she'd expected and start planning what to do in her gardens. She was looking forward to the serenity of working with the soil and smelling the trees and flowers around her. It would help her forget the troubles she was facing now with the uncertainty of her disease and, hopefully, it would also help her condition.

She watched the tree swallows pecking at the ground behind the house and sighed. What a strange turn of events. Her best friend was finally engaged to a wonderful man who Roni felt sure was the right one for Chelle. But at the same time Roni was diagnosed with a disease that had no cure. She shook her head as she continued to study the few new buds around the house. What a roller coaster ride this life was turning out to be.

Chapter 6

March 4 8:45PM

AUDRA searched through the infinitely painful flames for answers on how to release Minotti from Limbo. She found many entities as she searched through the dancing inferno, and she questioned every one of them, but no one seemed able or willing to offer any information. In fact, they seemed to do everything possible just to avoid her. She tried desparately to find the female entity who had explained to her what he was doing there in the first place, but her search proved futile. That particular entity had apparently chosen to hide from her and had found a successful way to do just that, but it only made Audra angry. Her fury grew, causing the flames around her to grow with it. She noticed how her rage attracted agony like a magnet and she watched as all the other souls around her suffered from the intense, antagonistic presence of that agony. She heard them cry out in pain, saw them use their hands to form an impotent shield against her advances, and she felt powerful from the effect she had, even in hell. She enjoyed it as she had on earth when she tore those helpless bodies apart and watched her victims writhe in pain, saw the fear on their faces, and the desparation in their eyes. She experienced the same feeling here, but on a level of intensity she could never have imagined. If she could cause all that with just a thought, could she free Minotti the same way? With just a thought? Would she be strong enough? Of course she would because she had an idea how to make certain of it. All she had to was take the energy from the souls she found as she moved around this dreaded place, absorb it into herself, and use it to strengthen her own will.

She had no way of knowing how strong Minotti truly was. Could he fight her attempts to bring him to her? Would he? Maybe, for some reason, he wanted to be stranded where he was right now. Well, that wouldn't do for her. She needed the power he possessed and she needed it now. By combining her will with that of all those around her, she would become his equal, stronger even. Then she could free him whether he liked it or not. That would have to work. But how would she drain the energy from these entities? It wasn't exactly like draining the blood from humans as she'd done in the physical. Or was it? She shook her head in frustrated anger. She didn't have the patience for all this planning. But she didn't have a choice, either. She was dealing with a being she'd already seen in action and she was smart enough to fear him, smart enough to assume there was much more to him than she'd witnessed. She had to think.

Audra allowed her anger and hatred to grow while her frustration fed it and gave it strength. Now she only had to figure out how to steal the very essence of the souls trapped here and make it all part of herself. She thought about it, looked around, and knew she would have to come up with a plan of some sort. She considered the weakness her fury was able to cause in those around her, how her anger made them suffer. Maybe she could use that same weakness of theirs to will their energy away from them and into herself. Would that work? Why not? It would have to work because she decided it would. Everything else seemed to happen as quick as a thought in this place. Why wouldn't this?

Audra began searching through the flames and the heat and the burning anguish for whatever souls she could find, whichever ones had still not learned to avoid her at all costs. Anything was possible here and she would make sure that what she desired would come to pass. This was another realm. This was not the physical. Anything was possible with the right desire, the right amount of power, and amassing a huge cache of power was Audra's number one priority. But absorbing all of the condemned souls into herself and releasing Minotti might not be enough. The more she thought about it, the more she thought it would be best to try to take his power and energy as soon as she was strong enough to fight him. She would have to be careful how and when she attempted such an endeavor, but she was certain she could do it. For now, however, she would be content to build her own strengths until the time was right to take away Minotti's. She had to stay focused on her main concern which was to achieve vengeance on Christian, Samuel, and whoever tried to get in her way in the process. The only one she might have a problem with was the angel, Jesse. He was the one who had put Minotti here and she was certain he would play a role in defending Christian and Samuel when the time came for her to battle them one on one.

First, she had to continue working on Roni, continue to push her illness further, watch Christian suffer in the process, all while she searched for the souls who hid among the flames.

* * *

Christian entered the kitchen shortly after Roni and Chelle finished talking. He'd heard parts of the conversation while he lay in bed, thinking about what was to come next in their lives. He didn't want to continue to exist unless Roni was by his side for as long as the normal human body could live. The very thought of her not even being there to look at, to talk to, to hold made his stomach queasy. She'd taught him so much, showed him a life he'd never known, and led him to a love he had never believed could be his. Now he feared the worst, the one thing he dreaded since the day he finally admitted to himself that he was in love with her. He feared how temporary this relationship would be if she never decided to join him in immortality, and he wondered how long the memories would last after Roni was gone. As more time passed it became apparent that Roni would not join him on his side of eternity and it was a difficult thought to accept. The only thing that made the idea of her human existence bearable was the fact that she still had sixty or seventy years left to live with him. But now, even that idea was gone. He couldn't help but wonder what it would feel like to watch her die, to be there when she was buried, to live in her house, alone. Could he even stay here without her? It made him sick to have such thoughts on his mind, but he couldn't stop them. As a vampire, loneliness was his reality and Roni was the dream that made the reality bearable.

He bent down to gently kiss her. "How are you feeling?" He rubbed her back as he stood beside her and wondered if she might change her mind, decide she didn't want to suffer the pain that might accompany what had already begun, and give his blood a chance.

Roni looked up at him and smiled a half-hearted smile. "What is this?"

He looked down at her, uncertain of her tone of voice. "What do you mean?"

"This," she said, waving a hand toward her back. "This isn't the way you normally act." She put her arm down and looked straight ahead. "Is this how the pity starts?"

Christian was taken back by her words. His heart stung from the insinuation they presented and he let his arm drop to his side. "I don't understand. I always touch you. It's not unusual for me to rub your back."

Roni shook her head and looked away.

"What's the matter with you?" Christian asked, sitting down next to her. He could feel a barrier between them that had never existed before. He wanted to know what she was really thinking, but he couldn't bring himself to invade her privacy by using his telepathy to find out. Besides, he didn't really need to. Her fear was quite obvious. "What's going on Roni?"

Roni shook her head and tapped her fingers on the table. "Nothing," she said. "I think I'm being overly sensitive now that I know there's actually a name for what's happening with my leg." She stared at the table, her face like a mannequin, then reached down to pick up Sammi, their white, female cat.

Christian put his hand over hers, then rubbed the cat's head. "That's understandable," he said. He did not want to discuss her diagnosis until she was emotionally stronger, so he purposely changed the subject. "Was that Chelle on the phone?"

Roni nodded.

"What did she want?"

Roni looked at him and frowned. "You still don't like her do you?"

Christian sat back, startled. This was not the Roni he was used to. "Of course, I do," he said. "As far as I'm concerned our differences were settled quite a while ago." He studied her face for a sign that would tell him the perfect thing to say in order to bring her back to herself, but she gave him nothing. "What's really on your mind?"

Roni took a deep breath and sighed. "Chelle and Joe got engaged last night."

It was a natural reaction for Christian to smile when he thought of all the trouble Chelle had experienced with relationships. "I'm happy for her. She's been a good friend to you. She deserves the kind of happiness we share." At the moment, such a statement was difficult, but maybe Roni would realize there was still so much to be glad for.

"Yes, she does," Roni said, gently setting the cat on the floor.

"Then why doesn't it seem as if you're really happy for her?" Christian had never seen Roni like this, so uncertain and evasive, in another world and obviously confused.

"She wants me to be the maid-of-honor." Tears began to form in her eyes before Roni finished speaking. "But they haven't set a date, yet."

Christian shook his head. "That's alright. It's terrific that she wants you as her witness. Why aren't you happy?" He would have thought Chelle's news would have taken Roni's mind completely off her own troubles and cheer her up.

"I am," Roni said, beginning to sob. "But what if I can't walk at all by then? What if this thing progresses so fast that I can't even walk down the aisle for her?" Roni put her hands to her face and began to cry uncontrollably.

Christian did not know what to do, but he moved his chair closer to her and pulled her into his arms. "Oh, Sweetheart, don't plan for the worst." He stroked her hair and kissed the side of her head. "You heard the doctor. You're in the early stages and there's no way of knowing just what will happen. Don't decide it's going to be such a bad case when you can't possibly know." He waited for a response of some kind, but only received her heartbreaking sobs. "I'm here, Roni. In whatever way you need me, I'm always here. I love you more than you could know. We'll get through this together one way or the other. It doesn't matter." Still, Roni said nothing and Christian wished he had the nerve to bite into her right now and make the pain and fear go away. He even felt his fang teeth move ever so slightly, but he controlled himself and kissed her again, instead. "Roni, whatever you need you'll have to let me know."

She nodded, but didn't speak.

"I mean it. You can't try to carry this on your shoulders and be strong when you're not feeling that way." He waited, but all she did was sniffle. His heart was begging her to ask him for the change, to ask for just a little blood to see what it might do. But he knew she wouldn't, and he hurt even more because of it.

"I love you," he told her, again, then pulled her closer. This time he was silent as he let her lay her head on his shoulder and release her true reaction to Dr. Reno's news; the reaction that she'd controlled until now.

* * *

Audra had finally found a stray soul who didn't seem to know enough about her to hide. It was so much easier to take the energy from another entity than she had thought it would be. In this realm, the whole being entered her, not just a part of it. But it made perfect sense. They were nothing more than energy, after all, and she found that by willing them to her she was able to will their entire existence to join with hers. It was mind-boggling and she was soaring with the heat of her new power, especially the knowledge she gained when the foreign entity became her. She absorbed their thoughts and their entire life force at the same time. In so doing, she learned how the other souls were fully aware of her plan and how, even here, in the most dreaded place imaginable, where the worst of all those who had failed in their physical existences were now forced to dwell, even here, they were petrified of her. It only fed her ego, the awareness of her rapidly growing strength, and she used it to hunt down the others. It wouldn't be long, now. Her patience was no longer needed. The conquest would be quick and, if she wasn't successful in absorbing Minotti's energy, then she'd have him by her side, working with her as she headed back to the physical to do the most damage she'd ever done in her two hundred years on earth.

* * *

"Christian."

Christian looked at Roni's swollen, exhausted eyes as he sat across from her at the kitchen table. Her face was blotched in red from crying. All he wanted to do was make her pain go away, but she wouldn't let him. He hurt for her, but couldn't do a thing for her. It didn't make any sense to him. Now, when she truly needed him, she pushed him away by denying the most valuable thing he could give her. A full, painless life. "What, Sweetheart?" He leaned on one elbow and caressed her hair while he waited for her to tell him what he wanted to hear.

"How would you feel if this. . . . disease . . . did get that bad?" She looked up at him for a moment, then let her vision shift to one side as if she were ashamed. "You will always be alive and healthy. Won't you be sickened to watch me go through that?" She tried to look at him, but her eyes moved to focus on the table, instead. "Won't you be embarassed?"

Christian squinted slightly as he tried to understand where such a thought would come from. Embarrassed? "How could I be?" he asked, watching her fumble with his hand. "I can't imagine true love allowing room for embarrassment over anything." He would only feel alone and empty if he lost her because of this illness, but he could never say such a thing to her. He could never add such a burden to her already scarred emotions. Never. "It's not like you're doing it on purpose." He quickly regretted saying such a thing because thought it would only make her feel worse. "It's not like you're playing a joke on me," he said, smiling.

She looked at him, her blood shot eyes frowning until she saw how hard he was trying to make her smile with him. "Maybe it's just me," she said. "Maybe I'm the one who's embarrassed to have an illness like this."

"That's because you're always so strong," he said. "You hide too much, but this is something you will not be able to hide. It will show on its own if it does get worse." He stroked the side of her face, then leaned over and kissed her on the forehead. "Don't look so far ahead. We have to take this one day at a time. One symptom at a time."

Roni smiled, wiping her eyes in the process. "I guess you're right. I'm probably jinxing myself just by thinking about it."

"You probably are," Christian said as he stood up. "Can I get you something from the kitchen?"

Roni handed him her cup. "Would you pour me another? The pot is next to the stove. I just made it so it's still fresh."

Christian took the empty cup from her and just looked at her for just a moment before he went to pour her tea and get himself a glass of wine.

* * *

Audra had no trouble locating the souls in hell now that she was absorbing the knowledge of their whereabouts along with the energy of the others before them. It was wonderful, invigorating, and so very powerful. Oh, if only she'd had this kind of power on earth she would never have been forced out. But this might be better. When she was still in her body she didn't know that her immortality did not depend on whether she was a vampire or not. She didn't realize that no one in the physical ever really knows that. Most people assumed that death is the end, but they are so wrong. Still, it was an intriguing idea that caused her thoughts to wander for a bit. Since all those mortals already expected their death to be the end, what would happen if she were already there, waiting to absorb their life force at the moment of death, before they ever knew what was really on this side? They would simply become Audra, and for them it really would be all over for good. Audra would become the ultimate power. She loved the idea and decided to try it as soon as the rest of her plan was already underway. There were enough souls floating around right now to strengthen her.

But what about Minotti? Did she need him now that she'd made this discovery? Could she absorb his energy right now from here among the flames while he floated out there in Limbo? His would be the ultimate power to absorb. And if this was hell, then the other side, where all the good-deed-doers go, must also exist. Could she get there and absorb all of their energy, as well? Oh, the possiblities were so exciting. She could run it all. She could even take the place of the One God that she had still never seen, the One whose true presence she now questioned. She could change everything in existence to be the way she wanted it. That would be the ultimate defeat. Yes, that's what she would do. But first she had to get back to the edge of the flames. Minotti's energy lay dormant in the middle of nowhere just waiting to be picked up and used. And Audra would make sure she was the only one to pick him up and use him.

Chapter 7

March 7 9:00PM

A flock of geese appeared alongside Christian and Samuel as they headed to Nantucket by their own powers of flight. The air was crisp and clear as if the seasons had already turned the corner into Spring. Christian found it invigorating as he looked around at the ice and snow that still held on to the ground below, reflecting the light of the moon and stars, while pools of water formed in the areas where the sun had warmed the ground during the day. He was looking forward to visiting Jesse Nestarius. Jesse was closer to Christian than his own brothers had been. He was beside Christian through his worst experiences, had saved Christian and Diana's life at different times. He had even saved Roni's life when Minotti poisoned her.

"I don't fly as much as I used to," Christian said. "This is wonderful. Look at these birds? If only Roni could experience this, she'd see the beauty in our existence."

"Her eyes are closed to it by her own choice." Samuel reached out to touch one of the geese, but the bird maneuvered itself just out of reach without taking its eyes from him. "You can't change her mind, Christian. It has to be her decision."

Christian nodded and watched for the island to appear while he listened to Samuel, but he did not respond. He wasn't ready to give up and watch Roni suffer, maybe even die sooner than she should. There had to be a way to help her.

"Diana did talk to her, again," Samuel said.

Christian looked at him, surprised. "And what happened? How did it go?"

Samuel shook his head. "No different. But Diana told me that Roni is actually feeling worse than she's letting you know about."

A pain shot through Christian's heart. "Worse? Why would she keep it from me?"

Samuel looked at him in disbelief. "If you'd use your telephathy you wouldn't be asking me that question." He shook his head. "My guess would be that she doesn't want you to know because she doesn't want you to push her into the change." Samuel looked around, then reached for the goose to his right one more time, but again, the bird moved away. "Funny, they fly with us, but they never let us touch them."

Christian looked at his friend and sighed. "I never try to touch them, Samuel. I leave that to you."

"I don't know why not," Samuel said. "Aren't you curious?"

Christian smiled. "The poor thing would probably lose its aerodynamics if I got too close. They know what they're doing. Give it a rest and just enjoy their company."

Samuel turned to him sharply and smiled. "There, you see," he said. "That's what I keep telling you, but you're not listening to me, either. Stop trying to make Roni be the way you want her to be and give it a rest. Just enjoy her company, enjoy your time together while you have it."

Christian deliberately gave him an angry look. "It's not quite the same thing."

"Sure it is," Samuel said. "Except that geese are not as important to you at the moment as Roni is. That's understandable, but the analogy still fits."

Christian shrugged his shoulders. "I suppose." He saw the top of Jesse's house rise up in the distance and he pointed toward it. "There it is. Does he know we're coming?"

"I'm sure he does by now."

"Yeah, you're probably right."

They finished the last few minutes of their flight to Jesse's front yard overlooking the ocean, and landed just outside the porch. Jesse was already seated on the railing, waiting for them.

"Hello, gentlemen," Jesse said, smiling as they approached. "What brings you here?" He pointed at the geese that continued their flight above. "Did you enjoy your companions?"

"Actually, it was quite a nice surprise," Samuel said, extending his right arm. "Did you send them?"

Jesse laughed and took Samuel's hand, then pulled him closer for a friendly hug. "Not exactly, but I wasn't surprised to see that they had joined you." He turned to Christian and hugged him, as well. "Glad to see you, too, my friend. It's been a little too long, once again." He motioned them to the front door. "Come inside. Tell me what's on your minds. I know this visit isn't just something you've done to kill time."

"You're right," Christian said as he entered Jesse's house. "We do have a specific issue we came to talk about."

Jesse gave them both a curious look, then shook his head and smiled. "Let me get us something to drink and we'll discuss it."

Christian watched as he walked to the kitchen, opened the refrigerator, and removed a bottle of port wine. Jesse poured three glasses, left the bottle on the counter, and returned to the living room. "To good friends," he toasted.

"To old friends," Christian said.

Samuel chuckled. "To being old," he said, a mischievous grin spread across his face.

They touched glasses, took a sip, then sat down. Christian and Samuel were seated on the sofa in front of the window while Jesse sat on the arm of the old wing-back chair across from them.

"Do tell," Jesse said. "What can I do for you?"

"Well, for starters," Christian began, leaning forward, his arms resting on his knees. "Roni and I received some disturbing news about her health a few days ago." The look on Jesse's face surprised him. It was as if Jesse already knew. Christian wasn't sure if he should continue, but he quickly decided to get his story told and see what Jesse had to offer. "She has multiple sclerosis. It's been causing a terrible pain in her leg." He briefly looked away. "And it's been causing her a huge amount of depression."

"And then some, according to Diana," Samuel added. "She and Roni have spent quite a bit of time together and Diana tells me there's more than Roni is letting Christian know about." He looked at Christian, then back to Jesse. "Diana said that Roni is ashamed to be sick."

Christian nodded. "Roni just told me the same thing a few nights ago. She's torn up about this whole thing. She's afraid I'll be embarrassed by her. To make it all worse, her best friend is getting married. She wants Roni to be the maid-of-honor and Roni's concerned about what condition she'll be in when that day finally arrives."

"Chelle?" Jesse asked, smiling. "That's wonderful news. I remember her from the incident with Audra. How has she been?"

"She's doing great, now," Christian said. "Her fiance, Joe, is a terrific man, from what I've heard. She's finally in love the way it's supposed to be." He shook his head as he looked across the room. "She's been through so much with her previous relationships, Jesse. I'm actually quite happy to see the way things are going for her, now."

"That's wonderful," Jesse said, sipping his wine. "Especially when I remember the tension that was always between the two of you. Quite a nice change." He placed the glass on the coffee table, sat back on the arm of the chair, and looked at both men before he continued. "Do the two of you recall when we went up against Gaetano Minotti and Roni was bitten by that serpent-like creature he had created?"

Both men nodded.

"Do you remember the poison that ran through her body and how hard you worked to remove it?" he asked Christian.

Christian nodded. He remembered the whole incident as if it had happened only an hour ago. "Do I ever? Are you telling me that the bite is what caused this illness? I thought it was a natural occurrence. Can it be healed?"

Jesse appeared thoughtful as he stood up and paced slowly, passing by them a few times before he sat back down. "No disease is natural," he said. They're all caused by man's foolishness and thoughtless actions toward their own home planet and each other. Humanity was meant to die of old age, nothing more." For a moment, he looked away as if he was lost in his own memories. "Still, what Roni has could happen to any mortal because the genetic potential is there in everyone now. It just takes something, some chemical, some occurence to cause it. In Roni's case, Minotti's poison was the trigger. I knew it that night in the church when it happened, but I couldn't be sure what disease it would cause to manifest. All I could do was wait and . . . . . . Now, I know that it has caused Roni's multiple sclerosis, based on what you just told me." He shook his head and shrugged. "As for fixing it? I don't know. I have limits and rules, as you both know. Roni hasn't asked me for help and I can only do so much of that sort of thing without a direct order. Nothing I do is without permission or, at the very least, Higher Knowledge."

Christian and Samuel nodded together as if their joint movement had been rehearsed.

"I will say this to you, though. I'm not surprised to hear about this." Jesse looked out the window behind them as he spoke. "I had a premonition that something was coming up, but this doesn't make a lot of sense compared to what I was told."

Samuel tilted his head to one side in question. "Isn't that when you see something in your mind? So what were you told and by whom?"

Jesse smiled in such a way that Chrisian thought he seemed to be embarrassed. What side of Jesse was he seeing now? Nothing ever surprised him about this man. “I have a very old friend who still resides on the other side,” Jesse said. “I hadn’t seen her in hundreds of years, then all of a sudden she appeared to me one day to warn me about a strong evil that is on its way. Not directly to me, but it is apparently something I will have to be a part of when it comes time to fight it. That’s about as specific as she got.”

Christian and Samuel looked at each other, then both turned back toward Jesse.

“What kind of evil could be worse than what we’ve already been through with Minotti?” Christian asked.

Jesse shook his head. “I don’t know, but Roni’s disease certainly doesn’t fit. At least not in any way I can determine right now. Still, I’m unsettled by all of this and I believe it all has something to do with Serella’s warning.”

“Is that her name?” Samuel asked.

Jesse nodded. “Yes, Serella Stone. She was a practitioner of the natural arts back in the thirteenth century. She and I were friends.”

“Were you an angel then?” Samuel asked. “Or were you human?”

Jesse laughed only a little. His face held a far away look, almost sad. “I was an angel.”

Samuel nodded, open mouthed, but didn’t say anything more.

“Anyway,” Jesse went on. “ Gaetano Minotti was around then and he decided he wanted to make her belong to him. She was a good witch, if you want to put it that way, but he didn’t like that. He didn’t like goodness in anyone, even back then.” Jesse reached for his glass. “That was my first encounter with him, but I lost.” Jesse appeared to feel the pain as he spoke. “Serella’s body died at his hand, but her soul ended up in a good place.” He looked away. “I took her home." He sipped his wine, looked at them, then took another sip before putting the glass down and leting out a deep sigh. "After that I came back because my purpose, as you know, is here with you and others like you. I didn't see her after that until a few days ago."

"So what would cause her to come see you, now?" Christian asked. "Did she warn you about Minotti when he kidnapped Diana? Did she warn you about Audra when she tried to kill me?"

"No on both accounts," Jesse said, shaking his head. The look on his face gave away his own uncertainty about her visit.

"Then why now?" Samuel picked up his glass and drank half of it in one gulp. "What kind of evil could be worse than either of those two?"

"Satan himself?" Christian asked, staring at Jesse.

Jesse shook his head and smiled. "No such entity," he said. "Satan was created as a metaphor for an entire mass of evil. An outbreak of evil, if you will. He, ... it, ... was another of humanities own creations just to make sense out of what was going on in the heavens." He held his arms above his head as if to punctuate his words. "But it was all happening right here." He shrugged, letting out another huge sigh as he did so. "If only mankind would learn how powerful their very thoughts are." Jesse stared at the floor in silence while Christian and Samuel waited to hear what came next, but Jesse seemed lost in his own thoughts, once again.

"What about the story of the angel created by God, who defied Him, and was sent to hell?" Christian asked, wondering what other stories weren't true if that one wasn't.

Jesse looked up slowly before he answered. "Man made. It's so complicated," Jesse said. "Even our Creator is so much more than you could ever comprehend. He is not just a kindly, old gentleman with immense strength to perform miracles. He isn't even a he. Our Creator has no real gender lines, no single name. He is literally everything you see. He is Love. He is everything pleasant and unpleasant. He is every lesson you learn and every thought you have. Your free will makes Him who He is. There was no hell until man created it and it only exists for those who were so evil here that they took the evil with them to the other side. Remember gentlemen, the way you live here is the way you will live over there, but the existence in heaven will be felt tenfold. Can you imagine how Audra or Minotti are existing in the next realm?" He shook his head as he looked toward the evening stars outside. "The pain they must be suffering there because of all the pain they caused when they were here is immense."

"Wouldn't they be destroyed?" Samuel asked. "I don't understand. I thought we were rid of them."

Jesse blinked, then looked at Samuel. "We are," he said. "There is a place over there where monsters like Minotti, Hitler, Ivan the Terrible, and Napolean go to chill out for a very long time. They're placed in Limbo because of their own sense of destruction that goes against the natural laws of creation as designed by the Creator Himself, or Herself, as some choose to see it. Every one of us is a creator and we're co-creators in different things that exist, but God, is the Great Creator." He shook his head as if to clear his thought. "The point is, everything is made of energy. Even God is a huge mass of ultimate, creative, emotional energy and everything in existence is part of Him, just like all the things you might create are part of you. Even if you make something, then give it away it still remains a part of you because the original thought is ingrained in your mind, in your soul, and will be with you for eternity because it came from you. God expects all that exists to be part of Him for eternity. There's only one problem."

"Yeah," Christian said, standing up. "Free will. He had to go and give that away."

"Well, yes, He did," Jesse said. "But the fact remains that without it, life here would be nothing more than a dictatorship with God as the head dictator. But that wasn't the plan. You see, God is free will itself. When He gave that gift away, He gave the largest part of himself that He could. He gave away His power, and with love He gave away His identity. But He is also everything positive, everything good. And there are many reasons we were even created in the first place, but the biggest reason is that a loving person is also a giving person, and if there's no one there to give to, then the love is wasted." Jesse paused as he looked at Christian and Samuel. "And remember, love isn't selfish either, just as God isn't selfish. He couldn't keep all that He had to Himself, but He had no one to give it to. Therefore, He created us and the world in order to have others to share His love and generosity with. He was not on a power struggle. He was not trying to create an army for Himself. Unfortunately, a few of His creations remembered being attached to Him. They remembered having the power to do and create whatever came to mind, and they did break away, they did try to get the full amount of power for themselves. That's when evil, or Satan, as some call it, was born." Jesse looked at them, then stood and took his glass from the table. "Another? Either of you?"

Both Christian and Samuel emptied their glasses, then handed them to Jesse to be refilled. Jesse went to the kitchen while Christian and Samuel remained in the living room.

"What do you think?" Samuel asked Christian. "Diana and I are supposed to go back to France for a bit on business, but I don't feel comfortable leaving the area right now."

Christian shook his head, continuing to watch out the living room window at the waves as they rolled over the ocean on to the sandy beach at the end of Jesse's front yard. The only signs of winter left visible here were the small patches of ice and snow left at the edge of the woods where the sun barely reached. "I don't know. But I still have to learn what can be done for Roni." He looked at his friend. "Don't worry about us. You and Diana have your own lives to take care of. You go back home and do what needs to be done."

"Doesn't it bother you that this Serella showed up all of a sudden to warn Jesse at the same time Roni started to have this illness develop?" Samuel turned to look out the window with Christian. "What if Minotti isn't really out of the way?"

"You heard Jesse," Christian said. "He's stuck in Limbo for a long time. It's out of his control." He shook his head. "No. It's got to be something else. But I do agree with Jesse. Somehow Roni's illness is part of Serella's sudden visit and the evil that is supposed to be approaching."

"How can you tell?"

"I don't know. I just feel it." Christian turned to him. "Don't you?"

Samuel stared at him for a few seconds before they were interrupted.

"Of course he does," Jesse said, handing them back their glasses. "But he can't explain it any more than the rest of us can."

Christian and Samuel exchanged a quick glance and Samuel nodded, acknowledging that he knew Jesse was right.

"Then what is the connection?" Christian asked. "And why would it be Roni and not one of us? She hasn't offended anyone. She hasn't hurt a soul."

Jesse was shaking his head as if he was upset with himself. "I sent Diana to you for safety that night," he said, looking at Christian. "If you remember, Christian, at the church that evening Father Larry was there with Samuel, Diana, and Roni."

Christian looked at him and shrugged.

"I don't think it was planned for her to take the hit from the serpent," Jesse said. "That strike was intended for Diana. She was the one he wanted this time. When Minotti went to take her with him, Roni jumped in front of Diana as a natural reaction to protect her. But since she was the one the poison effected, she is the one who is suffering, now."

"Damn," Christian swore, turning around to look outside, again. "It was all an accident that Roni took that hit." He ran his right hand over his head in frustrated anger. "And we'll never know what it would have done to my sister if she'd been bit as he intended. If I ever leave this realm, I will find Minotti on the other side and destroy him for this myself."

"Admirable," Jesse said. "But you are a vampire, my friend. It is quite unlikely that you will see the other side for a very long time. Put your anger to rest and save your energy for good things. Like loving

Roni. Support her. And I'll see if I can find out anything else about what's happening to her."

"Just heal her," Christian said, turning to him.

Jesse sighed. "I'll ask. But you might want to do the same."

Christian turned to look at him, and squinted. "I don't think so."

"And why not, Christian?" Jesse asked. "I've heard you pray before."

"Once. And that was because I was afraid for Diana's life."

"Well, now you're afraid for Roni's life, so start praying, again."

Christian drank some of his wine, then stared at Jesse. "This should never have been allowed to happen to someone like Roni in the first place. God should have stopped it."

Jesse shook his head. "That's not the way it works. I told you. It's too complicated to fully explain, but a set of rules were put in place to work naturally and they did. They always do. There are also rules for divine intervention, Christian, and the number one component is prayer. So, unless you want to sit back and helplessly watch this whole thing with Roni happen on its own, I suggest you start playing by these rules. Even I can only do so much." Jesse's eyes were soft and full of emotion. "Don't let your pride or your fear get in the way of what Roni truly needs from you. This is where your free will comes in, Christian. Use it the way it was meant to be used, to turn to Him who gave you the gift in the first place."

Christian hesitated a bit, then nodded. "All right. I will, but see what you can do as well. You're an angel, man. You're closer to Him."

Jesse smiled. "Don't underestimate yourself, Christian." He looked at Samuel. "Either of you. The more prayers, the better. And I'll see what I can do."

"Thank you," Christian said, finishing his wine. He turned to Samuel. "Are you ready to head back?"

Samuel stood, then smoothed down his coat. "Ready."

Jesse walked them to the door and hugged each of them before he opened it. "Don't forget what I said. I'll be in touch as soon as I have more information about the evil Serella is talking about, or as soon as I find out what can be done for Roni. Until you hear from me, keep your faith."

Both men nodded as they walked out onto the porch. They turned to wave to Jesse, then ascended into the night air to head back to the mainland.

Chapter 8

Mid-Summer 1252 A.D.

HE had been watching her through many life times, drawn to her soul's beauty, intrigued by its rapid development. Always choosing the same entities to assist her through the journey, Serella had finally reached the point of near perfection, and of course, Jesse could do nothing to share in her triumph for no other reason except to acknowledge that, as an angel, it was his calling to love and be loved, but only in the spiritual sense.

Though he had existed in the physical for many centuries, he had never fully been part of the human race. He had never felt the calling of the physical, never felt the desire to fully unite with another soul, until now. But he knew it was not allowed. He was an angel, stronger than most of God's other creations, though not the strongest of all angels. There was an entire hierarchy of celestial beings, all more powerful, more in control than he was even after millions of years in existence, but Jesse had never experienced anything like he had felt for the past few thousand years of watching the development of

Serella's spirit. Was it a mistake? There were no mistakes in the universe. Was it a test? The Creator did not test His children. They tested themselves. Then why did Jesse feel this way? He sighed as he continued to watch her harvest the herbs from her front garden, dressed in the sleeveless, summer dress she had created herself. She was alone in this life because of the death of her parents when she was just a child, yet so spiritually fulfilled in the company of nature. He watched her fill the baskets with mountain mint and lavendar, then her apron that hung down over her blue skirt with rosemary, thyme, and sage. For so long he'd wanted to truly know her, but it was not appropriate for him to become involved with a mortal until their spirit was ready and could accept his presence.

But Serella's time to interact with the angelic realm had come and he knew he must go introduce himself. It was time to guide her down the final path of her development in the arts of nature and the powers they possess, time to show her the few truths that were left for her to discover so her truest desires might be realized, allowing her to fully know the Creator.

Jesse walked out from the cover of the forest that surrounded the acres of land left to her by her father, and the small, log cabin he'd built before she was born. He watched her continue to pick the garden herbs, unaware that anyone was around, but with no reason to be concerned, either way. He saw the breeze gently blow the ends of her long, blonde hair around her face, then to the back of her neck, saw the sweat soak through the back of her dress, and marveled at the birds who stayed by her side and the wolves that came from the other end of the property to watch his approach with trepidation and concern for their beloved Serella. How could an angel feel this way about a mortal woman? It wasn't even supposed to be possible, yet it was happening to him.

Jesse felt a presence behind him and he stopped walking for a moment and turned slowly to see that two more wolves stood at the edge of the trees, poised to pounce if the need arose. They were beautiful to watch in their determination and self-assured dedication to the beautiful witch. Jesse respected that level of loyalty. He couldn't help but smile as he turned back around to face Serella, but the smile quickly vanished from his face when he saw that she was now watching him, too. He froze for a moment as he saw the light radiate from her deep, blue eyes. He was mesmerized.

"Might I help you with something?" she asked. "Lost, maybe?"

She spoke the words as if she already knew the answers, but enjoyed the game of teasing the traveler just a little.

"Yes," Jesse said as he continued to approach her, now at the very edge of the path that cut through to the other side of the herb garden. "My name is Jesse. I have come to see you." He knew he sounded like an idiot, but he couldn't help himself. He was still fairly new to the ways of the physical realm and no where near used to dealing with human beings, feeling the way he did about her.

"About what?" Serella asked, smiling sweetly at him; another tease.

Jesse stopped walking and stood before her, determined to take control of the situation before he completely botched it up. He was here for a specific purpose and he could not fail at something so important as to complete someone else's spiritual development and prepare them to re-enter the realm of the Creator. "I am here to further your training."

"Training in what?" Her eyes sparkled as she looked directly into his own. "Matters of the flesh?" she teased. "Or is there truly something else you had in mind?"

Jesse blushed. To think she would even discuss such a topic so openly with no second thought, no hesitation, and quite obviously no shame. What was he to do? "I am an angel," he said, trying to appear very proper. "I was sent here to further your studies in the true powers of nature as you have been practicing throughout this lifetime and many others."

Serella reached her hand up to his face and gently touched his cheek. He saw the wolves that still stood behind her, slowly lower their bodies to lay on the ground just at the edge of the trees, watching her but without as much aggression in the energy that eminated from them. He was relieved, though still in awe of what she was able to control without any effort at all. "They love me," she said as if reading his mind. "And I love them."

"They protect you," Jesse said. "That is quite obvious."

Serella smiled, took her hand away from his face, and bent down to retreive her basket of herbs, then placed it over her arm into the crook of her elbow. She pulled her apron up with both hands, then looked around the edges of her property at the wolves who seemed to await her desire. Suddenly, they all turned and went back into the forest as Jesse watched each of them move away. "Come in with me for a cool drink?" Serella asked. "I must hang these herbs to dry, but I would be most happy to talk to you while I do so."

Jesse looked at her and smiled. "I would enjoy that. Thank you."

She turned and headed up the stone path to the house, leaning over to pick up another basket on the way.

"Might I help you carry those?" Jesse asked, reaching to take the basket from her hands.

She released it to him. "Thank you," she said. "There are two more on the way." She nodded her head in the direction where two more baskets stood along the path.

Jesse saw them and smiled. "I shall get those for you, as well." He followed her to the house and set the baskets on the table in the kitchen where Serella had rolls of twine already set up with a knife nearby. The house suited her with all the herbs hanging in various places and the cat sleeping on the window sill. Serella seemed to float as she moved around setting the herbs down, then pouring him a cool drink from a pewter pitcher she had stored in the corner, in the shadows. "This should help cool you some," she said, gently handing him the wooden goblet. "If you feel as if you might like more, just help yourself." She pointed to the shaded corner where the pitcher stood. "I have much to do before nightfall."

"That is some of what I was sent here to discuss with you," Jesse said. "There is much I must teach you about the craft and nature, the workings of the universe and the afterlife. How the whole cycle of life actually works and why it all works the way it was created to. These are the things I am commissioned to teach you."

Serella laughed in such a way it made Jesse's heart beat faster as a wave of warmth seemed to encircle him. "I know why you are here." Serella began tying bundles of herbs together as she spoke. "And most of what you speak of, I already know." She smiled. "I must be honest with you, Jesse. I have been expecting you. Your presence does not surprise me at all."

Jesse was dumbfounded and curious at the same time. She'd been quite psychic in her prevous two incarnations and she was born with the same abilities in this life, only much stronger. Yet, it still took him by surprise that she was so honest about her knowledge. "I apologize," he said. "I should have known better."

"Oh, do not be sorry," she said as she placed a bundle to the side, then began another. "You are quite old as far as spirits go, but your knowledge of the physical is limited." She looked up at him. "Am I your first earthly assignment?"

Jesse looked down, blushing. "One of my first."

"Ah, I thought so."

"What does that mean?" Jesse asked.

"It means that I thought so," she said. "Nothing more, nothing less."

"What made you think so? Am I handling this so poorly that is was obvious?" Again, she was turning him in to a babbling fool, but he had no idea how she managed to do that to him. He knew it definitely could not continue if he was to be effective as a teacher. He had to get control of himself, somehow, and maintain it.

Serella placed the second bundle to the side and began a third. "No, not really. But it is quite obvious how nervous you are." She glanced at him from the corner of her eyes. "Why is that, Jesse? Why are you nervous?"

"I suppose I simply do not want to do anything wrong by you in teaching you what I have been instructed to teach you," he said. "It makes me nervous to have your future in my hands."

"Oh, why should you be so nervous?" Serella asked. "What is the worst thing that can happen? If you make a mess with my lessons, then I shall only have to come back again, begin another incarnation so I can learn what my teacher handled wrong. It certainly would not be a terrible crime. It would only be a minor waste of time, but then, nothing is ever truly wasted, is it." She smiled as she brushed the fallen leaves from the table into the palm of her hand and placed them in a bowl that she'd set on the side. "So how about if you simply begin my lessons at your leisure?"

"I think I should understand you better first," he said. In truth, he simply wanted to know her from her own words, from her own vision of her life. "It would, most likely, help me teach you if I know about your experiences, how you look at things, how you might interpret my own words. I am sure you know what I am trying to say."

"Why?" Serella asked. "Because I am a witch and you are an angel? That does not make much sense now, does it?"

"I never question the Creator's judgement," Jesse said. "He has His reasons for all that He does."

"Why would you not choose to ask questions?" Serella asked. "If you wish to truly know, there is no reason you cannot simply ask so you can learn. That is what all of life is about, is it not? I cannot imagine the Creator finding any fault in that."

Jesse nodded as he sipped his drink that tasted like very sweet fruit. "No, I suppose not. But I certainly would not want to appear as if I think I know better."

"Do you?"

"Do I what?"

"Do you know better?" she asked.

"No, I do not know better than the Universe," he said.

Serella stopped working on the bunches of herbs, sat back, and looked at him. "My dear, Jesse," she said. "How can you say such a thing when, in fact, you are the Universe. We all are."

Jesse was taken back in surprise, speechless. She knew so much already. What could he possibly teach her?

"We are all part of the Creator and She is part of all of us." She stood up, took her bunches of herbs, and began hanging them by the few empty areas that were left around the windows. "I can feel it when I walk through the woods or lay with the wolves in the forest. I can feel it when I bath in the stream down the hill or lounge in the sun in front of the house. All the smells, all the sounds. It all belongs to Her and to us. I feel so connected to Her all of the time." She looked at him. "How can it be possible that you do not feel all those things?"

Jesse thought for a moment. Who was the angel here? "I feel it when I am with Him," Jesse said. "When I am on the other side, in His presence, yes, I do feel it. And I feel it when I pray. But here on earth I see the hardships of the physical and I only feel pity for the trials all these souls have chosen to undergo. I understand that such decisions were made with their spiritual development in mind, but still, it is disheartening to see it happen. Suffering of any kind is nothing more than depressing."

Serella shook her head and frowned as if she were uncertain of his response. "You are an angel, Jesse. At least, that is what I thought I heard you say." She started to tie the herb bunches once more as she spoke. "You should know better than me how closely related all things are to the Creator, the Source. How can you not feel it when you are amongst the creations themselves? How can you not see it when you are looking at the physical manifestation of our desires, the Creator's desires? You are allowing yourself to be blinded by emotions, my dear man. That is not a good quality for any angel. I should think you would be quite a bit more impartial and so much more open to all that you see. You cannot just look at the physical as if that is all there is, Jesse. You cannot just listen to words and believe they really mean what you are hearing. You must look deeper than that for the truths. I am sure you are a wonderful angel and, most likely, very good at all you do, but here in the physical you are not seeing what lies beneath it all. Even hardships are surrounded in beauty."

"Where do you see that?" Jesse asked. "Beauty in hardship?"

"No, not in the hardship, itself," Serella said, smiling. "The beauty is in the possiblities the hardship presents. What can happen? What good? What bad? What lessons might be learned from it all? How do I steer the course in the direction I wish it to go? How can you not see the beauty in having control of your own destiny, in being part of the creation process itself?" She cut a length of twine, then placed the knife on the table and leaned forward, closer toward Jesse. "I asked for you," she said. "I asked the Goddess to send me an angel to teach me the greatest of knowledge so I might be closer to Her, and here you are."

Jesse did not know how to respond to her. "You asked for me?" He stared at her. She was so beautiful she could live as an angel in heaven, though her methods were not those of any angel he'd ever known.

"Well, not for you by name," she said. "I simply asked for a tutor to be sent to me who might teach me the ways of gaining Her confidence, of showing me how to connect to Her directly. So, it does not suprise me that She sent you."

"Please, would you do me the favor of referring to the Creator as I do?" he said. "You throw my consciousness off balance when you speak of the Goddess. It would be so much easier to talk on similar levels, with similar words."

Serella chuckled as she cut more twine. "There are many names for each human being. Why should the Creator not have many names? It all still refers to the same entity, so where is the confusion?"

"Human beings do not have many names," Jesse said to her. "Here in the physical they have one, their names given at birth."

"Do they not? What about a husband who calls his wife, 'Sweetheart?' Or a child who calls his mother, 'Mother?' Yet her given name might be 'Lita?' All three names refer to the same person and all those who know her are fully aware of her other names. It seems to me that if we can do such a thing and accept it, then the Creator deserves the same in return." Serella carried her bunch of herbs to the window to hang it. "So, if you choose to call the Creator, 'God,' and I choose to call the Creator, 'Goddess,' it still refers to the same entity and both of us know who we speak of. Where is the problem?" She turned to look at him with such a sweet expression on her face that Jesse's heart melted as if he had just seen the birth of the most beautiful child. Suddenly, her argument made perfect sense to him and he realized that she had just taught him something quite valuable, but something he should've already seen.

"I agree with you," he said, smiling. "Every soul has a name assigned to him or her at the moment of their creation, though they may have had many different names to identify them throughout their many lifetimes. I just never looked at it that way before. I apologize, Serella. You are right. I will not argue the point with you, again."

"No harm done, Jesse." Serella began to tie another bunch of herbs before she continued. "Though I must say that I am quite surprised to find an angel who does not know these things."

"Honestly," Jesse began, "I do know such things and I should have seen it before I spoke, but being in your presence confuses me."

"Why should that be?"

"I do not know," he said. "I only know that I do not have much interaction with most mortals so this is, somewhat, new to me, as you have already observed. I only hope I am able to be more open with you in the future."

Serella smiled at him. "I am sure you will."

Jesse took a deep breath and leaned back slightly. "Now, maybe I will be able to teach you what you were looking for when you asked for a teacher to be sent to you." He stood up and took the knife from her hand. "For the time being, I will cut the twine and you may wrap the bunches. Together we will get these herbs wrapped quicker and then have more time for lessons of the spirit."

"That sounds wonderful," Serella said as she began in earnest to use the remaining twine she had cut to wrap the herbs, while Jesse began the task of cutting more.

Chapter 9

March 7 11:30PM

JESSE stood at the door in his jeans and sweatshirt, staring at the darkness outside. He watched the moonlight play across the ocean waves and wondered what he was really doing here in the physical plane, but then, he'd been wondering that same thing since he'd first met Serella.

A shooting star quickly caught his eye and he sighed. All these centuries he believed he was here in order to help the worst souls in existence find their way back to God, but he had spent more time fighting serious evil than he had spent teaching the seriously sinful how to change. He took a deep breath and leaned on the door frame as he listened to the snow crunch under the weight of some unseen animal. What was happening? Was the earthly plane growing worse? Were things really getting that bad here? Maybe they were. Why else would Serella, a village witch he hadn't seen or spoken to since 1253, appear after all this time just to tell him that another strong wave of evil was on its way? Why would a visit from her be necessary unless whatever was coming turned out to be worse than what he'd already experienced from Audra Trivette or Gaetano Minotti? Jesse shook his head, then turned to walk into the kitchen where he poured himself a cup of tea he brewed from herbs grown in his garden during the summer months. He let the tea steep a few minutes while he looked out the kitchen window and reflected on all the things that seemed to be happening at once. There was just so much of it suddenly, including Roni's diagnosis of a disease which modern medicine has virtually no knowledge how to cure. He stretched his limbs and sighed. The millenium was here and so was the planet. It had not been destroyed as so much of the world feared it would be, but that was simply because it wasn't supposed to be. When and if that time came Jesse was supposed to be instructed, but he hadn't been. Unless,. . . . . . . Did someone forget to contact him, or was that Serella's job? Maybe that was her true message and she simply delivered it the wrong way. Language always did have a tendency to become garbled between the dimensions. Telepathy was truly the only accurate way to communicate. So why wasn't Serella using hers? It only made Jesse question her motives even more.

He took his tea to the door and stepped out onto the porch. He looked around, then walked down the stairs to the cold sand that lay between his house and the ocean. The air was chilled as late winter air should be, but it felt so fresh and clean. He shook his head and raised his eyes to the sky. He needed answers and he knew who would have them.

"Serella," he said to the night. Above him the clouds slowly parted to reveal the full moon in all her glory. "Serella," he said, again. "I know you're listening. You've probably always been listening," he mumbled under his breath. "But don't ignore me. We have to talk."

"And so it begins."

Jesse recognized the voice and turned toward it. "Serella," he said, surprised she had appeared so quickly. "I thought you weren't going to be around anymore."

She floated toward him, smiling. "I lied." Her waist length hair flowed behind her ever so gently giving her face a soft appearance. Softer than he remembered.

Jesse shook his head and looked away. "Are you here to help me or to mislead me?"

"Neither," she said. "I'm here so you know where I am."

"What do you mean by 'and so it begins?'" he asked her.

Serella smiled. "Just what I said. The questions, the paranoia. The uncertainties." She floated in pulsating movements. "All the things that evil sends as a prerequisite to its appearance." Her face suddenly held a look of desparation. "We need you here, Jesse. Your strength is needed on this side to fight this thing."

He turned to her. "I'm not going home yet, Serella. You have more than enough strength on that side. Mine is needed here if this evil is going to appear in the physical. Right now, though, I need to know why, after all these centuries, have you come to me? There were many other times you could have warned me. What's different now?"

She started to float backward, causing her crimson and rose colored garment to flow around in front of her. She was still smiling at him, but her eyes held a mischievous glaze. "I've always followed you, Jesse."

He watched her start to fade, but somehow knew she was teasing him. "You've always followed me, but never warned me. So why warn me now?"

Serella solidified quickly, her form taking on a more human appearance as she flowed close to him. "This time is the culmination of all that has come before. This time will require many sacrifices, Jesse. Many sacrifices in order to set things right."

Jesse stared at her, frowning.

"Don't look so angry," she said. "Sacrifice is as old as time. You know what it has done in the past. You know what it does today. It will be very necessary, now."

"What kind of sacrifice, Serella? And why?"

She smiled at him, but said nothing.

Jesse shook his head, frustrated. "What about Roni?"

"What about her?" Serella held her arms out, her ethereal garment flowing between the worlds as parts of it disappeared, then reapearred. "She is the weapon."

Suddenly, Jesse felt very uncomfortable. "The weapon? What kind of weapon?"

Serella looked out across the water. "I don't know," she said.

Jesse was disappointed. Now he knew she was playing with him. "That's what you said the first night we talked, but you've found quite a few answers in a very short time. And you've admitted lying to me about being able to come back. I mean you no disrespect, Serella, but don't be offended if I tell you that I don't believe you."

To his surprise, she began to laugh. "You do know me, Jesse. But I can only tell you so much. You know the rules. If the Creator wanted those on earth to know everything, she would tell them before they were incarnated so their time in the physical would be easier, smoother. But that's not the purpose of life, is it?"

Jesse looked away. "No, it's not," he said. "But I'm here to help these people. I'm not here to pass some kind of test. I'm not here for my own instruction or spiritual advancement. I'm here to be in service to others."

Serella waved a forefinger back and forth while her form hovered above the sandy ground. "That's where you're wrong, Jesse. Every entity is constantly learning. That includes you and me. Even though you're here to guide your immortal friends on earth, you're also learning in the process as they are learning from you. Just like you and I learned from each other."

Her words made sense and pulled so strong on his heart, but his better judgement made him question their validity. "Then what am I supposed to learn? What haven't I encountered already? And why would I be sent here for all these centuries to do a job I'm not prepared for?"

"Oh, but you are prepared for it," Serella said. "And if you think about it, you'll realize that you already know what's coming because it was inevitable."

"Your riddles are confusing me, Serella." He turned toward the ocean. "You're not telling me anything." In fact, she was piercing his heart with an emotional dagger.

Suddenly Serella was by his side, only inches from his body, staring at his face with a look of adoration in her eyes. "What do you want to know?"

He looked at her, his heart already beginning to heal by her nearness to him. "First, can Roni be healed? I know her disease was triggered by Minotti's venomous creation. Can it be reversed?"

Serella smiled. "Of course it can. Everything is possible, Jesse. You already know that."

"How?"

"Now, you see. You're asking a question you know the answer to in your heart. You can heal her yourself."

It was a trick. It had to be a trick. Jesse shook his head. "I'm not going home, yet. Those powers come from the side you're on. I'm not going home just to get them."

Serella shook her head and smiled. "Those powers are in you right now," she said. "It wasn't so long ago when you first healed Roni, now you think you can't do it, again? You're an angel, Jesse. Healing is part of your nature. Those same abilities live in everyone, but those in the physical don't believe in what exists on this side, so they don't believe in their own powers to heal, either. You've been here too long, Jesse. You're starting to think like them. I can see it would be for your own good to come back here." She looked away. "Even if it was only for a little while."

Jesse turned back toward the water and watched the moonlight ripple in the current. "I can't, Serella. I care for these people too much to let them down. I can't just abandon them and go home because it would be in my own best interests. It wouldn't be in theirs."

"Ah, but maybe it would."

Jesse gave her a quick, angry glare. "And maybe you can simply tell me what Roni needs."

Serella smiled. "All right, Jesse. For starters, she needs faith and confidence."

"In God?"

Serella floated higher for a moment, then settled back down only inches from the ground. "Faith in the Creator, yes. But faith and confidence in herself, too. She doesn't need someone else to heal her, Jesse. She is perfectly capable of healing herself. All disease comes from a place outside each of us. It's nothing more than just another form of energy, but we attract the energy of the diseases to ourselves based on what we do; based on the energy we exude. It all begins with a thought, followed by a single action that triggers the whole mess."

"But I thought Minotti triggered her disease."

Serella nodded, her silvery blonde hair flowing around the movements of her head. "He planted the poison, but Roni's thoughts determined if and how that poison would develop."

Jesse shook his head. "This is a disease that she has no control over."

"I know. But in reality, she does."

Jesse was already so frustrated over the whole situation that he was growing impatient with her. "Let's assume she doesn't understand that and cannot control it. Then what is the basis for this type of illness? What am I missing? She's a tender, loving, woman." Jesse was feeling inadequate because of his confusion. He was supposed to know all these answers. Maybe Serella was right. Maybe he needed to go home for awhile. Maybe he was really doing more harm than good here.

Serella nodded as if she understood, but her smile was almost motherly. "Roni has been very strong. Sometimes too strong." Serella placed her hand along the side of his cheek. "You know how diseases manifest according to the actions of the person they have infected."

Jesse stared at her, but said nothing.

"A disease that takes one's control is manifested in one who has always been controlling of others." Serella held her hand by his cheek for a few more seconds, then lowered her arm, allowing the tips of her fingers to pass through him. "That's what multiple sclerosis is, Jesse. It takes away its victim's control."

Jesse felt her essence blend with his when their auras touched and he felt the loss of her when she was no longer so close. He took a deep breath. "But Roni isn't like that."

"As I said." Serella looked across the ocean while she finished speaking. "She is a weapon. The disease is not being manipulated by her, but by the one who is using her. Roni's part in facilitating the whole process is her need to stay in control even when she really can't."

"Is that one Minotti? Is he the one manipulating this illness?"

Serella shook her head, the moonlight shining right through her whole being.

"Then who?"

She looked at him. "I don't know who, but I do know the entity must be evil. Only evil desires to control others."

"Then I'm back to my original question, Serella. Can she be healed?"

Serella smiled, light dancing from her eyes. "As I told you. Yes. Regardless of how the disease began or who is controlling it, she still has the power to heal herself, just as we all have that power to heal ourselves and each other. Roni only needs to be shown how. Humans have been raised to believe they're helpless. They should all be trained in the truth."

Serella's words had begun to make him sad and he looked away. "Yes, I know," he said. "But I don't know how to teach Roni." He looked at Serella. "Why don't you teach her?"

Serella shook her head and smiled as she began to glide backward once more. "I can't. You know the rules, Jesse."

"Don't hide behind your so-called rules, Serella," he said, but she ignored him and continued to move away. "Serella, don't you dare go," he said, but he watched her disappear into the atmosphere, anyway.

He looked down at the gentle waves that flowed to the shore under the midnight sky. What did she mean that Roni was a weapon? The only way a person would be a weapon was when someone else wanted to hurt whoever cared about them the most. In this case, Christian would be the one most susceptible to pain if anything should happen to Roni. But Jesse was there when Christian's biggest enemy, Audra, was destroyed a few years ago. At least her body was destroyed. The rest of her energy was supposed to be in Limbo along with Minotti where they would have no awareness of anything. He looked at the sky and thought about both of them. Granted, Audra would be free long before Minotti, but by then she'd have no desire to do harm. The whole point of putting her there was to cause her to lose the memory of what that kind of unnatural power felt like. Even Audra was given the base desire for good as part of her original creation and she was entitled to have it back. So it wasn't possible for her or Minotti to be behind what was happening to Roni. But if not them, then who?

Jesse turned and began to walk along the water's edge. In the distance a hoot owl sang its evening song to the world. Jesse smiled. Some thing's still existed as they were originally intended, pure and natural.

Then there was Serella. He didn't know what to make of her. He remembered the person she was in her mortal years, a good woman who was in tune to the feminine side of God, the true Mother Earth, and everything that existed. But all those centuries ago, her dealings with Minotti changed her.

Jesse stopped walking and let the freezing, ocean water gently touch his toes. There was so much he should tell Christian about Serella, the truth of what Minotti was after. All he ever wanted were her powers as a witch. He wanted to steal her abilities to control the natural surroundings, the weather, the wild life, everything. But Minotti's only reason for wanting such strengths was to use them against others when he felt it was necessary. Serella's practice was for the good of those around her and she refused to give in to him. When Minotti captured her the second time, he tortured her unmercifully. By the time Jesse was able to reach her, Serella's physical form had taken all it was able to. The only thing Jesse could save by that time was her soul. And he did. But the damage to her pure heart had been done. When Jesse returned to earth, Serella stayed behind, having chosen never to visit the physical, again.

So that brought Jesse right back to the original question he'd been wrestling with since her first appearance. Why now? Why wasn't Audra enough to bring her to him? What about Minotti? She didn't come to him either time, but now she was here. Jesse suddenly felt pain, like a dagger shoot through the center of his being. It couldn't be. He looked up to the moon and saw the millions of stars that had appeared with the retreat of the many clouds that had covered the sky at sunset. What if neither of them ever made it to Limbo? What if both of their souls were still very much awake? Jesse shook his head as he felt the dagger twist. It couldn't be. How could there be a break down in the natural laws, on that side, especially? He'd never heard of such a thing happening. Jesse put his hands to his head, then let his palms slide down across his cheeks. He sighed deeply. There was only one way to find out without going back to the other side himself. "Serella!" Jesse yelled to the night air. "Serella, you know what's going on! Come back here!"

As he expected, though, there was no reply. If his assumptions were correct, Serella was using a very serious situation to bring him back to the realm of reality for good. He had to admit he'd thought about it many times. He'd thought about her many times. The truth was, he had loved her very much when she was in the physical, and he knew she could easily convince him to stay with her in heaven where it was eternally peaceful. That's why she was playing this game with him. He was sure of it, now. If she didn't tell him what he needed to know, then he'd have to go home in order to find the answers himself. But was he strong enough to simply visit, then return here? Afer all this time he couldn't be certain, but he knew that right now he was at a point where he did not have a choice. If his suspicion was correct, he couldn't rely on Serella for help. He had to find out what was really going on here, and he had to know

now so he could try to stop Roni's illness and heal her from the damage that may have already been done. He took a deep breath as if he was fueling up for a long journey. Alright. So he'd take the chance and go back just for the amount of time he'd need to get the information, then quickly return. He could do it. He knew he was strong enough. He had to be. He would leave the physical for a short time, visit the Creator, find out the truth, then come back.

He turned and headed for the house, shaking his head in wonder. The work of an angel was definitely not what he'd originally expected.

Chapter 10

Late Summer 1253.

"THIS is amethsyt," Serella said, seemingly in awe of the crystal. "This one is very powerful in so many ways." She turned it over in her hands a few times, then looked up at Jesse. "Why does each crystal have certain powers?"

Jesse looked at her, fully prepared to answer, but the vision before him caused him to be momentarily speechless. He was intrigued with this beautiful woman. Try as hard as he might, there was no way he could determine whether this feeling was alright for an angel to be experiencing. What most impressed him was that for all the knowledge she had already obtained in her 24 years of life, she was still hungry for more. "Each crystal is endowed with individual powers because of the manner in which it was formed," Jesse said. "In order for each stone to be what it is, to have the powers it does, to have the unique properties found only in its type, it has to be created under certain conditions. Otherwise, it would not become the stone it is, but rather, it would become something else." He lifted the piece of amethyst and held it to the flame that burned from the candle on the table beside them. "In its formation, amethyst obtains the powers to heal and protect, to help us focus on a mental level, and to reduce anger or impatience. On a spiritual level, however, it connects the bearer to the spirit." He handed the stone back to her slowly. "And that is just for starters. The very process that causes such a crystal to look the way it does, to have its unique color, is the same process that creates its individual powers."

Serella looked at the stone, glanced up at Jesse, then put the crystal aside and looked at another. "This one is my favorite, though I truly do not know why." She lifted a foggy, pink stone and held it to the flame. "Rose quartz," she said. "I do not know what it is about this stone. I have been told it is the stone of love and romance, but beyond that I could not tell you much more."

"It is also a very strong healing stone," Jesse said. "Maybe the most powerful. It is peaceful and it gives the bearer a feeling of emotional balance." He looked deep into her blue eyes. "It helps you love yourself, but not in a conceited way." He touched the stone while it remained in her hand by the candle. "The energy it possesses is as soft as its color. It soothes and warms the bearer and allows you to be a soother and spirit warmer of others. It is part of the function of love."

"But they lose their color," Serella said, placing the stone next to the amethyst she had moved aside. "My mother used to tell me that the energy of the stone is weakened over time. Is that true?"

"Your mother was a very wise woman," Jesse said, basking in the glow of her smile.

"Strange," she said. "I do not see how something as strong and solid as a stone can lose anything." Serella rolled the piece of rose quartz around on the table. "What can I do to stop it from happening?"

"Did your mother not tell you that, too?"

She looked at him and smiled. "Yes, but I want to hear it from you. I thought you are here to teach me things. Is that not true?"

"Yes, I am," Jesse said. "But I am here to teach you things you do not already know."

Serella leaned across the table and placed a hand on his arm. "Tell me, anyway."

Jesse leaned back until her hand was no longer touching his arm and took a deep breath. "Then you must use your cleansing ritual to replenish the natural energy of the stone," Jesse said. "The Universe shall connect with you, feel your desire, your request, and replenish the original characteristics of the stone. Each of these crystals has a sort of personality that belongs only to them. You must nourish those feelings, even the feelings of what might seem to be an inanimate object, just as you would nourish someone you love." He gently touched her hand, then pulled himself away. "I must leave soon," he said.

"To go where?" Serella stood up from the table and went to take an apple from the basket of fruit by the window. "Where do you go at night, Jesse? Back to heaven? I see you walk away, but I have no idea where you live. You said you are here in the physical, but does that also mean you are trapped as I am?"

Jesse studied her face for a moment and watched as she bit into the apple, then waited for his answer. "Until you die, you are trapped in the physical," Jesse said. "That is true. I am here until I am summoned back home or until I choose to go back home for my own reason."

"And where is home?"

"On the other side where the true home belonging to everyone exists."

"No, Jesse. I mean your home here. Where do you live in this life?"

"Through the woods toward the next town," he said, smiling. "The walk is not long, really, but it is safe enough from too many prying eyes."

"Safe?"

"I do not get too many travelers going past my little house," he said. "For this mission, I need that sort of privacy."

Serella turned to him, a hurt expression on her face. "Is that what I am?" she asked him. "A mission?"

Jesse shook his head. "No, not any more, Serella. You have become my friend as well as my student." He hesitated a moment. "And you are becoming a most interesting teacher too."

"I enjoy teaching," Serella said. "I wish I had a little girl in my life to pass my knowledge to the way my mother passed hers to me, but I have not met the right gentleman, yet." She tilted her head and smiled. "Maybe that will change soon."

"You have plenty of time for that." Jesse did his best to ignore her sultry look. "The right young man shall come along when the time is right and you shall have your own children soon enough."

"Do you also know the future?"

"No," Jesse said. "You shall make your own future just as all humans are able to do. Every decision you make throughout your day sets the course for all that is to come next. Your possible future is constantly changed because you are always given new decisions to make. Some are larger than others, but they all make a difference in where you end up at the end of each life time."

"And when the life time is over?"

"Then you go home for a rest," Jesse said.

Serella released a short chuckle that sounded a bit sardonic. "Only to come back and do it again, anyway."

"Maybe," Jesse said. "Or not."

Serella turned to him. "Explain yourself, Jesse. You make no sense to me with this line of discussion. What are you telling me? That we do not have to come back if we choose not to?"

"I am telling you that you always have the gift of free will." Jesse started to walk across the floor as he thought about her question. "That simply means that if you do not wish to learn more, become better, perfect your spirit, your soul, then you may simply exist in your current state on the other side for as long as you like. But you must remember that it is the desire of your spirit to be reunited with the Creator. It is the desire of every spirit to experience that."

"You mean my soul," Serella corrected him.

"No," Jesse said. "I mean the third element of human life on earth. I mean the spirit."

Serella appeared puzzled. "Then what is the soul that my mother always spoke of?"

"Every human life is made up of three elements," Jesse said. "You have the body here in the physical that allows you to experiment and find ways to learn needed lessons. Then you have the spirit that always remains on the other side watching how those lessons are learned, monitoring your physical process and how you choose to progress along the many paths shown to you during your life. Then you have the soul which is the conduit between the two realms. The soul relays messages to the physical body. What humans call ideas or intuition. Where do you think those ideas actually come from?"

"It has always made me wonder," Serella said. "Sometimes I think of a thing and I truly cannot figure out how I thought of it."

"Those are the things I am referring to," Jesse said. "They come from the communication between the spirit and the body as we are lead through each lifetime."

"Then none of our ideas are truly our own," Serella argued.

"Not true," Jesse said. "Your spirit is you. Your spirit is who you have always been. It is your eternal connection to the Source, the Creator. All ideas, ultimately, come from the Creator."

Serella frowned. "Jesse, you are making it sound as if we are not individual people. As if there is only one entity that has ideas. As if the Creator is only loaning us our thoughts."

"No, Serella. Listen to me. There is only one Creator, one Source of Knowledge, one God, regardless of what name or title you choose to give Him." He spread his arms out. "All of us. All of life." He looked around the room and out the window at the darkness. "Everything is the Creator. And the Creator is everything."

"You are confusing me, Jesse."

"Just listen," he said. "You will soon see how true it is to your soul. Just listen and absorb what I tell you." He went to sit by the table, then turned to look at her. "God is lonely without us. He was always alone until He created us."

"She," Serella said.

"As we have previously discussed, the title you choose to give Him does not matter."

Serella nodded. "I apologize," she said. "I did not mean to interrupt you. I always think of the Great Mother as the Creator and when you say 'He'. . . . well, I understand why it bothers you so much to hear me say 'She'. I know we discuss it quite often, but I still need to clarify for my own thoughts, now and again."

"That is fine," Jesse said, admiring how the moonlight reflected off her hair as it shined through the open window. "If it is easier for you, then I shall do my best to refer to the Creator in the feminine when we are having these discussions."

Serella smiled. "Thank you."

Jesse saw the sparkle in her smile and wished he could look at it forever. "As I was saying, the Goddess created us to keep Her company, to let Her experience Her own creations through us. What we feel, She feels. What we see, She sees. And that works in reverse."

Serella nodded her head and smiled. "Oh, so what She thinks, we think. And what we think, She thinks. That's why Her ideas are really our ideas, while our ideas are really Hers. Because all of it happens at the same time. In truth, we are all one entity, part of the Creator, for real. I am fascinated."

"Yes," Jesse said. "And She is aware of all that we do and knows when we need Her help."

"Now I must argue with you," Serella said. "If She knows when we need Her help, then why does She not just help us? I would help someone else if I knew they needed my help."

"And so you have answered your own question," Jesse said. "How would you know if someone needed your help?"

"Well, they would have to ask," Serella said. "Or if someone was in trouble, I would hear them scream, or cry, or. . . . . . . something."

"Exactly," Jesse said. "Asking for help in words, screaming, crying, and so many other things are simply ways of asking for help. But if you never ask for it, you cannot really expect to receive it, can you?"

"But She already knows," Serella said. "We should not have to ask for help."

Jesse couldn't help but smile. "Then what about those people who always have to figure things out for themselves because they want to. Because they have a sense of accomplishment when they do it alone?"

"But how do they figure it out alone if the Goddess already knows and gives them the ideas how to accomplish a thing?"

Jesse laughed, arose from the table, and walked over to where Serella still stood. "You are a fast learner, my dear. You make me proud."

"What?"

"Think about it?"

Serella looked at him, an open question on her face, but it only lasted a few moments before she began to laugh. "I understand," she said. "With the Goddess, we never have to ask. We only have to listen and trust in Her and the answers to our dilemmas shall come to us in the form of thoughts and ideas."

"Wonderful," Jesse said. "I knew you would understand."

"Alright, then what about us being individuals and not just one big entity who is temporarily split into smaller ones."

Jesse took a step back. "I told you, Serella. She is lonely without us. It makes her happy to experience our relationships, our life journeys whether in the physical or the celestial. No one is ever truly happy alone."

"I am," Serella said.

"I know," Jesse said. "That is because your closest relationship is already with the Great Mother, as you called Her. You feel Her presence in the wolves that are around you every day, and the herbs you grow in your garden. She is always by your side and you are always aware of it. Think clearly, Serella, then tell me you are happy alone. What if you did not have all that surrounds you and fills your life?"

"Yes," Serella said. "I see the truth in your words."

"It is because you feel the Goddess beside you."

"Never more so than right now," Serella said, smiling.

"And that is precisely why I was sent here. If you are feeling a stronger bond with Her, then I am accomplishing my work."

"I still have to ask you, though." Serella turned to stare at the moonlight out the window. "Why is it that we do not remember our true home, our true selves when we come here? Life time to life time, we come here and are unable to remember unless we are raised in such a way that our parents assist us in the remembering." She turned to face him. "Why are we not born with that memory, Jesse? What kind of sense does that make?"

Jesse couldn't help but chuckle. "Some people are born to remember it all," Jesse said as he stood up. "But most are not because it would prevent them from experiencing the trials and tribulations, the joys and sorrows they chose to experience in each incarnation." He walked over to where she stood, watching the moonlight's reflection in her hair as he approached her. "How hard would you try to solve a problem if you knew that it truly did not matter since you would still be going home? How hard would you try to learn anything if you knew the worst that could happen is that you would simply have to come back and do it all over, again? Why would anyone bother to get it right this time? Or the next time?" He felt his hand begin to move toward the strands of hair that hung down her back, felt his pulse begin to race as he touched the furthest tip of blonde hair that lay across the pinkish-gray of her dress, then he stopped himself and turned away. "I will have to leave soon," he said as he began to walk away once more. "It has already grown quite dark and I will need a light to make my way as it is."

Serella turned to him. "I have no trouble allowing you to spend the night here," she said.

Jesse shook his head. "I cannot do such a thing. It would be indecent. I simply cannot." Serella approached him with the grace of a cougar approaching the kill and for the first time, Jesse was unsettled by her presence. "I cannot stay and I will not stay," he said, again.

Serella smiled, then softly shrugged her shoulders. "Suit yourself, Jesse. But it would only make sense. We have not finished with our studies for today, yet and I have much to do in the garden tomorrow. I would be much happier to continue teaching you about my studies in the nature arts and to go on learning from you about the powers of the spirit and the Goddess."

Jesse thought for a moment, looking around the room as he did so. He was truly in no hurry to be anywhere but here, in her presence, in her home, learning all there was to know about this beautiful woman, this beautiful soul. "Let us continue until we are too tired to go on," he said, smiling. "I can tell you that I have a few more hours in me."

Serella smiled. "That makes me happy, Jesse. Now tell me more about using our will to create something from nothing. I assume that all comes from the Creator, as well."

"Yes, it does," Jesse said. "That is exactly how She created the whole universe. It was just a simple thought that allowed her to do it all."

"And do I have that kind of power, too?"

"Everyone does," Jesse said. "But no one truly believes it. And belief is the key ingredient in making such things happen. But the credit for such things must always be given to the Creator. Anything that a human being does is allowed and made possible by God."

"Goddess," Serella corrected him, smiling.

Jesse smiled back at her. "Same entity," he said. "You know what I meant."

Chapter 11

March 8 12:00AM

JESSE returned to his kitchen and fixed himself a special cup of herbal tea: chamomile mixed with lemon verbena to relax and help him prepare for meditation with the Creator. Serella was playing games with him, confusing him, but he needed direction and answers. He knew he could choose to handle the upcoming situation however he saw fit, but he wasn't feeling strong enough these days. For whatever reason, he wasn't as sure of himself as he'd been in past situations. And there was no doubt in his mind that he didn't have all the information required in order to figure out what was going on with Roni and Serella's recent appearance. There were too many blanks and he needed them all to be filled in.

He finished his tea, then went to sit on the porch where there were no walls, no physical barriers of any kind to separate him from his destination. The cooler air would keep his body alert while his spirit traveled to the other side. Now that he'd decided to make the journey, he found himself growing excited with anticipation.

He sat in the lotus position on a carpet he kept out there just for times when he chose to meditate. He placed his hands, palms up, to rest on his knees, thus opening himself up to the journey. He watched the stars blink, listened to the water lap along the sand, and thought about home. The peace of that realm moved through him almost instantly and he felt the love that fed it as it enveloped his very essence. He closed his eyes and let himself go to the Source of all the calming warmth he suddenly found himself wrapped within. When he felt the ethereal gold cord that connected him to the Creator pull on his torso, he opened his eyes and saw it stretch far into the distance and disappear. The light was before him in an instant. A single ray appeared, then another, and another until he was surrounded by the purest clarity there ever was. It was not a color. It was clear; clearer than crystal. It was like nothing he had ever seen on earth because it only existed here with the Creator. Being in the presence of such perfection made Jesse miss his time in this magnificent place. He let himself soak it in and pampered himself with the luxury of where he was. He didn't rush his search for information. Rather, he allowed himself to be replenished with the energy that gave life to everything. And he was catered to as any servant of God would be after returning home. Right this minute all he wanted to do was stay and never leave again. Here, he was safe where none of the evil that he'd encountered on earth could reach him. Oh, to just exist in Heaven, forever. He sighed. That was not his purpose, but he was thankful for the acceptance he received with this long-awaited return.

He looked up into the depth of the light. "Father?" He waited. He did not hear a sound, but rather felt a nod of assent and knew he should continue. "I've come to you for guidance. As you know, I've been visited by Serella Stone who has warned me of impending evil approaching. Those in my care are in its path." He looked around at the clear nothingness that protected him. "But you know that," he said. Suddenly, it all seemed too complicated to explain to an entity who knew everything. He shook his head and looked back into the depth of the light. "What am I to do?" He waited, allowing himself to feel settled as the words came to him.

"You have done well so far," the Voice said. "You know I am behind your decisions. I am with you and every step you take."

Jesse smiled, his heart beat warm in his soul. "I know, but it comforts me to hear you say it. What about Serella? Am I to listen to her? What is her purpose in coming to see me? She distracts me." He paused, not wanting to ask too many questions at one time, but the answer came quick.

"She distracts you because you love her still," the Voice told him. "Do not be embarrassed. Love is not a sin, my child. *I* am not a sin. Serella visits you of her own free will and the knowledge she has gained in her search."

Jesse was surprised. "What search?"

"For information in order to protect and help you." A laugh seemed to emanate from somewhere within the energy that spoke to him. "She loves you too, Jesse, as she should."

Jesse waited, but did not receive any more information. "So, what she tells me is true? Then why does she play games with me? I only need to get my instruction from you. Why is she stepping in this time?"

There seemed to be a huge smile all around him before the Voice spoke. "Serella is only exercising the free will I gave to all of you. Do not be angry with her. Her intentions are good. She wants to help you, but she also wants you here with her."

"I know what she wants," Jesse said. "What do you want from me?"

"I want you to make your own decisions with a clear conscience and a good heart, Jesse. That's all I want."

"And what about the evil?" Jesse asked. "Am I to defeat this new problem that approaches?"

"Do you wish to?"

"Of course I do," Jesse said without hesitation. "I can't allow those under my guidance to be effected by it."

"Then do as your heart instructs. That's where you'll find my advice when you ask for it, as well."

Jesse nodded. "And what of Roni?" he asked. "Can she be healed as Serella said?"

Once again, Jesse felt the overwhelming smile that seemed to encircle his very being. "You already know it to be true."

"Then what will it take to make it happen?" Jesse asked.

Immediately, there was an enormous embrace of warmth like nothing he'd ever experienced. "The faith and confidence Serella spoke of."

"That's all?"

"It must be two-fold. Faith and confidence in me; faith and confidence in the knowledge that my presence exists in the self. These two principles are simple, but very strong, very effective when they're powered with honest humility. That's the only way they can bring about the desired outcome. That's what Roni must understand. There can be no underlying motive other than the truth and it cannot be for any form of evil. I will know."

Jesse nodded, knowing the one question he was here to ask still sat at the edge of his mind.

"Ask me," the Voice said. "I cannot impose my words unless you do."

Jesse felt himself take a deep breath back in his physical body on his front porch even as his spirit received a surge of strength from the energy around him. "Are Audra and Minotti still in Limbo?"

"No," the Voice said. "Audra never was in Limbo, but Minotti still lies there."

Jesse didn't understand. "Why wasn't Audra put there?"

"No one is put anywhere. Audra brought her own existence to this side as all my children do. She burns among the flames of her own anger and evil intentions."

"And Minotti?"

"He is in Limbo because there was no other place for evil of his kind. Even those who burn of their own choosing could not exist on this side with him in their midst. He is where he chose to be."

That was not the answer Jesse expected to hear. "Minotti chose to be in Limbo? How is that possible? Why would he?"

"Not chose in the way you are thinking," the Voice said. "He chose it by his extreme actions on earth.

You know I cannot destroy myself, Jesse. All energy is of me, including his. But only the energy that remains pure can be reunited with me, here where you are. Energy that becomes tainted must be made clean and so it is recycled until it becomes so. There is no other way. Energy such as Minotti's has no other place to go but where he is now. While on earth, he existed outside of everything around him. Therefore, while he's here he will exist outside of everything around him until he can be cleansed."

Jesse nodded. It was beginning to make sense to him, finally. "Then is Audra the one behind Roni's illness?" He felt the light around him grow.

"Audra manipulates the disease, but she did not create it."

"I understand," Jesse said. "But why is Audra involved at all?"

"Her desire is to hurt Christian through the one he loves the most."

"Why?"

"For sending her to this side."

Jesse thought about it. He could handle Audra if that was the only concern. "So Minotti will not be involved. He's under control. Is that so?"

"No."

"I don't understand," Jesse said, feeling frustrated. "If he's in Limbo, then how is it possible for him to have anything to do with this?"

"Jesse, you know that all energy is inherently good with a deep desire to purify itself so as to be with me where it all began."

Jesse nodded.

"Limbo is a place where energy goes, knowing it has to rest and pull itself together before it can go on. It's a place for the kind of life that has gone so far astray it cannot see a clear path to get back to the right way, so they stay there until the energy has dispersed on its own, gone back out into the universe, and been tranformed into other things. But energy such as Minotti's has no real desire to be cleansed so his time in Limbo is limited. He isn't existing there in order to be made clean. He is simply there because there is no other place for his energy to go in the meantime until he's ready to return to the physical."

Jesse shook his head, not able to accept what he was hearing. "You are the most powerful. You are the Creator of all, including Minotti. Why can't you control him while he's in Limbo?"

"Jesse. I gave you all free will, including Minotti. He still makes his own choices and if those choices lead to his own destruction, then so be it."

"But what about the destruction of others? That's what we're facing right now."

"I can't stop Minotti from doing harm any more than I could stop a human being from doing harm. It is still their choice and they make such a decision knowing in their truest self that it will return to them."

"But you have allowed your messengers to step in many times and prevent harm and disasters. What's the difference, now?"

"Calm down, my son. This is no difference. You and all my messengers are able to step in because of prayer. I have always said to simply ask. You know that. You have *always* known that. You are too close to this situation because of your great love for those who are involved and I commend you for it. It's what I would expect from you and I'm well pleased."

"Thank you," Jesse said, bowing his head in reverence. "But I feel inadequate to be able to handle this, now."

"You are well equipped. You have me. There is nothing else you need. Just do not forget to ask as so many others do. And be patient. My help is always there."

Jesse nodded, sensing that the time for him to leave was drawing near. "Thank you for taking this time with me."

The overwhelming smile surrounded him before the Voice spoke. "I have all the time that exists, Jesse. Never feel as if you are imposing. I am here for all of you."

Jesse felt the hesitation, but didn't know if it was a cue for him to speak.

"Is there something else?" the Voice asked.

Jesse thought for a moment. "I don't believe there is. Why? Am I forgetting something?"

"It doesn't matter," the Voice said. "If you think of it later, you know how to contact me. Just reach me through your heart."

Jesse smiled. "I will." He watched the light flicker, then retreat. When it was no more than a pin point, he directed his consciousness back to his body where it rested and waited on his porch. The re-entry was something of a shock when he opened his eyes and realized how small and confining his body felt now that he'd experienced the freedom of the spirit realm, once again. But he felt better knowing he could still travel safely between the worlds. In fact, he felt renewed and whole. On a physical level, he felt stronger than he remembered ever feeling since his earthly missions began. Even his emotions felt so much more under control.

He stood and walked to the stairs where he watched the first sparks of the early morning sun as it began its low ascent to the morning sky. It was symbolic. What he felt was a fresh start to all that he'd encountered with Serella and the many adversaries he'd dealt with in past years. Maybe he'd been too hard on Serella. Maybe he'd been way off the mark in trying to figure out what her true motives might be. The Father had just told him how simple it all really was. Serella had been spending her time looking for ways to help him. He had no right to be suspicious of her. Everything she'd told him was true. Well, almost everything. She was able to tell him much more than she did and she could've told him what she knew much faster than she did. He smiled. What if she truly didn't have all the answers? Just because she was on the other side didn't mean she knew all there was to know.

Jesse laughed out loud. "Oh, Serella," he said to the morning sun. "What have you been doing to me? You silly soul." The Father was right. He did still love her and he always had. And her feelings for him were still the same. Maybe their love wasn't so forbidden after all? What had ever given Jesse the idea that it was? Ignorance? He nodded to himself. Ignorance and his attempts to be perfect in God's eyes. "I understand, now," he yelled to the ocean.

He sat down on the top stair of the porch and sighed. Well, he knew what Serella was really about. But what about Audra? What about Minotti? From what the Creator had just told him, Audra was the biggest threat. Then why couldn't he get rid of the feelings of forebodence where Minotti was concerned? That's what he wanted to ask the Father. What were the chances of Minotti waking up in Limbo and deciding he might like to float around with Audra and others who exist in the flames? He could do this. And what would happen then?

"Father?" Jesse said out load. "What then?"

He waited, but only felt a gentle, morning breeze.

"Father, I'm asking. What are the chances of this happening?"

Again, he waited, only feeling the breeze, but this time it stung. Stung? A moment ago it was a cool, gentle breeze. That's it! The Universe was trying to get his attention. When did he stop listening to the words of the Creator through His creations? The wind. The sky. Things suddenly out of the ordinary. Minotti was out of the ordinary. There was no place for him, even on the other side of life. He was restless. Jesse could feel it. Minotti was up to something, but what? Jesse looked up to the sky. "Father, why can't you just answer me in words. What is Minotti up to?"

He waited, then suddenly on the arms of the growing breeze, he heard it. "Minotti is aware of everything," the Voice said. "Be alert."

Jesse stood up, the blood suddenly rushing through his veins as if it was being forced. It made his head temporarily dizzy and he grabbed the rail for support. The two of them? Working together? If Minotti was so aware of what Audra was doing to Roni, then what might it cause to happen if Minotti were to join forces with her? He had to warn the others. He had to let them know about his visit with the father. The one thing he knew for sure. Whatever this new situation turned into, whatever it took to resolve it, he could do this. There was no doubt about it, now. He was an angel and he was well equipped to do an angel's work.

Chapter 12

March 8 3:00PM

THERE he was. Floating in a void of his own creation just as Audra wandered through the flames of her desires, her own personal inferno. In a partial fetal position he lay, surrounded by nothing but open space. She stared at him in admiration for his evil strength. He was magnificent, and she would be, too very soon.

Audra began her first attempt to absorb Minotti's energy as she had done to all the souls who had crossed her path among the flames. But while the other souls gave in easily, Minotti's energy held its ground and would not allow itself to be moved or manipulated. Audra admired that even more. It showed the intensity of his will. Still, she tried again, concentrating with every ounce of strength she now possessed, but she could not budge his evil mass. In fact, the mere effort had already begun to drain her as if she'd actually been battling with him. But that couldn't be since he was not conscious of his predicament. Could he be this strong even in such a seemingly defenseless state? What kind of entity was he if he held that amount of power? Whatever he was, there was no doubt that Audra wanted him on her side, working with her.

Since she couldn't take his energy, Audra decided she might as well try to wake him and force his release from his prison in Limbo. If it worked, he'd be obligated to help her and he'd be right to repay her by helping her get rid of Christian and Samuel.

She floated amidst the blazing hatred and tried to will his spirit to come closer. There was no drain on her energy this time, but he did not move, either. He remained exactly where he was the first time she found him, and no matter how hard she tried to move him, she failed. She threw her arms up in frustration and shook a fist at him as if it was his fault she was getting no where. The frustration fed her anger, and her anger fed the malice that grew in her every time she heard her name mentioned by those on earth who had put her here. They shouldn't even be alive and able to talk about her. They shouldn't be aware of anything enough to be able to think of her. And she wasn't going to waste any more time on something she obviously wasn't strong enough to succeed at yet. Minotti could wait a little longer. She had to have his strength and she'd find a different way to get it. Nothing was going to stop her from having access to power of his caliber.

One more glance in Minotti's direction was enough to make her turn around and walk back into the flames in search of the strength left among the remaining souls she still hadn't found. Minotti could stay where he was for the time being. He wasn't in her way, and that was just as well for now.

* * *

"We had to do the family thing, first. But I think we'll be able to have a small gathering of friends to celebrate your engagement in about two weeks," Roni said, handing Chelle a glass of Pepsi. "How does that sound?"

"It sounds like fun," Chelle said. "But you don't have to go to all that trouble. I don't want you wasting your energy on this." Concern was evident in her face, even though she smiled when she looked at Roni. "We're just going to have a small ceremony, so we don't want to make all this preliminary stuff bigger than it has to be."

Roni sat in the living room chair and listened to Chelle do her best to hide her secret fears that a party would drain Roni of the strength she might need to get better. Their kind of friendship carried an unspoken shield of protection that never allowed hurt feelings. This was no exception. "I know, but we've been waiting for this," Roni said. "I'm as excited for you as I'd be for myself. I have to do this for you." She leaned forward and placed a hand on Chelle's. "I want to do this."

Chelle fiddled with the black drawstring that hung loosely around her neck and smiled. "Alright. Go ahead. I won't argue."

Roni was relieved. "It won't be any bigger than you want it to be. We'll have it here and only invite who you choose. Does that sound comfortable?"

"It does," Chelle said, taking a drink of her soda. "I'm even starting to like the idea."

Roni laughed, leaning back in the living room chair. "Well, that didn't take long."

"Oh, I really wanted something like that," Chelle admitted, sporting a sheepish grin. "I just didn't think it was proper to ask."

"Ask your best friend?" Roni pushed her chair away from the table. "Be serious, Chelle." She stood to grab the bottle of Pepsi from the counter, but just as she turned, her right leg gave out and she fell, hitting the kitchen floor with a terrible thump. The pain that shot up through the entire side of her body was excruciating.

In a moment Chelle was by her side helping her sit up. "Are you alright? What happened?" Chelle's arm came around behind Roni and held her in place where she sat on the floor.

"My leg," Roni said, pushing on the area of most pain. "The pain won't go." Roni began to cry. "This isn't supposed to be happening, yet. Dr. Reno said he didn't expect it to get any worse than it already was for a long time." Roni felt as if she was falling apart inside. She couldn't think straight all of a sudden and nothing made sense. She'd never expected anything like this to happen to her life and she was doing a terrible job trying to handle it. In fact,she wasn't handling it at all, but she didn't understand why.

"Here, let me help you."

Chelle began to pull her up, but the pain went through Roni like a bolt of electric heat. "No," Roni nearly yelled. "Just let me sit a minute." Her tears were falling non-stop, uncontrollable. "Why is this happening to me? This isn't right."

Chelle rubbed her back as she sat next to her on the kitchen floor. "I'm going to call Dr. Reno right now." She started to stand, but Roni grabbed her arm.

"No, not yet," Roni said. "Please, not yet."

Chelle sat back down and stared at Roni. "Why not? You're in pain, Roni. This isn't going to go away just because you want it to. You have to get serious about your health, now."

"Not yet," Roni said, again.

Chelle looked at her with a concerned expression spread across her face that only made Roni cry more. "Why don't you want me to call him?" Chelle asked. "Tell me, Roni. What's really going on here?"

Roni grabbed the arm of her friend's black, fleece jacket and did her best to control her sobs long enough to speak. It took a full minute, but finally her breathing was under control. "I don't want Christian to know," she said. "I don't want him to find out how bad it's getting."

"Don't you think he already knows?" Chelle asked, stroking Roni's hair to comfort her. "Even if he won't read through your thoughts, Samuel and Diana don't share the same morals as Christian. I'm sure one of them has told him."

Roni stared at the floor, realizing Chelle was probably right. "He hasn't said anything about it, if they did. I've been doing a good job hiding it from him, except for the night when he came home with Samuel and saw Diana helping me up. Other than that, I've been keeping it to myself pretty good."

Chelle shook her head. "Roni, you're only fooling yourself. You can't let it go and not do anything. And you can't really believe that Christian doesn't know. Even if he isn't reading your thoughts and even if Diana and Samuel haven't told him, he would still be able to sense it. And you're not doing anyone a favor by hiding it. You're going to have to get to the doctor so he can see what's causing this to happen so fast."

Roni looked at her friend. "There's nothing they can do, Chelle. Dr. Reno told me they can only treat the symptoms."

Chelle moved closer to stare directly into Roni's eyes. "Then let him treat the symptoms."

Roni said nothing, but looked at her friend and tried to clear the confusion that had settled in her mind. "Would you please help me to the chair?"

Chelle lifted her under the arms while Roni pulled herself up by the edge of the table.

"Would you rather be on the sofa?" Chelle asked her. "It would be much more comfortable and you could stretch right out and relax."

Roni looked at the chair that was close by, then at the sofa. "I can get to the sofa," she said. "The pain is going away slowly."

"Is it?" Chelle asked. "Or is it just getting numb?"

The smile that crossed Roni's lips was impossible to prevent. Chelle knew her far too well. "Just get me to the sofa."

Chelle shook her head and laughed, helping support Roni until she was comfortably seated in the living room. "Better?"

"Much."

Chelle went back to the kitchen and brought their Pepsi's in to the living room, then sat down at the end of the sofa near Roni's feet.

"Massage, too?" Roni teased.

Chelle slapped her ankle playfully. "You wish. You're on the sofa. Thank your stars I got you here."

Roni used her arms to prop herself up a bit, then glanced briefly at Chelle. She was feeling vulnerable in her weakened state and she knew it, but she was grateful for Chelle's friendship and there was no denying how lucky she was to have it.

"What?" Chelle asked, sipping her Pepsi.

"Nothing," Roni said. "I'm just very lucky to have a friend like you."

Chelle smiled and looked at her. "Ditto."

* * *

Audra stood among the empty flames, void of most of the souls who had come here to rest and spend their time in a self-imposed punishment. She had absorbed the living spirit of all those she passed on her way through, then stopped to peek in on Roni's condition. She wanted to try out her new powers, her new strengths and see how far she could push someone in the physical. She saw the two friends seated at the table and she watched them for a short time while she thought about what to do to Roni next. A slight heart attack? That might be fun. Or maybe she should make her black out and hit her head on the counter. She was enjoying herself so much as she was dreaming up ideas that she was startled when she saw Roni suddenly fall. How did that happen? She didn't have anything to do with it this time. Could it be that the mere desire was enough? The mere thought to cause more pain, more harm, was all it took for it to happen? Amazing! Things were so much simpler to accomplish from this side.

"Do not fool yourself into thinking you had anything to do with that little episode you just witnessed."

The voice came from directly behind her and was so deep and malevolent it made Audra cringe in fear. She didn't even want to turn around, but instead waited for some kind of devastating pain to pierce her, some kind of apocalyptic event to destroy her, but it didn't happen.

"What's the matter, Audra? You've been looking for me, calling to me. Did you think I didn't hear you?"

She turned around slowly, afraid of what she might see; afraid of what he might do. But she turned, bracing herself as she did so and there he was. Eyes so black they held no light. Thick hair that fell like a stately mane, wild around his face. But the demeanor, the entire field of life that surrounded him was, in reality, a field of death, so intense it made the flames around them seem to die into water. "Minotti." She just knew. He was everything she'd learned he was and more. Just being near him put the fear of annihilation into her, a feeling she had never known.

"Are you surprised?" His form shifted around her, seeming to come apart, pull her in to itself, then reform before her.

"I was told you were in Limbo for an indefinite period." Audra found it difficult to keep her thoughts focused, but she had to pull herself together. She had to show him that she was his equal and could handle a successful partnership with him. "Did you do that to the little wench, Roni?"

His smile was fierce with the look of a killer knowing the next step would bring his prey within pouncing distance. "That I did," he said. "Beautiful, wasn't it? Would you like to see more?" He turned as if to look toward a specific goal, but Audra stopped him.

"Not yet," she said. "First, tell me. How did you get out of Limbo?"

"Why is that important?" he asked, releasing a hideous laugh.

Audra looked at him, not yet knowing how to react in the presence of such power. "Are you that strong that the laws of the universe can't even hold you?"

Minotti stopped laughing and let his eyes bore right through her. "I use the laws of the universe," he said. "That is my strength. What you cannot change or control you must learn to use and manipulate. That is where true power comes from."

"Are you willing to join me. . ." Audra began, but Minotti silenced her by suddenly raising his hand.

"I already know what you are planning," he said. "And I will work with you to bring about the demise of those you bear your strong hatred for. But know this," he waved a hand across the flames and a picture of a man appeared before her.

Audra knew who the man was. She'd seen him before. He was there the night Christian destroyed her earthly body.

"When the time comes for me to meet with Nestarius, it will be him and me, alone," Minotti said.

Audra looked at the picture in the flames of Jesse sitting on his porch, then to Minotti. "I have no interest in him," she said. "Christian and Samuel are the two I mean to destroy."

Minotti waved the picture of Jesse away and the flames returned. "I know what you're up to. I've been listening to your thoughts since I first heard Christian's name enter your anger. I know everything you have done and everything you're planning to do."

"Then why didn't you come to me sooner if you knew all that?" She felt her anger boil around and through her. "Why did you let me go through all that I did calling to you and searching around for souls to absorb?" No longer did she feel intimidated or frightened by him. Now, she would just as soon kill him too, if she could. "I do not take lightly to being made a fool of."

Again, the hideous laughter bellowed from deep within Minotti's soul. "You make a fool of yourself," he said. "Never think you are smarter, than someone else."

Audra sent slivers of hatred through his spirit before she spoke. "It wasn't very smart of you to fight Jesse in a sanctified place. A church of all things. What were you thinking? You wouldn't be here right now if you'd been using your head."

Minotti gored her soul with his vision, then let go. "If I wasn't defeated there, then I wouldn't be here in the middle of all the power that exists. It's all at my disposal now. I have access to every metaphysical truth there ever was. I have access to all the possiblities in the universe and throughout eternity. What did I do that was stupid? I wasn't afraid of being defeated because I always knew it would only lead to my ultimate superiority." He shook his evil, ethereal head and turned from her. "You underestimate me as you have underestimated everyone you've ever known." He turned back to fully encircle her with his harsh essence. "But you will learn, my dear. Because I need your conniving intentions to meld with mine. We share a hatred and a purpose. Together, our strengths are more than any other entity, any other army of entities could ever hope to defeat." He stopped and hovered before her with the flames, now turned silver as liquid mercury, crackling and burning around them. "Together, my dear, we are truly invincible."

PART II

"Look to this day!
For it is life, the very life of life.
In its brief course lie all the truths and
realities of existence. . . . ."

Unknown

Chapter 1

April 27 4:00PM

RONI walked out to the back deck with a tray of spinach, feta cheese, and tomato au d'eauvres in her left hand and leaned on the door frame for support with her right. It was unseasonably warm for a late afternoon spring day and she couldn't help but enjoy the earthy scents that were all around in the fresh air. A cool breeze brushed by her as she placed the tray on the wooden table, then sat in a lawn chair by the deck railing next to Chelle. She felt better today than she had felt in the past few weeks and she was thankful that her new cane was able to stay tucked away in the bedroom closet.

"How are you doing?" Chelle asked, watching her movements with a concerned eye. "Feeling alright?"

Roni smiled and leaned back in her chair. She looked out into the wooded yard and marveled at the beauty of the April flowers all over that grew everywhere. "Better than I've been in a while," Roni said. "Are you enjoying your party? You should be mingling, not sitting here babysitting me." She patted Chelle's arm and looked right into her eyes. "I'm fine, Chelle. Go talk to these people. Your parents are here and you've hardly spent any time with them at all."

Chelle looked toward the other end of the deck where most of her family had chosen to congregate, and waved her hand through the air. "They're fine," she said. "They're all together and I have actually spent a few hours with my parents, my brother and his wife, and my sister and her family. I need to relax, now. This socializing thing is too much like work."

Roni laughed and shook her head. "You're too much," she said, checking around the yard for Joe. She located him at the edge of the trees where the woods began and nodded in his direction. "He seems to be fitting right in," she said, watching him joke with a few of Chelle's cousins.

"Oh, he fits in everywhere he goes," Chelle said. "He's just that type. I've got to tell you, though. I'm touched that your parents are here. I never expected them to travel all the way from Arizona just to come to our engagement party."

Another breeze drifted softly past them, ruffling the napkins on the table and brushing Roni's hair behind her shoulders. "I'm standing up for you," Roni said, glancing at her friend. "It's important for them to see it, to be there."

Chelle was silent, but the message was understood. Roni's mother was concerned for her daughter's failing health and didn't want to miss a moment of her life right now.

"What did you tell your family about why Christian is still sleeping?" Chelle asked. "Or didn't you tell them anything at all?"

Roni smiled at her overly practical friend. "I told them he's been doing so much to help me get ready for this party that he exhausted himself," Roni said, looking around to make sure no one was listening. "No one questioned that. Besides, he'll be awake soon. The sun doesn't bother him as long as it's diffused." She turned toward Chelle. "You know that."

Chelle nodded, but seemed to be more interested in something other than their conversation.

Roni turned to see what had grabbed Chelle's attention and was pleasantly surprised to see her old friend walk out on to the back deck. "Father Larry," she said, standing up to greet him. She could see the pain he felt in his joints reflected in his eyes as he walked gingerly toward her with the aid of Father O'Manley from St. Joseph's. Father Larry's face showed his age and his discomfort, but he still had that beautiful Santa Claus smile that everyone agreed had become his trade mark. "I can't even believe you made it," Roni said, leaning forward to hug him. "I'd heard you weren't feeling well."

Father Larry smiled at her, then looked at Chelle who had also stood to welcome him. She had just finished motioning to Joe to come join her when Father Larry reached his right hand toward her and took her arm. "This is my golden opportunity to bring Chelle back in to the arms of the church," he said, only half-joking. "You know I'm retiring in July." He looked at both of them as if he were waiting for a response. "My health has made it difficult for me to fulfill my duties and has limited all of my social activities, as well."

"I'd heard that about you," Roni said. "Who will be taking your place there?"

"Father O'Manley here has already been named to the position," Father Larry said, pride and pain mixed in his eyes. He turned to look at Chelle. "Congratulations on your engagement," he said just as Joe approached. "Father O'Manley told me you'd been in to make arrangements for the ceremony."

"Thank you, Father." Chelle pulled Joe close to her and looked at the two priests who stood before her. "We also told Father O'Manley that if there was any way possible to involve you in the ceremony, we'd like that."

Father Larry appeared surprised, but smiled, rubbing his round belly with his free hand. "I'd be delighted to make it one of my last official acts," he said. "It would mean so much to me. Thank you for asking."

Chelle and Joe nodded in unison. "You're welcome," they said.

"And this was supposed to be a simple ceremony," Roni teased them.

"Which brings up another matter," Father Larry said, teetering slightly where he stood.

Father O'Manley reached forward to steady him. "Why don't you sit, Father." He turned to face Roni as he helped lower Father Larry to a seat. "As you can see, we won't be able to stay long, but Father Larry insisted on being here for this celebration. He told me how close you've all been these past few years."

Roni and Chelle both returned to their seats as well. "And I'm glad you brought him," Roni said. "I know you must've gone out of your way to make sure he would be alright."

"Oh, don't make such a fuss," Father Larry said, positioning himself for comfort. "I'm just fine. But there is one matter I'd like to discuss with you, if you have a moment. This may not be the best time, but my time is so limited these days, that I'm forced to make good use of what I have available."

"That's not a problem," Roni said, smiling. "What do you need, Father?"

"Oh, it's not really what I need so much as it is what you and Christian might need," Father Larry said.

Chelle stood up and placed a hand on Father Larry's shoulder. "I think we'd better go talk to the family and leave you two alone," Chelle said. She motioned toward where the rest of her family sat. "I'll be right there if you need me, Roni."

"Thank you," Roni said.

Chelle nodded, turned around, and walked over to the other end of the deck with Joe by her side.

Father O'Manley stood up, too. "I'm going to grab a plate of food. Would you like me to put one together for you, too, Larry?"

Father Larry looked at him and smiled. "Of course, I would, Stephen. You already know that." He chuckled to himself, rubbing his belly with both hands this time.

Father O'Manley walked over to the tables that were set up on the lawn alongside the deck for the buffet and began to fill two plates at once. Roni watched for a few moments, then turned back to face Father Larry.

"Have you told him about Christian?" Roni asked, searching Father Larry for his reaction.

He looked at her, smiled, then looked away. "Not yet, I haven't. To tell you the truth, I wasn't sure how. I even thought it might be your place to tell him since it might never be necessary. I might just be jumping the gun a bit if I told him now. You could all get to know each other better and give Stephen, . . er . . Father O'Manley, a chance to like him as a mortal first. It might be easier." Father Larry shook his head and smiled. "I honestly didn't know how to go about it."

Roni nodded, looking toward the woods. "I expect he'll ask questions about us living together sooner or later."

Father Larry turned to her and leaned back, rubbing his belly with one hand. "Which brings me to another matter I wanted to discuss with you."

Roni pulled her pink cardigan tighter around her, then tilted her head slightly in question. "What is it, Father?"

"Well, my child," he said, looking around as if he didn't know exactly how to phrase what he wanted to say. "You and Christian are in a unique position with your Catholic upbringing and his . . . uh. . . . ," he looked around discreetly, then leaned toward Roni. "With his vampirism." He sat back up straight and cleared his throat. "And I'm retiring shortly." He looked up at her, his eyes fluttering nervously. "What I'm trying to say is that I'd like to marry the two of you."

Roni sat back and stared at him in shock and disbelief. "I thought you couldn't do that, Father. How would you ever register such a thing with the church?"

Father Larry smiled, obviously more relaxed now that his thoughts had been spoken. "I've given it much thought and I've come up with a valid solution. Christian is originally from a small town in France. For all intents and purposes, Roni, he's a foreigner. And since blood tests are no longer required in

Massachusetts, and since interfaith marriages are quite common and accepted within the church nowadays, I don't see that it would be a problem to register the whole marriage as just what it is. And it would prevent Father O'Manley from having reason to involve himself in your relationship, or from knowing the truth about Christian."

"Christian is Catholic, as well," she said.

Father Larry nodded. "I know he is, but we can't prove it. There were no records of that sort kept as far back as nearly six hundred years." He appeared thoughtful for a moment as he stretched his legs out before him. "It just seemed easier to handle it as an interfaith situation." He looked at her. "He is an American citizen, isn't he?"

Roni sat back and let out a small laugh. She could see the mischief in Father Larry's eyes and the pride he felt in having come up with a plan to bond the love she and Christian shared in the eyes of God. It was so crucial to Father Larry to create a marriage that would be recognized by the church and to protect Christian at the same time. "I imagine he must be," she said. "I never thought to ask."

Father Larry chuckled and waved a hand in the air. "Regardless, we'll treat this situation exactly as it is."

Roni was amused at the serious air Father Larry had about him. "And what is it?"

"Why, my child," Father Larry said. "This is simply a marriage between a Frenchman and a Roman Catholic American girl." He looked at her, so pleased with himself and beaming with excitement that Roni had to laugh out loud.

"Father," she said, "I love it. Now we just have to see what the Frenchman has to say about it."

Father Larry nodded. "He'll be awake soon, as you said. We can discuss it with him at that time, or at a later date if you wish. But I think it will be perfect."

"What made you think of this now, though?" Roni asked him. "We have discussed it before."

Father Larry shifted in his chair and smiled. "I'm getting old," he said. "I've reached an age where I am only answerable to myself and to God, and I don't see how either of us can find fault with honoring true love."

Roni was touched beyond measure. "Thank you."

Father Larry nodded, his eyes twinkling as he began to form the words, "You're welcome," but they were interrupted.

"Father Larry." Roni's parents were headed toward them.

Roni stood. "Father Larry, why don't you visit with my folks for a bit while I go check on the food rations." She looked around, then bent down closer to him. "And Christian," she whispered.

Father Larry nodded. "Good idea."

Roni looked up just as her mother approached.

"Do you need anything, Honey?" her mother asked.

Roni smiled and shook her head. "I believe I've got everything under control," she said. "But if you would just sit with Father Larry while I check to make sure, I'd really appreciate it."

"We'd love to," her mother said, taking a seat next to Father Larry while her father took the chair opposite them. "I'll be right here if you need anything."

Roni leaned over and kissed her mother on the cheek. "I know you will," she said. "You're always there."

Her mother blushed, then patted her gently on the cheek. Roni turned and headed toward the sliding glass door that led into the kitchen.

"That was fast," Chelle said, coming up beside her. "What was so important?"

Roni looked at her and squinted. "What makes you think anything was important? You could've stayed to talk."

Chelle shook her head. "Oh, no," she said. "I've known Father Larry a long time, too, you know. I could tell he had something he wanted to discuss with just you."

"OK," Roni said. "He offered to marry Christian and me." She felt Chelle grab her arm and stopped walking just as she approached the door to the kitchen. She looked at her wondering what caused the sudden reaction. "What?"

"Can he do that?" Chelle asked, a shocked expression on her face.

"I don't know," Roni said. "But he seems to think he can. He's retiring so I would imagine he feels he can do this one thing simply because he wants to."

"And he can," Chelle said, opening the door. "He's always been that way. Very determined when he sets his mind to something."

They walked into the eating area of the kitchen and closed the door behind them. It was quiet in the house compared to the voices and music that were going on outside. Roni turned back to see the party as an observer and saw how beautiful the pink and orange rays of the setting sun had become.

"Can I tell you something?" Chelle asked interrupting Roni's admiration of the evening sky.

"Of course you can," Roni said. "You can tell me anything. You know that. What's on your mind?"

Chelle looked nervous. She stood against the counter wringing her hands together and twisting her diamond ring around her finger while she looked at her friend. "I'm pregnant."

"You're what?" Roni felt her eyebrows raise and her eyes open wide. "Does Joe know?"

Chelle shook her head.

"Does anyone know?"

Again, Chelle shook her head. "Only me. And now you."

"How long have you known?"

"Since this morning." Chelle gave her friend a sheepish look that held a hint of guilt.

"Well, you're getting married so what's the problem?"

Chelle looked at her, then glanced out the window at Joe who had gone to sit by Father Larry and Father O'Manley. "None, I guess. Unless Joe isn't ready for it."

Roni leaned forward and hugged Chelle. "Well, I for one am very excited for you." She stood back up straight. "So you might have to move the wedding up a little. No problem. Maybe we'll all end up getting married at the same time."

Chelle gave her a serious look. "Don't laugh. We just might end up doing something like that."

"Something like what?" Christian inquired as he walked into the kitchen, leaned forward to kiss Roni, then stood and looked at Chelle. "You're expecting?" His smile was one of amusement as he smoothed his dark, shoulder length hair back with one hand, then leaned on the back of Roni's chair.

Chelle threw her hands up in the air and turned around, exasperated. "Make that three who know about it."

Christian laughed. "Well, don't you think you should tell Joe?" he teased.

"Stop that," Chelle said, frowning. "I wish you'd respect me and not read my thoughts the way you do for Roni."

Christian rubbed Roni's back and looked at Chelle. "I'm sorry," he said. "I just woke up and didn't get a chance to tune everyone out before your . . uh . . situation entered my mind loud and clear. There was nothing I could do about it."

"Well, remind me not to talk around you when you're sleeping," Chelle said. She stood up from the table and straightened her chinos. Then she took a tray of hot dogs off the counter, grabbed a bag of rolls, and headed for the door. "I'll take care of these for you," she said to Roni, then looked at Christian, a clear warning in her eyes. "Don't you tell a soul about this until I have a chance to tell Joe first." She waved the tray of hot dogs at him. "Do you hear me?" Her hazel eyes held a clear warning.

Christian nodded and laughed once more. "I hear you," he said, smiling.

Chelle opened the door and went outside, closing the sliding door behind her. Roni watched her as she headed toward the stairs that led to the buffet tables on the lawn and began to set the hot dogs out among the other trays. Roni felt a surge of love for her friend who always went out her way to make sure everything in Roni's life was as close to perfect as it could be.

Roni turned to Christian and looked up at him. "Father Larry had an interesting proposal a little while ago."

Christian looked at her for a few moments, then leaned forward to kiss her. "Did it go anything like this?" He took her hand and pressed it against his chest. The black, cotton T-shirt gave Roni a secure, warm feeling. When she looked back up at him, she saw his eyes were glistening and felt the love pour from him to surround her. "Marry me, Veronica," he said. "The only thing I want from all that could happen throughout eternity is to have you as my wife."

Roni stared at him, not knowing how to say all the things that raced through her mind like a waterfall. She felt a tear form and start to roll down her cheek. "Did you talk to Father Larry about this already?" she asked him.

He shook his head, never taking his eyes off hers.

"Then how did he know?"

Christian shrugged, still staring into Roni's eyes.

She stood there, melting into his vision as she tried to form the answer. She felt herself say it, but the sound of the words didn't register in her ears. Why didn't they?

"Because you said it with your heart," Christian told her.

"Hey, you're not supposed to do that," Roni chided him, smiling.

"But you wanted me to," he said. "It was different this time."

"I love you, Christian." She wrapped her arms around his neck and pulled him to meet her lips. "I'll marry you. If Father Larry can pull this off and it's right, then I'll marry you."

Christian pushed her gently away and bore into her soul with his sight. "And what if he can't," he asked. "I still want you for my wife."

"Because I'm sick?" Roni frowned, knowing that had something to do with this whole turn of events.

"Partly," Christian said. "But because I love you and have wanted this since we met. The only thing that stopped us was your desire to be married into your faith and believing it couldn't happen because of me. Now that turmoil can end if Father Larry is really willing to work this through for us." He touched her chin and held her facing him. "Even if he can't, I still want this to be."

Roni looked at him, knowing a decision was needed now. She looked outside at Father Larry who sat on the deck, surrounded by her family and Chelle's family and all their friends, in the center of attention as he liked it. She knew it would be alright, somehow. "It will work." She turned back to Christian. "It will work."

Chapter 2

April 28 3:00PM

JESSE sat on a dried out, drifted log that had washed up on the sandy beach in his front yard. Seagulls floated on the water while others wafted through the early morning air in search of food for the nesting season that had already begun. The air smelled of salt and seaweed, refreshing in the coolness of a pink, spring sunrise. He sighed. What was he doing here? For centuries it had been one battle after another. The worst of them started with Minotti in the thirteenth century when Serella lost her life. Since then, his activities in helping those around him were only intermittenly successful. He remembered when Larry needed help to settle his conscience and remain in the priesthood instead of leaving when he'd practically decided to marry. Larry would have questioned his marriage for the rest of his life and lived in guilt, always wondering if he'd done the right thing by God. That was not the way to spend one's time on earth.

Jesse shook his head as he watched a small group of seagulls land on the shore only a few yards from where he sat. He thought about Audra Trivette and remembered how she had filled Christian's empty life and his longing for love in the sixteenth century, but later played him for her own gain nearly killing him in the process. Jesse sighed. Then Minotti showed up for the second time, kidnapped Diana, and caused Roni's disease all in such a short period of time. These instances just seemed to grow more intense with each occurrence.

He looked across the water and sighed. What good was his presence on earth really doing? He just didn't know, anymore. Jesse put his foot up on the log and leaned his elbow on his knee. Now this whole thing with Audra reappearing at the same time he suspects Minotti is also close by, on the same side, against all those Jesse cares so much about. He shook his head. What good was he accomplishing here except fighting battles that could never truly end? He was tired and had begun to feel as if he was getting nowhere while he watched everyone around him suffer. What was he missing? What was he doing wrong?

Jesse reached over and pulled apart the hunks of bread he'd brought outside with him, then began to throw them in the water and on to the shore for the gulls. He watched them dive and chase each other for the prize possessions of food, then leaned his chin on his hand. Animals were supposed to fight. It was their nature of survival. But what about the life forms that were supposed to be intelligent? Maybe, that very intelligence was a curse for all of God's creations.

He stood up, threw the rest of the bread out for the birds and began to walk along the water's edge where it rolled softly on to the sand. His recent visit back to the other side made him feel calmer just to know he was able to go home whenever he chose and that the Ultimate would welcome him to stay for as long as he needed. It felt right, like it was time for it to happen. He couldn't deny it. He just might decide to go home to stay, very, very soon. It was what he truly wanted after all the centuries spent in the physical. But who would watch over the immortals in his place? He couldn't expect Larry to be there. He would be going home himself, soon. The rest of the humans would follow in their own time. The vampires were the ones he worried about the most. They held the deepest place in his heart because of all the things they'd been through, so similar to that of an angel who had served in the way Jesse had. He almost felt as if he had to provide for their futures before he'd be able to leave, but he also knew it wasn't his call. Whatever was done for them was up to God. He had sent Jesse in the past for that purpose. There was no doubt He would send another in Jesse's place when the time came.

He stopped and stood still, watching a seagull soar right at him. He put his hand out in front of him, then waited for the bird to land on his arm. When it did, he brought it closer to him. The seagull looked at him as if it were thinking, moving its head in sharp, quick motions. Jesse formed sweet bread out of the atmosphere simply from his desire to feed the bird, then handed it to the seagull. He rubbed the bird's head with his finger and waited for a signal that it was ready to go on its way.

"That's very special."

Jesse turned toward the familiar voice, releasing the seagull as he did so. "Hello, Serella. Have you come to bring me more bad news?" He started to stroll the beach again, not caring if she followed or not.

Serella quickly joined him, floating by his side as he walked. "I apologize if it always seems as if I'm no more than the bearer of sorrow," she said. "That is never my intention. It's unfortunate that it took a tense situation like this one to bring me here at all."

Jesse looked to his side, looked at her, and was struck by her beauty. "Then what is it this time?"

Serella held his gaze for a moment, then looked away. "There are some truths you need to know before Audra and Minotti are too deep in their menacing ways," she said. "Things I think you already know, but may have forgotten."

Jesse froze. "So they really are working together. Is Minotti out of Limbo?"

Serella nodded.

"I thought so." He hesitated a moment. "Now what?"

Serella motioned for him to join her as they approached a cropping of flat boulders that lined the edge of the water. "Now you sit and listen to everything I must tell you." She floated toward the rocks and hovered above them. "Things you need to be reminded of."

Jesse nodded and did as she suggested.

* * *

"Shouldn't we stop her?" Audra asked Minotti as they stood together on the beach watching Serella and Jesse.

"No," Minotti said, laughing. "She knows we're here. How far she is willing to go will be interesting and will tell us if she fears the risk."

"Does it matter?" Audra asked, losing her patience. "I have no interest in these. It's Christian and Samuel I want my vengeance on."

Minotti frowned. "My dear, Audra. You must learn to look beyond the obvious. This angel, Jesse, has been at the root of everything that has transpired since long before you and Christian ever met." He turned to face her. "It was he who reunited Christian and Samuel in order to protect him and destroy you."

Audra turned toward Jesse, fire burning deep within her. "How did he know he would need Samuel?"

Minotti laughed his dangerous, malicious laugh. "He's an angel, Audra. He's connected to the Ultimate Force in this entire universe just as you and I are connected to the other side of that force." He turned back toward Jesse and crossed his arms in front of himself. "His only problem is that he's been here among humanity a bit too long. He is uncertain of many things and he's grown tired. He is at his most vulnerable and can be easily defeated."

Audra turned quickly around and flashed a menacing look at him. "What does that have to do with me?" she asked. "All I care about is seeing Christian and Samuel's souls destroyed for all eternity, their hearts broken for good. I don't care about this Jesse."

Minotti shook his head, his black eyes bored through her. "Well, you'd better," he warned her. "He's been their protector and guide. But without him, they're all finished." He laughed. "Now, you tell me. Who would you rather go after first?"

Audra gave him a nasty smile. "I enjoy watching Christian squirm every time Roni's illness grows worse," she said.

Minotti grumbled under his breath. "You play your game with Roni," he said. "You have all the fun you like. But don't take your concentration from the core purpose."

"Which is?"

Minotti stared at her for a brief moment before he spoke. "To destroy all of them."

Audra nodded, smiled, then turned toward Jesse. "And what about her?"

"Serella?" Minotti laughed, but it did not sound as convincing as she would have expected. "What about her?"

"Does she matter in all of this?"

"She might," Minotti said, turning toward her. His face displayed a shadow of concern.

"Why? Who is she, really?"

Minotti's aura turned gray with uncertainty. "The only entity whose thoughts we can't discern," he said, still watching Serella.

"We can't pick up Jesse's thoughts, either," Audra reminded him.

Minotti turned to her. "Jesse's on the physical side, Serella is on our side. I don't worry about the physical because you can see what they're up to. But here, where we are, it is easy to mask your thoughts and your whereabouts." He gazed at Audra as if to warn her from further discussion. "For now, you should enjoy knowing how to come into the physical like I've taught you and get used to maneuvering here. You'll need the dexterity, later. But you can practice another time. Use it to play with Roni." He turned back to watch Serella and Jesse as they sat on the rocks and talked. "Go now, if you like. I need to replenish my own strengths." He looked at her and smiled. "Trust me."

* * *

"What truths are you referring to?" Jesse asked, watching Serella's ethereal movements.

"Ssshhh." Serella put a finger to her lips and smiled.

Jesse nodded.

"When I came to this side that day many years ago, I vowed never to go back to the earth realm," Serella said. "It was my choice as are all of our actions. I didn't want to be tricked by the likes of Gaetano Minotti ever again. I didn't want to be corrupted by that kind of energy. Make no mistake, Jesse. It almost happened back then." She drifted about before him as she spoke. "I wanted to stay here where I felt it was safe, where I could be true to my spirit, myself."

Jesse felt a pang of sorrow for the fear she must have felt at that time, but after all he'd seen, he fully understood. "And was it safer there?"

Serella smiled. "Always."

Jesse nodded. "Go on."

"But I missed you." Serella appeared genuinely sad. "I missed our talks and the feelings we shared. I missed your presence." She looked at him, her eyes appeared to be moistening. "And I wanted so much to go to you and beg you to come home, but I was only newly returned myself and still going through a period of resting from the ordeal I'd been through in the physical. The entities who accompanied me through that time advised me to speak with the Almighty for advice because you are an angel, after all, and under Her direction."

Jesse couldn't imagine her before the presence of God, but he smiled. "And did you?"

She nodded. "She is wonderful to talk to. She listened as if I were the only being in existence and She advised me to make my own choices, but She told me I'd need to understand the nature of what you were doing here before I could make such a choice." Serella paused a moment as if in thought. A flock of seagulls landed nearby and stood as if they too were listening intently to her story. She looked at them and smiled, then turned back to Jesse. "When the Creator was finished explaining to me all that was expected of you, She advised me to think about my decision, but told me that whatever my choice was, it would be acceptable."

Jesse nodded. "Yes," he said. "Free will." He looked up to see Serella watching him as if she had already known he would say exactly what he had just said.

"I thought about it." She went on as if he hadn't spoken. "And I realized that I couldn't come to you ever because I would only get in the way. And I couldn't come back, either, because I'd have to go through a whole new incarnation and start from the beginning, forgetting everything from my previous lives." She stared at him. "Forgetting about you."

Jesse didn't know what to say. He was an angel, his first loyalty to the Creator. This was not a situation he ever expected to find himself in.

Serella shook her head as if she were shaking rain from her hair. "My decision was to stay close to you, Jesse, without ever letting you know." Her gaze made his heart ache for her. "And I did."

"Then what was all the talk about not being allowed to cross back and forth without permission?" Suddenly, Jesse felt betrayed. "What did all that mean when you told me you didn't know certain things, then later you told tell me you lied." Serella's smile only made Jesse angry. "Ever since you showed up I've been confused."

"I appeared to you after all these years because I knew the danger you and all you love are facing. I knew what has headed this way." She glided toward him and hovered inches away. "I love you," she said. "I always have." She reached out and let her arm slide right through his heart. "Now you know me for real."

Jesse nodded. He felt her truth, her love for him, her reason for staying away and not accepting another incarnation. And he knew he could trust her. "Yes," he said. "Now I know you for real."

Serella smiled and removed her arm from his chest.

"Is the Father alright with your decision to cross between the worlds?"

She nodded.

Jesse looked out across the water. "He is very accepting. More so than I remember. Maybe I have been here too long."

"You only stayed because you care so much for these vampires," Serella told him. "And they do live a long time."

Jesse looked at her.

"But even they don't really live forever," Serella said. "Not in the physical."

Jesse nodded. "So now what happens? What is the plan? What are Audra and Minotti up to?"

Serella shivered visibly when Jesse mentioned the two evil adversaries. "Audra wants vengeance on Christian and Samuel for destroying her body in the physical, for taking away the chance she had at her dream of some sort of ultimate, vampire power."

"And Minotti?"

Serella focused her attention on him, but said nothing.

"What?"

She looked toward the sky, then back at him. "He only wants vengeance on you."

Jesse leaned forward, his arms folded on his knees, and lay his head against them. He felt Serella's soft touch brush against the back of his head and he sighed. "I'm not up for this," he said.

"Yes, you are."

He looked at her. "I'm not, Serella. I'm tired."

She smiled and brushed the aura of his cheek. "I know. That's why I'm here. I can help from this side. But it is going to be complicated."

Jesse shook his head. "What's the use? We're fighting a losing battle, Serella. Minotti will just show up later and we'll fight, again. Even worse, he'll show Audra how to do the same now that he's teamed up with her."

Serella floated back a bit and reached out to him with determination in her eyes. "Is it better to give up and let them win? I know you remember what that would do to the world on both sides. I'm not prepared to let everything be corrupted. I would think you'd feel the same."

"I do." Jesse silently pleaded with her to understand what he felt, the spiritual drain he was experiencing, the confusion. "I just don't know how much I can contribute to the fight this time. I felt so strong while I was in God's presence," he said. "Now I feel drained, again, and I haven't done anything about this new situation."

"Look, Jesse." Serella appeared suddenly stern. "You have never been alone in all of this and you aren't, now. In fact, you have more help available to you than ever before."

"And a bigger problem," Jesse said. "There's Roni's health, too."

"A way to weaken Christian."

"What?"

"Minotti planted that seed when he struck out at Diana during the battle at St. Joseph's," Serella said. "He knew Roni's nature. He knew she would take the hit for Diana."

Jesse looked at her, stunned.

"That's right," Serella said. "He also knew he would lose that battle."

"Then why instigate it?" Jesse was growing more confused by the minute. He was an angel. He was supposed to understand all these things. What was wrong with him?

"Because his power would be stronger from this side and he knew it," Serella said. "The core of good is not in the physical. It's here. Just as the core of evil is here. That's where Minotti wanted to be, but he could only be brought here through the power of the Almighty. No mortal could have ever killed him."

Jesse simply nodded, speechless.

"He's here for one reason, Jesse." Serella's entire aura flared up and shone an intense passion. "To take over control of all evil energy, everywhere. And his first priority is to get rid of you simply for his own satisfaction. It will be the only time he will leave himself weak enough to be destroyed forever, permanently. You are his Achilles heal."

Jesse smiled in spite of himself. "And Audra knows all this?"

"No, she doesn't," Serella said. "Minotti is using her, as well."

"For what?"

"For the power of her destructive intentions toward those you love," she said. "He knows how the emotions weaken those in the physical. He's counting on that to weaken you enough so that he can easily get rid of you and go on to his ultimate goal quickly."

"So what do we do?"

Serella's entire aura softened and she glowed as she moved closer once more. "We wait."

Chapter 3

Early Autumn 1253 A.D.

JESSE heard a a frantic banging on the door that woke him from his sleep and made him desparate to react. He rose, wrapped his robe around himself, and hurried to the door. He opened it and was surprised to see Serella standing there, knocking her fist in the air as if she was still making contact with the door. Suddenly, she looked up, saw him standing there, and quickly began to fall before him. He caught her immediately and carried her into the room where the evening candle still burned. He laid her on the bed, covering her with the blanket he'd been using only moments before. Her hair was rumpled and she was covered with bruises, but from what, Jesse could only guess. How on earth did she ever find him? She'd never been to his home, though he'd told her approximately where he was located. Still, traveling through the forest in the pitch dark at this hour of the night might account for all the scratches and bruises that were so evident on her body, but what had caused her to make the trip in the first place?

Jesse lit a fire in the small fireplace while Serella rested in his bed. He placed a large pot of water to cook over it. She would need some herbal tea to settle down when she awoke and he needed the hot water to clean her wounds before he began to dress them so as to prevent them from getting infected. He went about preparing what he might need depending on how bad the wounds turned out to be, tearing up small shards of fabric, locating a clean towel, and placing a cup nearby on the side table with a ball of catnip and lavendar ready to be submerged when she awoke.

When everything was in place on the table she was still asleep so he began to inspect only the areas of her body that could be seen without being too intrusive. He saw that many of the cuts were quite deep, but most had already begun to scab over. All he could do was wait for the water over the fire to boil before he could do anything for her, but his concern over what caused her condition was growing worse. What could have done this to her? Or who?

As he thought about it, he was struck by the fact that she came to him when she was in trouble. It touched his heart more deeply than he could've imagined. All at once he knew. He was in love with her. He couldn't deny it, but he didn't know quite how to handle feeling this way. He loved her in a way he'd never experienced before. Was this a test? What was he supposed to do with this experience? It was completely unexpected.

He walked to the window and stared into the darkness of the woods around him. "Father?" he began. "What am I to do with these feelings I have for her?" He wrung his hands together, then leaned on the window sill. "What happened to her?" He saw the moonlight's reflection in the eyes of some woodland creature that was close to the ground and wondered how Serella made it here without getting bit or eaten alive, but he quickly remembered the loyalty the wolves all seemed to have for her and he realized that they had probably protected her all the way. So why was she in such a frantic state so as to collapse in his arms when he opened the door? He inhaled deeply, intending a sigh, but smelled the heat from the water on the fire and walked over to check its progress. Steam rose from the pot and Jesse decided not to wait, anymore. The water was obviously quite hot enough so that he could begin to clean Serella's wounds.

He poured some of the water in a small bowl, leaving the rest for tea, placed the torn cloths in the bowl, then carried it over to the bed where Serella still lay unconscious. He began to clean the wounds on her hands and arms, then covered them with salve made from crushed willow bark, chamomile, garlic, and mullein. For the deeper wounds, he added echinacea root and feverfew to the salve before placing a cloth over the wound, then tying it in place. He treated her facial wounds in the same manor, then hesitated when he rinsed the cloth he'd been using to clean the cuts before proceeding to her neck. When he turned toward her, she sighed deeply and the light in the small room glowed on the deep cut across the top of her chest where blood still oozed and glistened in the candle light. He placed the cloth back in the bowl and stood up. He couldn't do it. He was an angel. He was here for an assigned purpose, to help those with unusual destinies and lead them down the right path, to guide them in what was good and right. Serella was a witch by her own choice and that was why Jesse had been asked to work with her, to make sure she didn't use her powers for bad ends, to teach her why she should never do so. He was not supposed to fall in love with the student.

He stood up and looked down at her laying on his bed. Her arms and face looked much better now that they were cleaned, but the gash across the top of her chest was not going to heal on its own. He sighed, closing his eyes as he released the air from his lungs. He lifted the bowl from the floor and carried it to the front door where he intended to throw the water out and start with a fresh pot of boiling water, but he heard Serella's voice.

"Do not go, Jesse." Her voice was faint and weak, but it was enough to make him stop.

"I shall be right back," he said. "I am going to through this water out." He turned around to reassure her, but she had already lost consciousness, again. "You rest," he whispered, knowing she couldn't hear him.

He turned around and, holding the bowl in one hand, opened the door with the other. To his surprise, standing only ten feet away was a man he'd never seen before. The man's very presence was quite ominous and he appeared to be shrouded in black, the color of protection. But what might he need protection from? Jesse walked out to face him and dumped the water to the side. "Can I help you?" he asked the man. Being so near to the intruder allowed Jesse a closer feel for the man's aura and Jesse knew in an instant that this man was nothing but evil.

"So, she ran to you, did she?"

Jesse's growing discomfort made him want to turn and run, but he knew something wasn't right with him. If this man had caused Serella's pain, then Jesse would need to know why. "Explain yourself," he said. "What are you doing here?"

"She shall be coming back with me," the man said.

"Who are you?" Jesse asked.

"That is no concern of yours," the man said. "Serella belongs to me and I intend to have her back."

Jesse saw the darkness in the man's soul as he looked into his eyes and he was frightened. "No human owns another," he said to the man. "And slavery is not practiced here, so whatever property you feel is belonging to you, take it up with the town magistrate. In the meantime, leave my property." He turned and headed back toward the door of his house, expecting a blind attack as he proceeded.

"This is not over," the man said. "I shall not enter the home of an angel, but Serella shall not be here forever, either."

Jesse stopped in front of the door and turned around when he heard the strange man refer to him as an angel. How could he know? "I have no idea who you are," he said, " but I do not expect to see you on this land ever again." With that Jesse backed up through the door and closed it before allowing the trespasser to say a word in return.

Serella was still unconscious, so Jesse went to the fireplace to pour more of the hot, steaming water into the bowl and prepare a new batch of cleansing supplies to finish cleaning her wounds, especially the one on her chest. The unexpected visit from the stranger had shaken him more than he thought anything could. He'd never been involved with such an intense, evil presence as he'd just experienced. If that was what had frightened Serella enough to come running all the way to him under such conditions as the darkness and the forest, then Jesse fully understood what she must have been feeling, the desparation that was so apparent on her face when he'd first opened the door. What had that man done to her? Jesse's mind began to race with all the possibilities, none of which he wanted to envision or find out to be true.

He stood up, carried the fresh bowl of water over to the bed, and began to clean the wounds on Serella's neck. They were mostly surface scratches, all of which had already closed and only needed to be cleansed, then treated with a little aloe.

Jesse began to rinse the cloth out in preparation to begin cleaning the wound on her chest, but saw movement from the bed. He looked up only to see Serella watching him. "How are you feeling?" he asked her.

"Better," she said, her smile quivering. "Safer."

Jesse stared at her for a few moments before he spoke. "Who was he?"

Serella looked away. "One of the wealthiest merchants from the next town over," she said. "His name is Gaetano."

"He is not from England, I take it."

Serella shook her head. "No, he is not. I was told he is from Sicily and is actually in England because of those goings on with King Henry and the Pope."

"What might that have to do with Gaetano?" Jesse asked.

Serella winced when she tried to reposition herself, then settled back down and sighed. "All I know is that Gaetano and King Henry are friends. King Henry is trying to buy Sicily for his son, Edmund. Beyond that, I did not care enough to ask anymore."

Jesse couldn't help but notice the blood that was still running down her chest, shining in the light, and wondered how to approach the job of cleaning it up for her, but she reached over and took the cloth from his hands. The disappointment must have been evident on his face because she smiled an understanding smile.

"Let me start this," she said, already beginning to wipe the oozing blood from around the wound. "But you will have to finish it." She looked down at the wound, touched it with her other hand, and winced in pain. "I think you will need to sew it closed for me," she said.

Jesse watched her movements being very careful not to look in the wrong direction and he nodded his head in agreement. He could see the depth of the cut when she touched it and he was amazed that she hadn't already bled to death. "How did all this happen?" he asked her. "Did he do this to you?"

"Not exactly," Serella said. "Most of it happened as I was trying to get away from him." She looked deep into Jesse eyes, then placed the towel back in the bowl where Jesse had placed it next to her on the bed. "I had to get away from him," she added.

"Serella," Jesse said, sighing. "I can feel that there is so much more to this than you are telling me. Please, I cannot help you if I am not given the whole story."

Serella began to clean the blood that was around the open gash in her chest, then briefly inspected the wound. "It will have to be sewed," she said.

"I know," Jesse said. "And I will gladly take care of that for you when I have finished disinfecting it for you, but you must stop changing the subject. I have to know the whole story with the Gaetano, gentleman."

Serella flashed him an angry glare. "He is no gentleman."

"Then tell me the whole truth about him."

Serella handed him the towel and laid back on the pillows. "Alright. It is now your turn to finish this job," she said. "And I will tell you whatever I know about him."

Jesse rinsed the towel in the bowl of water, noticing that it was still quite hot and began to clean around the wound itself. No more dried blood remained, but fresh blood continued to run across her chest. He had to get the wound closed, and fast, but he had no needle or thread available. He looked at her, saw her watching his movements around the wound, then around the room, and he knew a miracle would have to happen or she would die. "Close your eyes, Serella."

She didn't ask any questions. She simply smiled, then closed her eyes as he'd asked her.

He placed both hands directly over the wound and felt the warm blood spread across his palms. "Father," he prayed to himself. "I ask you to please send your healing energy through me to this woman in order to close this wound and save her life." Jesse felt his body warm immensely, felt the surge of power begin at the top of his head and run through to the bottom of his spine until his whole physical being was buzzing internally. He willed the power to move up through his arms, into his hands, and out to cauterize the wound. His hands were like hot coals and he smelled burning flesh, but he continued until he knew the process was complete. He removed his hands from the wound over Serella's chest and sat back. It was closed. The bleeding had stopped, but a large section of skin had been badly burned. He looked at Serella and saw that she was still smiling. "You can open your eyes, Serella."

She looked at him and took in a deep breath. "Thank you," she said.

"Did that not that hurt a bit?" Jesse asked, amazed that she didn't cry out or scream.

"I am quite certain it would have if I had not thought to meditate through it," she said. "But the worst is over. It hurts now, but once you rub a bit of aloe juice on it, the burning sensation will go away and I will feel as good as ever."

Jesse took his supplies to the table and cracked a leaf of aloe on the way back. He handed the leaf to her. "You do it, please."

Serella gently took the aloe leaf from him, squeezed a bit of juice on to her fingers, then began to rub it over the areas of burnt flesh.

Jesse watched her for a short time, but her movements were far too erotic for his senses here in the physical and he turned away. "Now, tell me the rest of the story about Gaetano," he said. "What happened to you tonight?"

"Honestly, Jesse. I do not know the whole story of what he is scheming, but I do know that he wants my powers as a witch in order to achieve some plan of his own making."

She continued to rub the aloe, but Jesse sensed that the leaf needed to be cut smaller. He turned back toward her and took it from her hand, tore it into two pieces, then handed one of them back to her. "Just tell me whatever he said to you and we can try to figure the rest out from there."

"Well," Serella began. "As I said, he is somehow trying to help King Henry obtain Sicily for his son, but why he would even care, I do not know. Once this deal of his is complete, he will be returning to Sicily. There seems to be some sort of plot for war that he is also a part of just for the blood shed of it."

"What could his interest be in blood shed?" Jesse asked. "Is he a dangerously ill individual?" Serella laughed a sardonic laugh that felt as if the mere sound of it took on physical form and stabbed through Jesse's body. He'd never seen such a side of her before and it tore him in two, emotionally.

"He is a vampire, Jesse."

Another jolt went through Jesse's soul and he felt his eyes grow huge in his head. "He is what?"

"He is a vampire." Serella handed him back the leaf she'd squeezed down to the thickness of a maple leaf and took the fresh piece from him. "That is why you have never seen him before." She only had a small amount of burnt skin left to treat and she began squeezing the juice from the new piece of aloe. "He comes to see me only after the sun has set. He never stays long, then he goes on his merry way to hunt." She looked at Jesse. "The wolves do not like him," she said. "He has been the main reason they surround my property as they do. I have never seen him that often, until recently. And I never knew too much about him until recently, either. It is only because he is preparing to return to Sicily and he needs my powers before he goes."

Jesse went to the window and looked out, trying to find a plan to stop him. "He cannot just try to own you, Serella. And he certainly cannot take from you the gifts our Creator gave to you."

"I think he might like to argue that point with you."

Jesse turned to her. "No matter what else happens," he said. "I do not think you should be spending your nights alone while he remains in the area."

Serella looked up at him and smiled "Well, I cannot very well spend my nights with you, either."

"Do not play this game with me," Jesse said. He was angry over what Gaetano had been doing to her and angry at the rules of the day that prevented him from being able to protect her in person. A decision had to be made. "I shall be staying at your house," he said. "Your life is in danger." He walked over to sit on the bed beside her. "Serella, we are far enough from town that no one will even know you are in any kind of trouble. Do you really think the townsfolk might know whether or not someone is staying at your house in order to protect you?" He shook his head. "You might possibly be dead for days before anyone even knew something had happened to you. And if he took you with him, then no one would ever know a thing." He looked at her, straight into her eyes. "I will not allow that happen to you. I am here to teach you, but I am also here to protect you."

"Jesse," she said. "I have been taking care of myself for a very long time."

Jesse held up his hand in order to silence her. "If you could have taken care of this situation yourself, then you would not be here right now. I do not want to hear another word. I am going to put a few things together in the morning and then I shall be moving in with you until that monster of a man is finally gone."

Serella began to object, but Jesse silenced her.

"I will not hear it," he said. "Part of my purpose is to fight evil and I felt that man's evil from a short distance away. If he has already been able to do this much harm to you, there is no telling what else he might attempt. Shall I wait until he has finally killed you before I take measures to prevent him from doing so? I think not."

"I appreciate your concern," Serella said. "But I do not want to be the cause of a scandal that might grow around us. I simply want him to go away and leave me alone."

Jesse sat on the bed beside her and took her hand in his. "My dear, Serella," he said. "I wish that for you, as well. But you can believe that it will not happen as you desire simply because you wish it. These matters must be handled. He must be made to go away." He laid her hand on the bed beside her and stood up. "Now rest and let your wounds begin to heal. I shall make you a cup of tea to help settle you. We can discuss this further in the morning."

"Thank you," Serella said. "I do not wish to be a problem for you."

Jesse placed a finger across her lips. "Sshhhhh. Rest."

Serella laid back on the bed and Jesse went to get a cup to begin the tea.

Chapter 4

April 28 7:00 PM

CHRISTIAN entered the living room where Roni sat, waiting for Chelle to arrive. She was rubbing her leg as she'd begun to do quite often recently, stopping here and there to massage a particularly painful area. He sighed. Why wouldn't she just let him heal her? Part of him wanted to take Samuel's advise and administer some of his own blood to her while she slept, but the other part of him didn't want to risk changing her against her will. She'd hate him forever because of such a deception, especially if it were to back fire. No, he couldn't take that chance.

"When is Chelle expected to be here?" he asked, sitting beside her on the sofa by the window.

Roni looked at her watch. "Any minute, now. She's running a little late, as usual." She smiled. "But it's giving me a few extra minutes to massage my leg."

Christian placed his hand over one of hers while it was rubbing one of the sore spots that seemed to plague her so often these days. "Not feeling too good today, I see." He looked up at her and saw the warning in her blue eyes.

"Don't even say it," Roni told him. "I'm not considering it and that isn't going to change."

Christian removed his hand from hers and looked at her. He hoped she would see the hurtful feelings in his eyes. "I wasn't going to say anything," he told her. "I would have asked if there was anything I could do for you, but. . . . " Chelle's vigorous knocking on the door interrupted him mid-sentence.

Roni stood up and went to open it. She was using her cane again this evening, but he noticed how she also leaned on the chair for additional support when she passed it. He didn't have to pry telepathically to know her condition was worsening much faster than Dr. Reno had thought it would, but it made Christian a bit suspicious about why it was happening the way it was. He hoped Jesse would be able to get back to him quickly with an answer on how Roni could be healed. The incident at St. Joseph's church kept popping into his thoughts. Christian could see it all so clearly, now. He remembered walking into the church and seeing Roni laying in the aisle as if she were dead.

"Hello, Christian," Chelle said as she entered the house.

He looked at her, shook the painful memory away, then stood up. "Hello, Chelle." He smiled. "Have you told Joe your news, yet?"

Chelle shook her head. "No, but I'm planning to tonight." She looked at Roni and shrugged. "The sooner the better. At least if he decides to move to Russia alone I won't have wasted a ton of money on our little wedding."

"Always sarcastic," Christian said, shaking his head.

Roni reached up and kissed him on the lips. "We won't be long," she said. "We're just going to look at dresses."

"For both of you?" Christian asked, smiling.

Roni nodded. "For both of us." She looked at Chelle, who shrugged her shoulder in an encouraging manner as if there was more she wanted Roni to tell him. Roni turned to him and smiled. "Chelle had a brilliant idea to have us exchange our vows during her and Joe's ceremony while I'm standing up for them." She tilted her head sideways, still smiling. "If that's alright with you."

Christian hugged her and nodded to Chelle. "Whatever it takes to make you my wife and have it done in the church at the same time is fine with me." He held Roni at arms length and focused on her. "I told you. I don't care about all the traditional things. I only care that we will be united forever. Don't take my words lightly, Roni."

She smiled and gently rubbed the side of his face. "I know," she said. "I think I'm just feeling a little insecure right now with all this. . . . " She looked down at her legs and her cane, then back up at him. "What are you planning to do while we're gone? Anything interesting?"

He nodded. "I think I might run over and visit Jesse. I haven't seen him in quite a while and I'd like to let him know our good news as well as Chelle's." He nodded in Chelle's direction. "That is if it's alright with you, Chelle."

Chelle waved a hand in the air as if to show him he shouldn't even have worried enough to ask. "Go ahead. Tell your friends. Just don't tell Joe."

Christian made an "X" across his chest. "Scout's honor."

"Oh, like you'd ever be a boy scout." Chelle chuckled. "That's rich. A vampire boy scout. I love it." She turned to Roni. "Are you ready to go? I'm going to start laughing so hard pretty soon, we'll never get out of here." She opened the door and waved good-bye to Christian. "A vampire boy scout. I have to remember that one."

Roni shook her head as she turned to give Christian a final kiss before joining Chelle in the car. "Don't mind her. You know she really loves you."

Christian nodded and smiled. "As much as I love her." He held Roni tight against him. "Be careful. Do you hear me? And if anything happens you know to just think to me and I'll be there."

"I know." Roni picked up her purse from the table by the door, turned to blow Christian a kiss, then left.

Christian heard the engine start up, heard the car roll along the loose pieces of gravel in the driveway as the girls pulled out and headed down the road. He quickly checked the house, then locked up, rose into the air, and headed for Nantucket to see if Jesse had any insight regarding Roni's condition.

* * *

Jesse was sitting on the weathered old rocking chair when Christian landed on the beach and headed toward the house. There was a troubled look on Jesse's face that caught Christian off guard. He'd never seen such a look from Jesse before. With Roni's illness, Chelle's marriage to Joe, and Father Larry's early retirement it felt as if there was something in the air, of late, that was turning everything around. It wasn't just the changing things. Christian had seen much change in his centuries on earth. There was something else happening that just didn't feel quite right. It bothered Christian that he couldn't put his finger on it. It wasn't all bad, especially in Chelle's case, but it was all opposite from the way things had been. Maybe Jesse would be able to help him understand what was going on.

Jesse looked up and waved to Christian when he was nearing the stairs, but his smile was forced. Christian said nothing until he reached the top of the porch and sat down on the railing across from his friend.

"What is it?" he asked Jesse. "You look upset."

Jesse faced the ocean and shook his head. "It's nothing." He turned toward Christian. "What brings you out here? I haven't seen you since Samuel came to visit with you last month. Is everything all right?"

Christian watched Jesse carefully, then looked away. "Not exactly." He shrugged. "Honestly, I don't know. Roni is on the defensive with everything I say lately."

Jesse's reaction startled Christian. His eyes opened wide and he seemed curious in an exaggerated way. He turned his attention to Christian as if he'd just told him Audra came to visit.

"What is it? What did I say?"

Jesse shook his head. "How is Roni? Besides defensive, how is her health?"

"Getting worse and fast," Christian said. "That's why I came to see you." Christian stood and turned to watch the evening, spring sky. "Her doctor didn't seem to think this was all going to happen so fast. He told us there would be plenty of time before we'd have to face her symptoms becoming worse."

"But?"

Christian turned to face his friend. "But she's already using a cane to help herself walk." He ran the fingers of his left hand through his dark hair and looked away. "She's constantly rubbing her leg because of the pain. And before she left the house with Chelle earlier she was using the chair for support because even the cane isn't enough help, anymore." He turned toward Jesse, holding his arms out in front of him. "It's only been a month and a half," he said. "Of all the people in the world, why is this happening so fast to Roni?" He waited for an answer, but Jesse stared at him as if he was lost. "All this because of what happened at the church."

Jesse looked at him and nodded.

"Damn," Christian said, whipping around to begin pacing again. "All because Roni jumped in the way to protect Diana."

Jesse nodded. "It's her nature to protect others before herself. And Minotti knew it."

Christian stopped walking and turned slowly toward Jesse. "What do you mean he knew it? What are you telling me?"

"I'm telling you that the thing Minotti sent out from himself to attack Diana was really meant for Roni all the time." Jesse leaned forward, still watching Christian. "I had another visit from Serella not too long ago. That was after I went home to visit with the Creator and get whatever answers I could. They were both most helpful and I believe I now know exactly what has been causing all of this and why."

Christian approached Jesse in a cautious manner, not sure what to expect from this woman, this witch that he'd never met. "And?"

"And the Father told me what's going on and how you're all involved." Jesse leaned back in his chair and motioned for Christian to be seated, too. "And Serella filled in the blanks for me after that initial visit. You're not going to like it any more than I did, but you're going to have to listen."

Christian pulled up a chair from the corner of the porch and sat down beside Jesse. "Ok. Let's get this over with. What now?"

Jesse smiled and shook his head. "My feelings exactly."

* * *

"What do you think?" Chelle asked, holding up a plain white dress with very little embellishment. "Is this something for me or something for you?"

Roni laughed and shook her head. "Neither. You'd want more decoration and I don't wish to wear white."

"But we're both getting married."

"That's not the point," Roni said. "It's your wedding. Christian and I are exchanging our vows at your wedding because we simply want to commit to each other in the church. This way it will be easier for everyone. Father O'Manley will marry you and Joe, while Father Larry marries Christian and me. It will work out beautifully."

Chelle nodded. "OK. So this dress is out." She hung the dress back on the rack and began searching through the other ones. "What do you want to wear?"

Roni turned to her. "You know, it doesn't really matter. It's your wedding so let's go with the colors you want and work from there." She took a deep breath and smiled. "I still can't get over this whole turn of affairs. I never really thought Christian and I would find a way to be married like this. It's mind boggling and I don't think I've adjusted to it yet."

"Well, adjust," Chelle said, laughing. "Father Larry has always had a soft spot in his heart for you and he has grown to appreciate Christian in a way no one would ever understand, unless they knew Christian."

"What do you mean?"

Chelle stopped rummaging through the dresses and turned her attention to Roni. "Take yourself out of the situation and try to imagine a priest and a vampire being friends the way those two are." She shook her head. "I know it's more than *I* would have ever thought possible."

Roni smiled and nodded her head. "I know what you mean. I never would've expected it, either. Christian was the one who went to see Father Larry in the first place. I didn't have the guts to tell him I was living with someone, not to mention that I was living with a vampire."

"Most people aren't as close to their local priest as you are close to Father Larry," Chelle said. "He's been like family to you since you were a little girl. He's played a big role in your life. Not everyone can say they've enjoyed the same privilege." Chelle turned back to continue her search through the wedding dresses. "Now me? Father Larry and I have a distinct fondness for each other, but it's nothing near what you and he have had." She looked at Roni once more. "You're actually very lucky, you know."

Roni looked at Chelle and smiled. Suddenly, a pain, gripping and terrible shot through her entire right side. It was like nothing she'd ever experienced before. It doubled her over, debilitating aches, forced her to lean on the rack for support while her purse slipped off her shoulder. She saw the contents strewn across the floor, saw the amethyst crystal laying on top of her credit cards, and her purse laying on its side. The pain grabbed at her again and caused both legs to give out entirely. Roni fell to the floor. Her head slammed against the table she'd been standing near and the room began to spin around her. She felt her whole body growing numb, then weak, and the fear began to set in.

"Oh, my God." Chelle was at her side in an instant. "Are you alright? Roni, say something."

Roni did her best to nod as she reached up to steady her head. "Just dizzy," she managed to say.

"Someone call 9-1-1," Chelle yelled. "Hang in there, Roni. We've got help coming. I'm not going anywhere."

"Christian," Roni said. "Think for Christian."

"We'll get him, too." Chelle's one hand moved across Roni's arm while the other gently caressed her hair. "Don't you worry. I'm a nurse, remember. You're in good hands. I'm not leaving your side."

Roni felt herself nod, hoping her friend was right, but before she could say another word, the lights around her all went out and the experience was gone from her perception.

* * *

"So you see the situation we're all in," Jesse said, looking intently at Christian.

Christian shook his head and ran his fingers through his hair. "So Audra isn't really gone, either? And this is all some sort of spiritual vengeance on all of us?"

Jesse nodded. "Not to mention the play for power Minotti is undertaking, as well. This is very serious."

"And where does this friend of yours, this Serella, fit into all of it? Can you really trust her?" Christian wasn't sure what to make of this woman spirit, but he trusted Jesse with his life.

Jesse sat back, and began to rock in the chair. "Honestly, I'm not sure, yet. Ever since my visit with the Creator I've found it easier to accept what she says and to see the truth behind her words. I think I was a bit paranoid before that. After not hearing from her for so long, I couldn't figure out what brought her around all of a sudden. But it all makes sense, now. And something tells me she is going to be the key to either our success in getting out of this all in one piece, or the death of all of us as we try." He looked up at Christian. "My heart trusts her but. . . . ," he shook his head. "I just don't know, yet."

Just then, Christian jumped up with a start and looked around.

"What?" Jesse asked. "What did you feel? What was it?"

Christian turned to him. "Roni," he said. "She's in trouble." Christian was already in the air and on his way to her when he heard Jesse's voice behind him.

"I'm going with you."

Chapter 5

April 28 11:00 PM

CHRISTIAN looked around the sterile atmosphere of the hospital corridor. The off-white painted walls and shiny linoleum made him feel as if he were in a laundromat for humans. He looked at Chelle and admired her calm exterior, but he knew how worried she really was. He'd been watching her pace the halls while the doctor ran his tests on Roni. She was the one asking all the update questions and pestering the nurses for progress reports. All the things Christian should have been handling, Chelle was taking care of like it had always been her duty. He admired her for her professionalism, but most of all, he was touched by her devotion to her friend. "I guess that's all we can do for now," he said, turning to Chelle. "Thank you for acting so quick and taking care of her."

Chelle nodded and smiled. "She's my best friend, Christian. She means as much to me as she does to you."

Christian nodded, but said nothing. He still couldn't believe this was happening.

"She'll be sleeping the rest of the evening," Chelle said. "There's not much any of us can do except let the family and friends know what's going on. I've got some of her belongings locked up in the car, her purse and stuff. I'll drop them off at the house tomorrow, unless there's something you can think of that she might need."

Christian shook his head. "Nothing I can think of. I'd like to stay the night with her if that's possible, though," Christian said, still trying to stay calm in the midst of all the sudden turmoil. He never thought the idea of losing her would cut him as deeply as this incident had just done to him. He felt stripped of himself, vulnerable and alone. He couldn't lose her. He couldn't even stomach the thought of it happening some time in the future. He ran his fingers through his hair as he tried to shake off the somber feelings. Something had to be done to stop this nightmare.

Chelle put her hand on his arm and smiled. "I'm sure the doctor will try to talk you out of it, but they don't know you won't be sleeping, anyway. I don't think they'll chase you away under the circumstances. I'll talk to them before I go. Maybe it'll help."

Christian nodded. "Thank you."

"No. Thank you for coming so quick." She looked from Christian to Jesse and smiled. "Even though I'm trained for this, it still hit me hard once we got her to the hospital and I wasn't needed, anymore. Then I had time to think about it and I'll admit, I was scared." She turned to look at the door to Roni's room. "I still am."

"It's natural," Jesse said to her.

Chelle turned to him. "We haven't met, have we?

I know I've heard Christian mention you a few times, but I don't remember meeting you."

Jesse smiled and shook his head. "No, we haven't met."

Chelle looked at Christian with a question in her eyes.

"This is a very old friend, Jesse Nestarius." He turned to Jesse. "This is Roni's best friend, Chelle Gambert."

Jesse nodded once to show he understood more than the simple introduction explained, then he reached out to her and took her hands in his. "Roni will be all right," he said.

Chelle gave him a look of doubt. "She's got more wrong with her than tonight's bump on the head. She won't be OK."

Christian watched as Jesse squeezed Chelle's hands a bit tighter, looking into her face the whole time. "If you believe in your heart that it's possible for her to be alright, then she will be."

Chelle nodded, mesmerized and unable to speak as Jesse slowly let go of her hands and moved his gaze away from her. She took a deep breath as if she'd just awoke, and looked around, her eyes shifting quickly from side to side before she spoke. "I suppose I'll go home and call Joe so he knows what's happened."

"That's a good idea," Christian said. "I'll get a hold of Father Larry, Diana, and Samuel. Should I call Roni's parents or will you?"

Chelle shook her head. "She's your fiancee`," she said. "It's your place to call them. It'll give you a chance to get used to doing the regular son-in-law type things." She smiled, but the exhaustive worrying was still evident in her eyes. "Why don't you let me call Father Larry and Father O'Manley, instead."

Christian nodded, but looked at the door to Roni's room for a brief moment, wanting desparately to be by her side. He sighed, then turned back toward Chelle. She was looking continuously from him to Jesse and back again, a thought obviously forming that she either didn't know how to voice, or wasn't sure she wanted to.

"I'm not a vampire," Jesse told her, smiling.

Chelle nodded once, then looked away. "I'd better get going." She grabbed her jacket and purse, dug for her car keys, then glanced up. "I'll talk to you later, Christian." She turned to Jesse. "It was nice meeting you. I'm sorry. I've got to run."

Jesse smiled and nodded as Chelle headed for the door. He turned to face Christian.

"Don't even say it," Christian said. "I felt it, too."

Jesse nodded.

"She's got something to do with all of this mess, but she wasn't even there at the church when Minotti attacked Diana."

"It's not just her," Jesse said. "It's Joe, too."

"What role could Chelle and Joe possibly have in all that's coming up?" Christian asked. "It doesn't make any sense? They're not even part of what's already happened."

Jesse shook his head. "All I know for sure is that we both have to trust our instincts right now and my instincts were clear as crystal when she looked at me. Serella will have to fill us in on the details as this unfolds, but in the meantime we have to keep a sharp eye. And you had better let Samuel and Diana both know everything I've explained to you. There's no doubt they're both already a part of this. Especially since Samuel was there the night you destroyed Audra's body."

Christian looked down the hall toward the room Roni had been assigned to once she was out of the emergency room. "What about Father Larry and Father O'Manley?"

Jesse smiled and sighed. "I don't know, but my feeling is that Father Larry's role in this is as big as Serella's." He stared down the hall for a moment. "But how?" he practically whispered. "All I can say is that I hope she comes up with more answers, and soon. I know what my instincts are telling me. Now I want to know the rest of the 'why's' behind those feelings."

Christian looked at him trying to camouflage the most unsettling thought he'd just had. "Father Larry is very sick, himself."

Jesse nodded.

"Any part he'll play in this will probably kill him."

Again Jesse nodded, but this time he studied Christian. "What are you thinking?"

"Well, Serella suddenly appeared because of the seriousness of what Minotti is up to," he said. "His power is on that side. Serella is on that side, too, but does she have the power to fight someone as ruthless as Minotti? How much power would it take to actually get rid of someone like Minotti once and for all?"

Jesse shook his head. "I don't honestly believe she has the courage based on what happened between them in the past. She was one of the most powerful witches of her time. But after what Minotti did to her. . . . . . . well, he pretty much broke her spirit and her courage. She wouldn't even allow herself to be reborn to a new incarnation."

Christian nodded. "Is it possible that the only way to defeat him once and for all will be with power from the other side?"

A look of understanding and fear suddenly crossed Jesse's face. "I don't think I like where this is going," he said. "Are you trying to tell me that you think we'll all have to be on that side in order to have any effect on him? That isn't even possible unless all of you are dead. I don't think God has that in His plan. I can't even imagine it."

Christian smiled. "Well, maybe you'd better ask Him. From what you've already told me, there isn't too much in His plan that isn't already in one of our own. If we're shaping our own lives and destinies then we have to find way to shape a life without Minotti ever being part of it, again. At the very least, you might want to ask the Father for His viewpoint on this whole mess. That is, if He'll even give it."

Jesse closed his eyes for a moment and let out a sigh of resignation. "If I have to. But I can tell you that He will leave the decisions up to us individually. Even if the only way to destroy what Minotti and Audra are working to create is for all of us to be on their side of existence, it will still be up to us if we want to fight the battle that way. The Father will never tell us that we have to die in order to do what's right. He'll never make those decisions for us. And He'll never try to force us to make those decisions, either. Free will, Christian. Don't forget."

"But wouldn't He at least advise us?"

Jesse shook his head. "No. He would never make our decisions for us. Once we knew what His advice might be, the decision would already be made based on the advice and not on our own motivations or desires. And He will never deny us the chance to determine the course of our own actions." He looked at Christian. "I've already been there, Christian. I know."

Christian looked at Jesse and nodded. "I understand what you're saying and it's frustrating." Christian ran his hands through his hair,then looked at Jesse. "Then it's up to us to figure it out and decide how we choose to deal with it."

"That's right."

Christian turned away from Jesse and ran a hand through his hair, once more. He stood still, looking at the floor for a few moments as if studying it. Then he turned slowly toward Jesse. "How does Serella feel about meeting the rest of us? Do you think she'd agree to it?"

Jesse looked at him. "What are you thinking?"

"If we're all in this together, then let's all work this out together."

"I don't know," Jesse said. "She's been so far removed from the physical for all these years. I'm sure she has no real desire to have any contact with it at all."

"Can you try?" Christian asked. "Will you ask her how she feels about it? Tell her how I think we might really need her. She's the only one on that side right now who can keep us informed on what's going on. We need to know so many things that only she can tell us. She has to meet with us. It wouldn't be right for her not to."

"As I told you," Jesse said. "She went through an awful lot with the physical and she isn't too anxious to ever be a part of it or any of its inhabitants again."

"But she's in touch with you after all this time." Christian reminded him. "You might be the only one who can convince her how important her involvement might be."

"Let me try to get in touch with her first," Jesse said. "It's quite unusual for entities from both sides to deal directly with each other in such a manner."

Christian laughed. "It's unusual for vampires to deal with angels, too, but it happens every day." He turned and threw his arms up in the air. "Heck, this whole situation is quite unusual. Don't you think?"

Jesse turned slowly toward him. "Point taken, my friend. Go make your calls to let everyone know what has happened to Roni. I'll see what I can find out from Serella. I'll contact you as soon as I have answers."

Christian put his hand out to shake, but Jesse put his arms around Christian and hugged him. "Stay safe." He patted Christian on the back, then turned toward the elevator which was already open.

Christian said nothing. He simply watched his friend board the elevator knowing he was already on his way home the minute the doors were closed. He went back to Roni's room to check on her. She was asleep, but he sat in the chair next to her bed and held her hand. His heart ached. So close to having her as his wife, and now this. He was sad and angry at the same time. Why now? How could he ever be free of Audra and Minotti? He shook his head, then leaned forward to rest it on the bed beside Roni. It was his own fault for changing Audra in the first place. He'd been so lonely in those days, that he made himself believe she loved him. It was what he wanted to believe even though his instincts told him different. He wasn't too good at listening to himself back then. He was weak. Roni's love had made him strong enough to fight Audra, but he never expected her to return. Or to be teamed up with Minotti after all they'd gone through getting rid of him.

Christian sat up and watched Roni sleep. "You will be my wife," he told her. "No matter what happens, I love you now and always." He stroked her forehead with the palm of his hand and felt the tears form in his eyes. "I know I'll have to live without you one day, but not now. Not this soon, Roni." He massaged her arm, running his hand down to her wrist, then looked into her face once more. "You have a lot of living left to do, and I promise you, I'll do whatever has to be done to protect that for you." His chest felt like it was being torn wide open, his pain was so intense. "You're too good, Roni. You don't deserve any of this." He watched her, but there was no response, no movement of any kind except the rise and fall of her chest as she circulated the life giving air around her. Christian leaned forward and sighed. "I love you more than my own life," he said. Then he stood up, kissed her on the lips, and disappeared.

* * *

Audra laughed hysterically while she stood at the foot of Roni's bed and savored every agonizing moment of Christian's pain. The thin veil between the two sides of reality gave her perfect cover where she could choose to be seen when and only when she chose to allow it. How perfect it all was working out. She watched Christian lay his head on the pillow beside Roni's. She saw his eyes fill with tears and she felt the flames of her hatred burn around her. In Christian's weakened emotional state, she could take him single handedly and there was nothing he could do this time. Christian would be so easy to destroy right at this moment. But that wasn't exactly the plan, just yet. She wanted him to suffer, and he was. So far it was already working beautifully.

Audra was already dead and now she knew her essence was eternal. That knowledge alone gave her more power than she'd ever dreamed possible. There were no time constraints; nothing to stop her, ever. She continued to laugh from the insanity the growing power had given her. It was too awesome to be believed. Minotti was a fool to be concerned about Jesse, when Christian and Samuel were the ones she needed to destroy. As an angel, Jesse was eternal. Minotti had all the time in the world to take care of Jesse. But vampires or not, Christian and Samuel could still be destroyed, and the evil they must have done before they decided to become boringly good still lingered in their karmas somewhere. That energy would only add to Audra's own and it would strengthen her evil resolve. By destroying Christian and Samuel, Audra would see a double victory in one shot. Self-satisfaction through vengeance, and self-empowerment through the absorption of their souls. Then she'd be on to bigger and better things. Like Minotti.

Chapter 6

April 29 2:00 AM

CHRISTIAN sat in the atrium at the hospital and sent his telepathic feelers out to Diana and Samuel, hoping they had not gone back home to France, yet as they were supposed to. He hoped the few legal matters they needed to handle could wait. Well, the very worst case scenerio could be that maybe one of them stayed in the states while the other went back. He shook his head. That was very unlikely. They seldom travelled separately.

He leaned forward, placed his head on his hands, and stared at the ground while he waited to receive a message back from either of them and he remembered Roni's family. There wasn't much he could do to notify her parents at this hour of the night. He knew where they were staying while they were in town, but he didn't know them well enough to wake them like this, nor did he feel comfortable doing so, even though the situation called for such measures. His fingers tugged through his hair while he thought about them and tried to put himself in their position. If it were his child, he'd want to know they were in the hospital, regardless of the time. He nodded to himself, leaned back, and sighed, knowing he had to tell them what happened. But how? If he simply knocked on their door, but they still didn't wake up, then what? He could call them on the phone, but they might have shut the ringer off or they could simply ignore the call. And he couldn't very well just appear in their room like a stalker or burglar. They didn't even know he was a vampire.

He dreaded having to do this. Still, he knew he had to try. But before he did, he decided to make one more attempt to reach Diana or Samuel before heading toward the Holiday Inn in Dedham.

* * *

"I will advise them through you," Serella said, her long hair cascading around her. "It isn't right that all those mortals should be in contact with me. You know how I feel about that. I don't trust them."

Jesse shook his head. "You're wrong, Serella." He looked at her and pleaded with his heart. "If what you're telling me is true, then it will save time if you talked to them directly instead of going through me. The only thing wrong about your contact with mortals of any kind is your fear of them, but you have no reason to fear these mortals. You know better. Minotti wasn't a typical mortal and you know that. He wasn't even human and you knew that, too. You're still a very gifted witch, Serella. Why don't you use some of your power to protect yourself and those involved in all this?"

Serella turned away just an inch, but it was enough to show her discomfort.

"You're stronger than that," Jesse told her. "You have always been stronger than that, but you've chosen to run from yourself. What happened with Minotti is in the past. Holding on to those memories and that fear will only cause them to weaken you." He leaned toward her. "Don't let it happen that way. We need you more than ever." He reached out to her. "I need you. I'm facing my own uncertainties. I don't think I can do any of this without you. You're strong, Serella. You've got to accept that about yourself and start acting the part. Even if you won't do it for yourself, do it for me. I'm weak, Serella. Right now, I'm weak." He lowered his head, ashamed of his failing abilities as an angel.

Serella nodded, briefly closing her eyes. "I know you are."

Jesse looked up at her. "Then you must also know that I can't even be strong for any of the others either."

"I do know that, too."

"Then how can you turn your back on how badly your talents are required?" he asked. "How can you turn away form doing the good you had always dreamt of doing when you were here on earth? This is your chance, Serella. This is a time when you are seriously needed."

Serella smiled. "I know that, too."

"Then you'll be available to all of us?" he asked, tentatively.

She nodded once more.

"Good." Jesse smiled and released a heavy breath.

"But I don't know how much I can do," she said, floating in and out of sight. "This is a force to be seriously feared, Jesse. I may be putting my own existence on the line for you."

"Then don't do it," Jesse said. "I'll find another way."

"I will do it," Serella argued. "You are the only one I would put my very existence on the line for."

"I don't want you or anyone else to ever do that for me."

Serella floated toward him, her arm outstretch toward him. "Jesse," she said as her hand touched his face. "It is still my choice. You cannot make such a decision for me."

Jesse looked at her, saw the love in her eyes, and felt himself blush. "I know I can't," he said. "But I can't allow it."

"You have no choice over my decisions," Serella said. "So, please relax and let me do this one thing for you."

Jesse nodded. "Alright," he said.

"But there's something else you should know." The look on her face had grown serious and fearful. She appeared to be dreading what she was about to tell him.

"What's that?" Jesse asked, not sure he wanted to hear, but knowing he had to. "What did you learn?"

Serella hovered a bit higher, then floated closer to him. "More help will be needed from this side, where I am." She appeared to be waiting for an answer before she went on.

Jesse shook his head. "Christian and I have both been afraid of that. We suspected that to be the case, but I cannot commit to returning until this is over," he said. "And neither of us can expect the others to give their lives for this cause. The whole purpose of fighting this it to prevent them from losing their lives. No. There must be a higher level of assistance here, as well. I know I have to stay and so do they."

Serella nodded. "I understand. But still, there must be more help on this side."

Jesse studied her expression, her eyes, her aura. He saw the energy around her grow in shades of dusty rose and lavendar, then shrink to shades of gray. She already knew the answer to the dilemma. "Who?"

Her eyes told him before her voice spoke. "Father Larry."

Jesse felt cold chills run through him. Somehow he knew Father Larry would be leaving soon, but he never saw this coming. "Why?" He couldn't bring himself to say anything more.

Serella reached out to touch his arm. If only he could feel the physical sensation of her hand. Still, the warmth was there and that was good enough. He looked deep into her eyes. "Why him? Why now?"

Serella looked sad. "I understand how you feel, Jesse, but you knew he was coming home shortly."

Jesse watched the small waves roll onto the rocks. He nodded. "I did, but not this soon. Not yet."

"He isn't supposed to go just yet," she said. "But neither Audra nor Minotti can be destroyed, otherwise. Their energy is eternal as all energy is. All that can be done is to find a way to change the way their energy flows, the way it's channeled." She hovered around until he looked at her. "Their energy flows against the Creator, Jesse. It must be rerouted, redirected. They are both very evil, very negative. You know how the cycle of life works. Energy is reformed, reshaped, taught through thousands of lessons until it is trained to flow back to the Creator. That's what brings us back in contact with the Source of life. That's what all these lessons here on earth are about."

"I understand that," Jesse softly said.

"Good." Serella clasped her hands together. "Then understand this. All energy must follow the path of its own choosing because of the great gift of free will. But every so often a mass of negativity develops that eventually becomes an Adolf Hitler or a Stalin. Those two, because of their own choosing in life on earth, are still unconscious in Limbo while their negativity weakens. Right now, however, we have something worse. Much worse." She pulled her arms close to herself as if she needed the security of their nearness. She appeared to take a deep breath in preparation. "We have Gaetano Minotti, and he controls his own Limbo. That's something that has never been done." She looked at Jesse, imploring him with her eyes to see the severity of the situation. "And he is planning to add the strength of Audra Trivette who is the epitome of one who knows no conscience. There is no controlling them as things are right now."

Jesse looked at her, anger growing inside of him. "Then what can Father Larry do by going back early?"

Serella turned away, gliding toward the water before she stopped. "He's only part of the solution," she said. "His sacrifice will be even larger than his earthly life." She turned to face Jesse. "But even he has to make the decision himself."

"What are you saying?"

She moved a little closer, then stopped. "One of us will have to tell him the truth of what is happening, and give him the option to come home now in order to help. It must be his choice."

Jesse shook his head, unable to believe that this had all grown so far out of control. "And if he does? Then what?"

"If he does," Serella began, then hesitated. "Well, then we might have a chance to force the energy that is Minotti's spirit into a different kind of Limbo, one even he can't control or get out of."

Jesse nodded, completely understanding what she meant.

* * *

Night went on as usual with the clear, spring sky full of active stars shining down on all those who slept soundly at home. But Christian still sat outside the hospital waiting for word from either Diana or Samuel and wondering what to do. Try as he might, Christian couldn't figure how this whole situation with Roni might've been prevented unless she would have allowed him to administer his own blood in to her veins. Even now that could fix everything. Maybe. He wrung his hands together as he thought about Roni laying on the floor of the church that night. He should never have let her go to the church with Diana. But he never expected Minotti to show up. They all thought they'd be safe in a sanctified place until Christian was able to return from Jesse's house where he'd gone to discuss how to get rid of Minotti. Christian shook his head and leaned forward, staring at the budding rose bushes in the moonlit garden.

"Christian."

He looked up to see Diana and Samuel materializing before him.

"We came as soon as we got your message." Diana quickly approached and sat beside him. She hugged him, then sat back. "What happened?"

Christian shook his head, took a deep breath, and sighed. "She fell when she went with Chelle to look at wedding dresses," he told them. "The store called 9-1-1 and the paramedics brought her right here. I was at Jesse's when it happened." He ran his fingers through his hair. "She's been unconscious for a few hours, but the doctor told us her vital signs were stablized."

"What the hell is going on?" Samuel asked, sounding angry. "This is all happening so fast. There has got to be a way to get this all under control."

Christian nodded. "I thought you two would be back in Mirande, France. I'm glad I caught you before you left."

"I am, too," Diana said. "We were still in Taunton when I felt your contact."

"Do they know what caused this?" Samuel asked.

Christian nodded. "Her legs are too weak to support her," he said. "Her balance is out of line because of the disease. It's all because of the disease."

Samuel began to pace rapidly back and forth along the cobblestone garden path. "Change her, Christian. This is ridiculous!"

"I can't," Christian shouted. "It's frustrating, I know. But if it's this frustrating for you to watch it all happen, then just imagine how I feel. But honestly, Samuel, I would rather enjoy fifty or sixty years with her love and respect even if she's ill, then turn her against me because I deceived her, even if it cures her for eternity. What sense would it make to go against her wishes just to heal her when it would push her away from me? No. I won't do it."

Diana rubbed his back and smiled. "And you shouldn't." She glared at Samuel who turned away and continued to pace. "But you should be with her, Christian. Not sitting out here wallowing in sorrow.

Even if she's unconscious, part of her will know you're there."

"I know," he said. "But I still have to let her parents know what happened. I told Jesse I'd take care of that while he contacted Serella." He looked at Samuel. "Did you tell Diana about her, yet?"

"He told me," Diana said.

"Good."

Samuel stopped pacing and stepped forward. "Did he reach her?"

"I don't know." Christian looked up at the third floor windows and found Roni's room just by the feel of her presence there. "He'll let me know when he does. In the meantime, I have to go wake up Roni's parents and tell them she's here in the hospital."

Diana shook her head. "No. There's nothing they can do. It's after three o'clock in the morning." She rested her hands on his arm. "Let them sleep, but call the hotel and have a message left that they'll get first thing in the morning. Make sure you explain that you wanted to spend the night at the hospital with Roni and you didn't want them to be awakened in the middle of the night, since Roni is stabilized and there is nothing they can do, anyway. It will show them you are trying to be considerate of everyone's needs and true to your love for their daughter."

Christian looked at her, smiled, then nodded. "I like that better," he said. "By her side is the only place I want to be, right now."

"And that's where you should be." Diana stood up. "We'll be staying at the house in Taunton. The things we have to take care of back in France can wait. This is more important." She turned to Samuel.

"I agree," he said. "Is there anything we can do for you in the meantime?"

Christian nodded. "Yes. Let Jesse know we spoke and find out if he was able to talk to Serella. Ask him what has to be done, if anything."

"I will," Samuel said.

"Would you rather if I stay with you for a little while?" Diana asked.

Christian looked at her, then at the entrance to the hospital. "If you don't mind, I could use your company."

"Then I'll stay."

Samuel bent down to kiss her. "I'm going to find out what Jesse wants us to do. You both know how to reach me." With that, he was gone.

* * *

Audra stood at the foot of Roni's hospital bed and watched her chest rise and fall with each breath, IV fluids being pumped into her as she slept. What next? Maybe a little more central nervous system damage would make Christian squirm. Audra didn't think his heart was breaking enough, yet. Roni's mishap at the store worked as it was intended. It was exactly what was needed to keep Samuel from leaving the area so he would be available to support his friend. That made everything easier since it would soon be his turn to suffer as well. As soon as both Christian and Samuel were sufficiently drained of joy and strength she would pull both of them into herself at once so that neither would be able to go to the other's defense. They'd be too busy trying to save themselves. She laughed. It didn't matter what Minotti said. Jesse meant nothing to her. It was Christian and Samuel she wanted vengeance on. Let Minotti fight his own battle. It wasn't her concern.

Chapter 7

April 29 9:00AM

FATHER Larry relaxed at his desk in the study and watched while Father O'Manley sat across from him taking notes. Fully aware that this would be one of the final times he would be able to enjoy making wedding preparations from his office, Father Larry savored every moment with a mixture of joy and sorrow in his heart.

"What next?" Father O'Manley asked, looking up at him.

Father Larry scratched his head and thought a moment. "I believe it would be best to have Roni and Christian take their vows first so that Chelle and Joe's exchange will be the final thing remembered from the ceremony." He rubbed his belly and smiled at Father O'Manley. "After all, it is their wedding."

Father O'Manley shook his head, then proceeded to write down what Father Larry had just said. "Done. And then?"

Father Larry chuckled. "Why, then we do the recessional so everyone can go to the celebration." He turned to look outside, still chuckling softly to himself. "It is a beautiful day, don't you think, Steve?"

Father O'Manley nodded. "Yes it is, Larry. Did you want to go out for a bit? Is that why you mentioned the day?"

Father Larry turned his chair around and nodded. "I think that would be splendid, but we should plan to have lunch. That would give me time to wrap up a few more things for the day."

Father O'Manley sighed, then looked at Father Larry in a curious way. "Are you alright with me taking over as pastor of St. Joseph's?"

Father Larry leaned forward, his elbows on the desk, and smiled. "There is no one better for the position, my friend. I'm very pleased."

Father O'Manley smiled a sheepish smile. "I'd better be getting a few of my own chores taken care of," he said. "Does noon sound like a good time to head out for a few hours?"

"It does, indeed."

Father O'Manley stood and looked at Father Larry. "If anything comes up, just call or send Cora to get me."

Father Larry nodded.

"Did I hear my name?" Cora stood at the door, her stately Irish attitude permeated the room making her appear as if she were the matron of a boarding school, until she smiled. Then the room lit up with love. "Talking about me again, Fathers?"

Father Larry let out a joyous laugh. "As a matter of fact we were," he said. "But it was all good, Cora, as usual."

Father O'Manley stood near her at the door. "I'm just leaving for a little bit," he said, then walked past her and headed up the stairs to the rooms on the second floor.

Cora watched him walk by, then turned back to face Father Larry. "Jesse Nestarius is here to see you," she said.

Father Larry's face lit up in happy lines. "He's here now?"

She nodded.

"Well, send him in, Cora. I haven't seen my dear friend in so long." He tried to stand, but found it very difficult to combat the pains that crept through his chest and down through his gout infested legs.

"Sit, Larry."

Father Larry looked up to see Jesse standing beside Cora in the doorway.

"I'll leave you two alone," Cora said, backing out of the room. "I'll bring a pot of tea in shortly."

Father Larry raised an arm to signal that her offer was accepted. "That would be wonderful." Then he turned to Jesse who stood before him on the opposite side of the desk. "Would you be more comfortable sitting near the fireplace?" Father Larry motioned toward the cushioned chairs that were positioned across the room.

Jesse looked toward them, then turned his attention back to Father Larry and sat down in one of the chairs by the desk. "This is fine for now."

Father Larry wasn't sure how to interpret Jesse's answer. He was more accustomed to Jesse being relaxed and comfortable, informal and easy going. This wasn't like the Jesse he'd known all his life. He sat back in his chair, rested his hands on his stomach, and looked at his friend. "What is it? Something is wrong. That's quite obvious from your expression. Let me help you."

Jesse smiled, but did not take his line of sight from Father Larry. "That's exactly why I'm here," he said. "I need to deliver a message. And you will have to make a choice."

Father Larry leaned back in his chair and took a deep breath. "You sound cryptic," he said, smiling. "You know Jesse, you are the only man I know who never seems to age. What is your secret?" He laughed, then reached behind him where he kept a small refrigerator with a pitcher of orange juice. He poured himself a glass, then turned around to face Jesse. "Would you like some?"

Jesse shook his head, still holding his serious expression. "We really must talk, Larry. I need your full attention."

"And you have it." Father Larry took a big gulp of his juice, then placed the glass on a ceramic coaster. "What is it that has you in such a tragic frame of mind that you cannot even relax with an old friend?"

Jesse crossed his legs in front of himself and folded his hands on one knee. "As I said, I have to deliver a message."

Father Larry chuckled. "Angels deliver messages." He laughed. "But then, I always said your friendship was a gift from God." He took another drink of juice. "What is the message?"

Jesse looked at Father Larry, his face softened almost to a smile. "You will be going home soon."

Father Larry tilted his head to one side and smiled. "I am home, Jesse. I'll only be retiring soon. Then mayble I'll be able to relax, finally, and continue with the Lord's work in a different vein."

Jesse nodded. "You will continue with the Lord's work, Larry. But how you do it will be your choice."

Father Larry shook his head, feeling uncomfortable with the way his friend was behaving. "This isn't like you, Jesse. What has happened? Is something wrong?" He thought a moment. "You said you were delivering a message. Who is the message from?"

"God."

Father Larry took a deep breath and quickly reflected on his life. He thought of the vampires who had become such a large part of his later years. He thought of Roni's childhood and her recent disease. He thought of his own mistakes and how many times Jesse had been there to support and advise him, to pick him up and guide him to better decisions, and suddenly it all made sense. "I've always been curious about you," he said. "There've been times when I thought I knew you like I know my own brother. Then there were times when you were a mystery to me." He leaned forward and shoved his juice glass aside. "Tell me the truth. You've been with me all my life. But who are you really?"

Jesse smiled and stood. As he did so, he began to glow in beautiful hues of soft blue and white that dazzled everything in the room.

Father Larry fell back against his chair and took in a huge breath. "An angel," he said. "All these years I've had an angel right here in the flesh, by my side, and I never knew it."

Jesse nodded. The colors of light that surrounded him began to fade. "You've always had a good and true friend by your side, Larry. That's all you ever needed to know." He sat down. "Until now."

Father Larry shook his head, not understanding. What was so different now besides Roni's illness and the upcoming weddings for her and Chelle? Those were good things. Could that be it? It didn't make any sense to him. "I don't understand."

Jesse looked past him, out the window where the sun shone brightly on the budding spring flowers. "Roni's illness isn't just a human disease," he said. "It was caused when Gaetano Minotti attacked her right here in St. Joseph's that night Roni and Diana were brought here for safety from him."

Father Larry shook his head. He'd been unconscious through most of the fight because Minotti had played with him like a volleyball. All he ever knew of what happened that night was what he'd been told later. "I remember when Minotti went after Diana and Roni jumped in the way to protect her," he said. "And I remember Christian showing up in the church when Roni was already lying on the floor. Everything after that happened so fast, and before you know it, I woke up in the rectory." He looked at Jesse. "In fact, you were carrying me there."

Jesse nodded.

"Then what really happened that night?" Father Larry knew his suspicions were true. He always felt he hadn't been told the whole story, but the look on Jesse's face told him it was all going to come out now.

"Minotti did everything he could to get everyone out of his way so he could leave with Diana," Jesse said. "But he never really cared if he left with her or not. All he cared for was pulling as much good energy away from those around him and holding it into himself until it was converted to bad. He needed the extra strength to carry him to the other side and still be in control of himself when he went through the punishments of his own design."

Father Larry shook his head. "I hear what you're saying, but I don't understand. There is only heaven or hell on the other side."

"In simple terms that's true," Jesse said. "But our actions here determine the degree of our personal heaven or hell once we cross over."

Father Larry nodded to let Jesse know he understood.

"Minotti knew that his personal hell was so severe that he would end up in a different place called Limbo. All evil ends up there when it is so deep that even hell cannot hold it." He leaned forward. "You see. We are all eternal beings, Larry. But we are able to experience many different lives if we choose. Those in heaven or hell are allowed to come back for various reasons. Those is heaven come back to purify themselves even further so they can be rejoined with the Creator in a state of perfection. Those in hell return to break through their bad karma and convert the negative energy they've been carrying around for all of time." He stared at Father Larry and shook his head. "But those in Limbo have allowed their own evil selves to grow through lifetime after lifetime until it has grown out of control and must be forced to rest until the bad karma has drained away and been converted to other forms of energy."

Father Larry shook his head. "Now you're losing me," he said. "There is only supposed to be one lifetime here."

Jesse smiled. "You know the truth. You know the interpretation of the words of Jesus. You know what they really meant. Catholic priests have always been told the truth. It's only the parishioners who were ever kept in the dark, which I have disagreed with from the very beginning." He shrugged. "But it wasn't my decision."

Father Larry stared at Jesse. He'd barely heard a word he said. "I still see you as my friend." He looked at Jesse and knew that he felt the truth in his heart about his friend's nature years ago. "I must force myself to remember that I'm talking to an angel." He chuckled, feeling more at ease.

"As I was saying, Minotti knew he wasn't going to win the fight that evening, but he didn't want to." Jesse leaned to one side before he continued. "He wanted more power and he knew the power he would have if he died and crossed over with the ability to control the ramifications of his centuries here on earth." He hesitated. "It seems to have worked. Roni's illness was given to her and is now being controlled by one from the other side as well."

"Someone else?" Father Larry asked. "Not Minotti?"

Jesse nodded.

"Who might that be?" Father Larry asked.

Jesse gave him a concerned look, then sighed. "Audra Trivette," he said.

"The one Roni was so concerned about when she first met Christian?"

Once again, Jesse nodded.

"Where does she fit into all this?"

"She is almost as evil as Minotti," Jesse said. "Just younger. Her motivation is only to get back at Christian and Samuel for removing her from her immortality here on earth, but Minotti is using her to absorb the souls in hell and from wherever else she might find them. When he's ready, he will most likely absorb her into himself. All he wants it to seek vengeance on me for my part in the fight at St. Joseph's and his defeat."

Father Larry shook his head. "But I thought he wanted to be defeated so he could cross over to the other side and have more power."

"He did."

"But I don't understand."

Jesse smiled. "It's the confusion that evil brings upon itself, Larry. It makes no sense. It looks for reasons to be angry, to cause pain. There is no rationale behind it. Evil only looks for power and control of every kind. Nothing more."

Father Larry looked at Jesse for a moment and thought of that night. "So it was you who defeated Minotti?"

Jesse shook his head. "I only fought him."

"Then how was he defeated?"

Jesse sat in stillness and sighed, then looked at Father Larry and smiled. "By the Son of the Highest Power."

"Jesus?" Father Larry shook his head. This was too much. It wasn't even possible. "Now you've gone too far, Jesse. That's blasphemous."

"The truth is the truth, Larry."

"But it couldn't be. If that were the case, why would Minotti be allowed to have that kind of power once he got to the other side?" He leaned forward on the desk and heaved a sigh. "God is the most powerful."

Jesse nodded. "But even Minotti was given the gift when he was born."

"Free will?"

"Free will."

Father Larry sighed once more. "And he used it this way and was allowed to."

Jesse sighed. "He played by the rules of the universe, even though he never played by the rules of ethics as laid down by the Creator."

Father Larry looked up at him. "Now what?"

Jesse sat back in his seat and straightend himself up. "Now we need a decision from you. There is only one way to handle the kind of energy Minotti has become and that is to force it to be changed from evil to good. There is no time to let him sit in Limbo until it diminishes as has been done with so many others through time. Minotti already removed that option. The only way to fix this whole situation is to have all good, positive entities of love on the other side ready to hold and sustain that energy until it can be passed to another incarnation with souls who are aware of what is happening and are prepared to deal with it."

"You mean a rebirth?"

"Yes. And it may not even work."

"So, what do you need me for?"

"Well, as I said, you'll be going home soon."

Suddenly, Father Larry understood what Jesse meant.

"I've been sent to ask you if you are willing to return sooner than you would need to if your time here were to simply run out on its own." Jesse looked at Father Larry with love and understanding in his eyes. "There is another one on the other side who will need the help of someone close to the situation and whose soul is clean and devoted to the Almighty."

"That's me?" Father Larry smiled, then sat back and rubbed his stomach. "What does this entity need my help for? Is it another angel?"

"Of sorts," Jesse said. "The power of your love is stronger because of your ties to the families involved.

It is that kind of strength that is needed for this purpose. Physical strength means nothing in that realm where nothing is physical. It's the power of your heart that makes things happen, the power of energy and desire."

"So I will have to keep Minotti a captive until a child is ready to be born?" Father Larry was puzzled. "Is that what you're telling me?"

"It's more involved than that," Jesse told him. "There will only be a fraction of earth time for this to happen so the power must be there at precisely the right moment. The child has already been chosen, but the parents must be made aware of this first and they must make their own decision as to whether or not they want to take on this responsibilty. All the conditions are right, but the decision is not God's to make."

Father Larry nodded. "Let me get a few things in order. When will you know the parents' decision?"

"Soon, I hope." He looked at Father Larry. "I'll let you know."

Father Larry shook his head. "It doesn't matter," he said. "My first obligation is to my God. I'm His whenever He needs me." He felt the tears begin to form in his eyes from the thought of leaving everyone he loved behind, and from the love he felt from the Father. He was overwhelmed. "Make it fast." He looked at Jesse. "When it's time, please make it happen fast."

Jesse leaned forward. "It will be." He stood and walked around the desk to where Father Larry sat. He stooped down to hug him.

Father Larry felt the warmth of his arms and closed his eyes. When he opened them, Jesse was gone.

Chapter 8

1243 AD

JESSE loved the early evening, summer air. The warmth, the scents of life, the damp nights that blossomed once the sun was fully set. He felt the coolness begin to descend and smelled the beginnings of moist wood as he walked through the forest, in and out of the light that was left before the moon finally took its place for the night. The setting sun showed its dimming rays through the trees, creating beautiful colors against the lush, green leaves. He looked down at the glistening foliage that carpeted the ground where the last rays of the day were still able to touch them and watched the chipmunks chase each other over the few rocks and into the little entrances to their underground homes. He listened to the last songs of the birds before they bedded down for the night and sensed the approach of the evening animals as they began to stir, awakening for their midnight rounds. He'd never had a preference for which season he might enjoy the most, but this year was different. This year he was seeing it all, experiencing it through Serella's eyes and the summer was taking on a charm of its own. The way she moved, the grace of her fingers as she inspected her herbs for new growth, her fruit for ripeness, her flowers for aphids or black spot. He could see the sun shining off her long, blonde hair as if she were standing before him at this moment. He could see the gentle summer breeze as it moved single strands behind her as she walked. She would be forever embedded in his mind and in his heart.

This evening was exceptionally beautiful with the cool, evening air so warm and moist as he walked along the well-worn path through the trees that he'd created over the past few months from visiting Serella. He loved his time with her, loved the parts of her life that she shared with him. Her knowledge of the natural arts was impresive and she was so willing to give that knowledge to him, never questioning whether he might already know such things. She didn't seem to care. She just wanted to teach him all she could about the stones, the herbs, the animals, and the trees. Someday he'd probably tell her that angels knew pretty much all there was to know, but for now, he just couldn't do that and take away all the fun she was having at playing the role of his teacher. He laughed as he thought about it. He was here to teach her, and he had, but he couldn't stop her from enjoying the times when she told him about the special way she cooked her food with the herbs she grew, or the jewelry she made with all the stones she collected. He loved the lessons and he loved the woman without question, but he still didn't know how to approach the subject so he could tell her. He didn't even know if he should. He was an angel. What would happen to him? Jesse shook his head as he stopped to relax and watch a racoon in the distance making its way through the woods. That poor little guy beginning to scrounge around for food like all the other wild animals did during the daylight hours. Now it was his turn. "Good luck hunting," Jesse said softly as he watched him move away.

Jesse took a deep breath before he turned to finish his walk to Serella's. His feelings for her were only one of the many burdens their relationship had put on his shoulders. Feelings he'd never planned to have, never dreamed could happen to him. What was worse, he'd already had two more run-ins with Gaetano at Serella's home and quickly discovered that this was no ordinary man they were dealing with, vampire or not. He suspected that Serella knew more about him, than she'd said so far, but Jesse was not going to push her for information she was, obviously, not yet willing to give. But it bothered him, continuously, to think that Serella's life was in danger every minute that he wasn't with her. Even now, this one day that Jesse had gone back to check on his own home, he couldn't help but wonder what might happen. Still, he had to make sure his house continued to appear lived in so no unknown passersby from town might begin to wonder if he was alright and look for him only to discover that he'd been living at Serella's house for the past few weeks. Jesse could not do that to Serella's reputation, so he'd continue to maintain his own house for as long as it might be needed. Nothing had transpired between Serella and himself and he intended to keep things proper and wholesome, but his feelings for her were growing and he feared that his physical existence would get away from him being so much in her presence. Still, it was the only foreseeable way to protect her from that man.

Gaetano reeked of evil intentions, evil desires, and destructive, deadly needs. Rarely had Jesse encountered such a degree of malice and it frightened even him these three times he'd come face to face with the demon. There was more unnatural about him than just his vampirism which he never showed signs of. Jesse wondered if he practiced the black arts against Serella's white witchcraft, but Serella had told him that she'd never heard such things about him. She did, however, admit that she was very aware of his evil nature. The third visit was the most frightening of all when Gaetano openly threatened her life if she didn't make herself his, but each time he showed up to claim her for himself, she turned him away. Jesse hadn't been able to get those events off his mind and he wasn't sure how to protect her, if Gaetano showed up, yet again. Each time he appeared Gaetano had found new and different ways to sneak around, even avoiding the wolves, which had unnerved Serella to such a degree that she hadn't slept for three nights afterward.

So many thoughts were running through Jesse's mind as he approached her house that he'd hardly heard her scream. What grabbed his attention was the incessant howling that seemed to be everywhere. He heard the canines and began to walk faster, sensing the urgency in their cries. When he reached the first line of wolves at the edge of the forest, he heard her scream, again and began to run for the door without a second thought as to what the wolves might do to him. Fortunately, the howling stopped when he reached the front door and ran in. What he saw not only caught him off guard, but frightened him in a way he had never thought possible. Serella was lying on the floor, her clothes torn, with blood was running from all parts of her body. Her hands and feet were tied behind her back and Gaetano stood beside her, a many-tailed whip in one hand and a garden hoe in the other. Both were dripping with blood. Gaetano looked at Jesse when he ran in the room and froze. A smirk on his face told Jesse all he needed to know.

"What have you done?" Jesse yelled as he ran to Serella's side. His pulse was racing and he knew it was already too late to save her physical life.

"Do not waste your time," Gaetano said, a proud smile on his face. "She is as good as dead."

Jesse stood up and faced Gaetano, both fists clenched at his sides as he tried to maintain his composure. "I thought you wanted her for yourself," Jesse said. "Why would you do this to her if she meant so much to you?" He started to cry against all of his own efforts to stay strong. Disbelief and pain ran through his soul. "Why did you have to do this to her?"

Gaetano laughed a hideaous, evil laugh and stood back in a relaxed manner. "I did not want her, you silly, innocent. I wanted her powers, nothing more."

Jesse grabbed at Gaetano's shirt, poised as if to strike out with his fist.

"From an angel?" Gaetano goaded, then laughed. "I have always been able to bring out the worst in others."

Jesse felt his dignity begin to wither and his soul start to shrink. What had this evil man done to him? 'God help me,' he thought. 'Keep me strong.' He looked at Gaetano. "And what purpose did this serve?"

"I am satisfied," Gaetano said.

Jesse stared him down for a few, brief moments. "Is that all?"

"Well, of course, she could have given in and none of this would have happened." Gaetano began to walk around the room as if he were strutting in front of a crowd of admirers. "I did not have to torture her until she died. It could just as easily have stopped if she would have simply relinquished her powers to me." He stopped walking and turned to Jesse. "But since she chose not to give me what I asked for, then I decided she cannot have them, either." He looked down at her as if she was nothing more than an animal carcass. "I have seen to that."

"Not if I can help it," Jesse said. He leaned down and undid the ropes that bound Serella's limbs, but her body simply rolled over to the side, no life left in her shell. Her chest was not moving and Jesse felt no breath when he placed a hand across the airway from her nose and mouth. He looked up at Gaetano. "She just screamed. I heard her."

Gaetano's eyes had fire in them as he stared at Jesse. "What you heard was the last sound to ever come from her. Now, I am going to take the powers from her soul, since her body chose not to oblige me."

He began what Jesse thought to be a meditation, but he didn't wait to be sure before he sat down next to Serella's lifeless body and began the process that would separate his soul from his body and take him to the other side, once again. Immediately, he saw her hovering over her empty, physical self, staring at what was left of her life on earth, then at him with frightened energy all around her. "Come with me," he said, holding a hand out to her. "Quickly. He can only follow us so far. Come with me, now."

Serella reached a hand to Jesse and their energy connected. Jesse felt her fear flow into him and he immediately empathized with her. "Am I dead?" she asked. "This is not fair."

"No, it is not," Jesse said as he pulled her along. "But we have no time to waste, Serella. He is going to try to cross over long enough to take your powers from you on this side. That is all he wanted."

"I know," she said.

He felt her spirit's energy tighten and felt the fear in her grow stronger. "It will be all over soon," he said. "We only have to get through this tunnel and a little beyond before you will be safe, forever." He felt her tug on him, turned to look at her, and saw Gaetano right behind them. "That cannot be," he said. "What is he? How did he get here so fast? That is not supposed to be possible."

"He is a vampire," Serella said.

Jesse pulled her along through the tunnel as he let her words sink in. "Yes, you told me. But there must be more to him that simply that, though it does explain why we only saw him at night. That makes sense. But still, the terrible energy I felt from him was worse than that of any vampire I had ever run across."

"All I know is that his vampirism was the method by which he was able to get in my house without being detected by anyone," Serella said. "Not even my beautiful wolves."

"How long did you know this?" Jesse asked as he watched the dark tunnel borders move quickly past.

"I knew it all along, but I could not make him stay away. He was always hungry for power and that is all he has been trying to do is collect as much as he was able." She tugged on him, again. "He is catching up to us, Jesse. We have to hurry."

Jesse sent a plea for help to the universe and felt his angelic powers grow stronger immediately. "We shall be alright," he said. "God is working with us. Just have faith and maintain our connection until all is safe. That is all we have to do." He looked back to check on her and saw her nod in agreement. "Good. We are almost there." He turned back around and saw the end of the tunnel approaching and the foggy mist that always lingered beyond that. "Do you see that?"

"The mist?" Serella said. "Yes, I see it."

"Gaetano cannot go through that area without being diverted to his own personal hell for all of eternity," Jesse said. "Or until he chooses a new incarnation. Either way, the minute Gaetano exits this tunnel of life, he shall be stuck on this side, but he shall never be able to follow you to your destination."

"Where am I going?" Serella asked.

"To a wonderful, peaceful place," Jesse said. "But even if Gaetano ends up passing all the way through the tunnel, you shall at least, be safe and your powers shall still belong to you."

"I have no care for my powers," Serella said. "Look at the horror they just caused me. And all I wanted to use them for were good, beautiful things. Look what it did to me."

"Do not think of that," Jesse said. "Your powers are a gift. One that you shall surely retain because of the huge sacrifice you just made to keep them pure."

They approached the mist and Jesse felt the calm that emanated from The Source of all Life. When they were in its center he felt Serella slow her progress and he turned to her and watched her approach him on her own. She was floating through the celestial surroundings of the other realm. Already she appeared to be right where she belonged. She was as natural a being in the celestial as any angel he knew, but he couldn't see what had caused her progress to slow down. "Is something wrong?" he asked.

Serella's arms were outstretched as if feeling the atmosphere. And she was smiling. "It is beautiful, Jesse." She looked around.

"You are beautiful, Serella."

She looked at him and suddenly, she was wearing the most beautiful dress in shades of rose and crimson. "What?" She looked at her ethereal clothing, then up at Jesse. "I feel wonderful, Jesse."

"And you deserve to." Love filled his heart and he wanted to embrace her, but couldn't. "Enjoy the feeling while you are here, Serella. One day you shall go back to the physical, but you must be fully rested, fully replenished of strenth before then. This is your time to heal."

Serella reached a hand toward him. "I plan to never go back," she said. "I already know that this is where I want to stay."

"You have not crossed over fully, yet," Jesse said. "Wait until then to tell me what you shall end up doing."

"Why? Is it bad?"

"No," Jesse said, laughing. "It is even more beautiful than what you see right here."

"I have no need of anything else but this feeling," she said. "The serenity is wonderful." She closed her eyes and let herself exist in place while Jesse watched her. "I have not felt this free before."

"This is not all there is," Jesse said. "But you shall have to move on so you can fully heal."

She opened her eyes and looked at him. "Come with me."

He wanted to.

"Jesse," she said, reaching a hand to him. "You do not have to go back, do you?"

He touched her hand, wanting desparately to stay with her. He could. Now that he was back he knew the Creator would allow it. That's what free will was for. It gave him that right to make his own choices. But should he? How would he feel if he were to abandon his current mission of taking care of the unusual souls on earth and helping them find the better paths to follow in their lives? Wouldn't it be selfish if he were to put his own desires ahead of those of the mortals who so desparately needed his help?

He looked at her, again. "I cannot, he said."

"Yes you can," she said, her eyes sparkling as she brushed her spirit hand across his cheek.

He gently moved her form away from him, his soul tearing apart as he looked in her eyes. "I have the work of God to do, first," he said. "That comes before everything else and I cannot go against that truth." He reached a hand out to her and felt her anguish course through him. "It is my truth, Serella. It is what I was created for."

"But I love you, Jesse."

His heart broke, his soul melted, he wanted to give up everything he was destined for in a split second of love's great anguish, but he felt his spirit self be calmed from within and around and knew the Father was proud of His child. "And I love the One, Serella. More than anything or anyone else I have ever known. All of those souls in the physical are part of Him just like you and I are. My duties are to nourish the Creator and enable Him to continue bringing new life energy to all of existence. That responsibility is so much more than just taking care of one soul that has already gone home to safety." He felt her heartbreak, her disappointment, but he knew, now, that he was right. "You are home and you are safe." He took a step toward her. "Come with me, Serella. "I need to see you safely to the other side."

Serella looked at him, a question in her eyes. "We are on the other side," she said. "What else is there to see?"

Jesse took her hand for the last time. "Heaven."

Chapter 9

April 29 2:00PM

CHELLE and Joe entered the hospital room where Roni had been taken the night before. Only two visitors were allowed in the room at one time, so Roni's parents had gone downstairs to the lobby to let Chelle and Joe could go up to see her. That was when they learned how her condition had worsened.

"Now remember," Chelle said to Joe. "We have to keep her smiling."

Joe nodded as he motioned for Chelle to enter the room first.

Roni lay in bed, her face obviously swollen from crying. Chelle did her best to ignore the sight. "Hey, Lady. If you didn't want to go shopping, all you had to do was say so."

Roni looked at her friend and gave her a half-hearted smile while Chelle bent down to hug her.

"How're you feeling?" Chelle asked, releasing her, then turning to sit down.

Roni shook her head. "My body doesn't want to do what I'm telling it to do." Tears began to form in her eyes.

"That's because you push it too hard," Chelle joked. "It's revolting against you."

Roni stared at her.

"I'm sorry," Chelle said. "That was a dumb thing to say."

Roni was silent.

"On a lighter topic," Joe said, stepping forward. "We're going to be parents." The smile on his face was huge and proud, as if he'd just seen his son win an Olympic Medal.

Roni seemed to liven a little, a genuine smile crossing her face as she used her arms to lift herself up. "That's wonderful news," she said. "You seem mighty happy about it."

Joe reached forward to help her position herself, then sat on the bed beside her. "I'm thrilled, Roni. I can't tell you how full I am inside right now."

He looked at Chelle with such love in his eyes, it warmed her heart and made her fall in love with him all over again.

"I'm about to have a wife I've only been able to dream of, and a child just when I was beginning to think that would never happen because I wasn't married." He reached over and took Chelle's hand, then lifted it to his lips and kissed the back of it.

Chelle looked at him and whispered, "I love you, Joe."

He smiled then turned back to Roni. "We wanted to come see how you're doing and let you know that Chelle told me about the baby and I'm so happy I can't even hold it in. I think I'm going to want to announce it in the church after we exchange our vows."

With the mention of the wedding, Roni's face dropped. Chelle knew she had to do something to reassure her best friend that nothing was going to change. "You're my maid-of-honor no matter what happens, Roni." Chelle put her hand on Roni's arm. "I don't care if we have to have the ceremony right here in the hospital. I don't want anyone else."

Roni turned toward her. "Pick someone else, Chelle. I'm getting worse." She looked away. "I won't be able to walk down the aisle."

"That's not what the witnesses are about," Joe said. "They're there to back you up in the eyes of God, to attest to the fact that you know exactly what you're doing as you're taking those vows. They're there to prove that we're of sound mind when we commit ourselves to each other." He shook her arm, just enough to make her turn to face him. "The witnesses are not there to put on a show for everyone." He stared at Roni, his face a mask of serious intentions. They're there to share in our joy and attest to the fact that we know what we're doing."

Roni smiled. "Thank you."

Joe nodded, his face softened, and Chelle thanked God for bringing him into her life.

* * *

"Thank you for lunch," Father Larry said as Father O'Manley helped him into the car. "Would you mind stopping at the hospital on the way back so we can check on Roni?"

Father O'Manley handed Father Larry his cane then took a step back. "Not at all," he said. "That very idea had crossed my mind, as well." He closed the car door, then walked around to the other side and got in behind the wheel.

The hospital was only ten minutes from the restaurant and before they knew it they were walking down the hall looking for room three forty seven. It was around the corner when they got off the elevator and only two doors from the emergency exit at the other end of the hall. When they reached it and peeked in, Father Larry was surprised, but pleased, to see Chelle and Joe already there.

"Well, well," he said, chuckling softly as he entered the room. "I would've thought you'd be off somewhere making arrangements for your big day." He looked over at Roni and saw she was sleeping.

"We're going to take care of some of that later. We wanted to stop in to see Roni first, though." She looked over at Roni as she lay sleeping, then turned back toward Father larry. "The nurse just came in a few minutes ago and gave her a sedative to help her sleep," Chelle said. "They said she had a restless night and a mighty hectic morning with all the tests Dr. Reno had them running on her, but when the news came back about how much worse it has all gotten and they told her, well, she's done nothing but cry. She didn't look good when we got here."

Joe joined Father O'Manley in helping make sure Father Larry was seated comfortably. "Ah, that's wonderful," Father Larry said, feeling content in the cushioned chair. "I was hoping to be able to chat with her, but her rest is much more important. I'll just sit for a minute and talk with you two, instead. That is, if you have the time."

"We do", Joe said. "But, I thought only two were allowed in the rooms. How did you manage this?

Father Larry and Father O'Manley exchanged glances, then smiled. "That's true," Father Larry said, rubbing his belly. "The hospital policy is only to allow two visitors per room, but we're here visiting so often, and so many times it's for much worse news than this," he said, looking quickly at Roni. "We're allowed in so we can comfort the family and friends and, of course, the patient."

"We're not going to cause a raucus," Father O'Manley said, smiling. "That rule was made to avoid such an event. That's not why priests are here, though, so in a way it doesn't apply."

Joe nodded, but said nothing. Instead, he looked at Chelle, smiled, then glanced down at where her hand rested against her stomach. His gesture did not go unnoticed and all at once, Father Larry knew who the chosen child was that Jesse told him about. It felt so right it made him want to cry from joy. God's timing was so perfect it was absolutely amazing. Now he just had to make sure Chelle and Joe could make a conscious decision to raise a spirit like Minotti and guide his development in a new incarnation. And he hoped someone would be there to witness if he got the answers Jesse said God would need to hear.

"So tell me," he said, glancing back and forth from Chelle to Joe. "What are your plans for a family, or do you have any?"

Chelle smiled and looked at Joe who smiled back, then turned to face the priests. "Actually, Fathers. We have discussed it. In fact, we're even discussing names."

Father Larry smiled and let out a soft chuckle. "That's wonderful," he said. "Are you hoping for a family soon after the wedding?"

"Well," Joe began. "How does nine months from now sound?"

Father Larry did his best to act surprised. "What? Already? Then maybe we should speed this ceremony up a bit." He laughed, aloud, throwing his head back a bit, then quickly recovered his composure. "No, next month will be soon, enough. No one will know and you'll still look to be your slender self in your dress." He sat up a bit and cleared his throat before he continue. "Tell me. Are you planning to raise them in any particular manner?"

Chelle nodded. "Don't worry, Father. Our child will be raised as we were raised, according to all that is good in God's eyes. And we'll try to get them to church. I know I haven't been to faithful in attending, but that can change." She looked at Joe, then at both priests. "I appreciate all you're doing for Roni and Christian, too. Their own marriage means so much to them." She rubbed her friend's arm before she continued. "What would happen if we asked Roni and Christian to be godparents?"

Father Larry felt his heart begin to pound. A vampire as a godfather in the Catholic church. But it made sense. It had to be if Chelle's child, this formerly evil entity, was to be raised under strong, watchful eyes throughout the night as well as during the day. Especially when the child grew older and more independent, more able to hide his or her comings and goings. It had to be. It would be the only way. Who else could be there in the blink of an eye to stop it from doing wrong or from being negatively influenced by wrong-doers. "I think it's a wonderful idea," he said. "Is there any reason you've chosen them?"

Chelle nodded. "It's a gut feeling Joe and I both had. Like destiny. I can't explain it, but it's really strong."

Joe squeezed her hand and looked at Father O'Manley. "I can't explain it either, Father, but for some reason it feels right. I think it's because of everything Roni and Chelle have been through together. They're closer than sisters and always part of each other's lives. But it feels like it's more than that, even. I don't know. It just feels right."

"And what about Christian?"

Joe shook his head. "There's something about him." He looked at Chelle. "I see the way he bickers back and forth with Chelle sometimes, but there's a strong, mutual respect there. You can see they'd do anything for each other as if they were family. I don't know the whole history of Roni and Christian, but I do know that I like him, and I admire his devotion to her. If he and Roni were only a fraction as devoted to their godchild as they are to each other, it would be a blessing for us as parents of that child."

Father Larry felt his emotions well up and he found he had to swallow hard before he could continue. "That has to be one of the most beautiful testimonials to the choice of godparents I've ever heard." He took a deep breath and turned to Father O'Manley. "Father O'Manley, would you mind taking a walk down to the cafeteria to get me a glass of orange juice?"

Father O'Manley nodded, then left the room.

"Very quickly before he returns," Father Larry said to them. "I need to ask the two of you something, but you have to listen close and think carefully."

"You sound so serious, Father." Joe leaned forward slightly. "Go ahead and ask."

Father Larry cleared his throat, not certain how to approach the subject, but he knew he had to try. "What if you were to find out there was a special reason you had to protect your child from the ways of the world? Would you be able to handle that?"

"What do you mean?" Joe asked. "All parents have to protect their children from the ways of the world. It's a given."

Father Larry hesitated, searching for the right words to say this. "You know that as a Catholic priest I cannot condone anything that goes against the doctrine of the church. But I have always had an interest in reincarnation." He looked at Chelle, hoping she would realize there was more to this topic than the obvious. "What if you were told directly, that you were raising a child whose soul was very evil in its last incarnation, but is now under your care to redirect it and change its evil energy to goodness." He looked at both of them, noticing the stunned look on Joe's face and the acceptance on Chelle's. "Could you do it?"

Chelle answered without a moment's delay. "Absolutely."

Father Larry looked at Joe.

"Is this a test?" Joe asked.

Father Larry laughed and did his best to make light of Joe's concern. "No," he said. "It's just a question. But a serious one. Some children can be so nasty no matter how hard the parents try to teach it right from wrong. That would be a very serious challenge. So, I'm wondering how you might handle such a situation, should it happen to you."

Joe was looking at Chelle, seemingly amazed at her quick response to Father Larry's question, but he nodded.

Father Larry could see the doubts on Joe's face, but he knew the answer had to be one of certainty in order for their plan to work. He certainly didn't want to leave his physical life early for nothing. "Would you?" he asked, again.

Joe smiled, leaned forward, and rested a hand on Father Larry's arm. "It's the way we were raised," he said, putting an arm around Chelle. "It's the way our children will all be raised. We'll do whatever has to be done in order to make sure they're not only raised right, but that they understand the importance of all that we teach them."

Chelle nudged him in the ribs and smiled. "Children? Now there's more? I haven't even delivered this one, yet and you've already got us having more."

Joe leaned over and kissed her forehead. "We aren't even married yet, either, but my love for you keeps growing." He turned to Father Larry. "If Chelle can be so certain in her heart not to question your concern, then I love her enough to follow her instincts and trust her judgement. Whatever kind of child we're blessed with, we'll do everything we can to make sure he or she is raised the right way. Whatever it takes, it'll be worth it."

Father Larry felt his heart fill up. Across the room he saw a hazy form begin to develop. He thought he was seeing things until he recognized the fuzzy outline of Jesse. He smiled at Father Larry and whispered a, "Thank You," that only Father Larry could hear. Then he was gone as quickly as he had appeared. Father Larry knew then that all the necessary decisions had been made and they had been witnessed by the perfect soul.

"Here's your juice, Larry." Father O'Manley entered the room with a glass of orange juice and placed it in Father Larry's hand.

"Thank you." Father Larry took the glass and drank almost half of it before he put the glass on the nightstand. He turned to Chelle and Joe and smiled.

"Will you let Roni know we were here? We'll see her family on the way out."

Chelle and Joe nodded in unison. "We'll be leaving soon, as well," Joe said. "We only have a few things to take care of today, but it's going on three o'clock. We should get started now that we know what's happening with Roni."

Father O'Manley and Joe helped Father Larry stand up. Then Joe went down to the nurses station and returned with a wheel chair for Father Larry. "They should have brought one of these to you when you arrived. I'm surprised they didn't."

When Father Larry was seated, he turned to Joe. "You're a very thoughtful young man," he said. "Hold on to that quality. It feeds your soul."

Joe nodded. "I know, Father. I've been told that before. It's how I try to be. But thank you for saying so."

Father O'Manley took the wheelchair and led Father Larry to the elevators. "That's one, beautiful couple," he said. "God must be pleased."

Father Larry took a deep breath. "I'm sure He is, Steve. I'm sure He is."

Chapter 10

April 29 7:00 PM

JESSE stood at the edge of the sandy beach and watched the waves roll toward him. The voices of Christian, Diana, and Samuel were easily heard from where they sat together on the porch behind him, but Jesse needed a few minutes to himself before Serella appeared. It was the first time he could remember feeling fear in a very long time and he knew it was another indication that it was time for him to go home. Angels should never be afraid. Their very nature dictated the power that was at their disposal to protect them from such thoughts, such doubts. Still, Jesse felt a very human emotion that was not supposed to be a part of who he was, not at all who the Father intended when he was created. That emotion was Fear.

Jesse looked back at his three friends and felt Christian's anxiety over not being with Roni at the moment, he felt Diana's concern for her brother's happiness, and he felt Samuel's well-meaning intentions to change Roni and put the entire matter to rest for two people he cared so much about. Jesse knew he'd have to keep an eye on him until this was all over because Samuel's blind loyalty might cause more problems than they already had.

"Jesse." It was Serella's voice, but it had a quality of uncertainty about it.

"I'm here," he said. "And I know you're uncomfortable."

There was no response.

"I'm here, Serella. Just tell me when you feel ready."

Water lapping at the shore was the only thing he heard, so he turned back toward the ocean, breathed in the salt air, then went to join the others on the porch.

"Well, what's happening?" Samuel asked. "I mean, I know what we're here for, but where's Serella?"

Jesse smiled. "Patience, Samuel. She's coming. You must remember that she's been on the other side for as long as you've been immortal. Minotti is the reason she has refused to return to the physical. Allowing all of you to see her at one time is not a decision that came easily to her. Again, it's because of Minotti that such a decision was even necessary. You see, with him on that side now, there is no where for her to go to be away from him."

"What about back to this side?" Diana asked.

Jesse shook his head. "This is not where reality lives. All energy exists in the celestial where reality and eternity coexist. The awareness of the soul becomes clouded here and entities in human form are no longer able to see the two realms simultaneously. But over there, nothing hides the reality of all creation. Full knowledge is open to everyone, and with knowledge comes power. Those in heaven are hidden from those on earth. But those on earth are hidden from no one on either side. Serella would be in even more danger if she were to accept a new incarnation because she would be born with the knowledge of truth, but she would forget it all before she reached puberty."

"Not necessarily," Diana said. "It depends on who her parents might be."

Jesse nodded. "That's true, but people change. She's not willing to take the chance that they'll actually become the kind of parents they seem able to become. She has very little faith in things of chance since her encounter with Minotti."

Diana nodded. "I know what you mean."

"I'm ready, Jesse." Serella's voice was nothing more than a frightened whisper, but there was a determination wound through it that was unmistakable.

Jesse nodded as he faced the three on his porch. He felt Serella's presence approaching from the other side and he looked to his right. "Diana, Samuel, and Christian," he said. "This is Serella Stone."

Suddenly, there she was in her aura of crimson and dusty rose hovering almost a foot above the sand. She smiled, and Jesse was pleased to see them all smile in response.

"Thank you for coming to talk with us," Diana said. "You don't know how much this means."

Serella nodded. "Yes, I do," she said. "That's why I'm here."

Jesse felt the awe eminating from the others, felt their unspoken questions, and stepped forward. "We'll take this meeting at your pace, Serella."

She nodded and smiled as if to let him know she understood and accepted his words.

"Has anything else developed?" he asked her.

She looked at each of them in turn, then glided a few inches closer. "Audra has been working on Roni almost non-stop," she said. "She is determined to go through with her own plans for revenge regardless of what Minotti tells her. She has little concern for what he's asked of her. Even worse, she's so consumed with her own agenda that she doesn't have any idea what his plans for her might be. Her concentration has been on Roni and the effect her failing health has been having on Christian." Serella hovered closer to Christian, watching him intently. "Don't worry, Christian," she said, facing him with a smile that was meant for only him. Then she backed up a few inches and glanced at each of them, again. "Minotti, however, has been on his own mission, traveling through all parts of reality to see what he is up against. He is quickly absorbing all the negative energies he can trace and growing stronger by the moment. His final burst will be when he approaches Audra to take her into himself." Serella looked at Jesse. "She is strong. Only Minotti is stronger at this time, but he will win against her because she is deranged and doesn't think beyond what she sees or chooses to see."

"That has always been her downfall," Jesse said.

Serella nodded slowly, causing waves of crimson to light the air around her.

"If that happens it will make our chosen mission more difficult to accomplish," Serella said. "And we may lose."

"Wait a minute," Christian said. "What kind of strength do we have on our side? Just who's here now? The five of us?"

Serella looked at Jesse. He sent her his hearts reassurance to go on, then nodded.

"No, Christian," Serella said. "All good forces and positive energy are there with you, ready to give all of us their strengths and come to our aide regardless of which side of reality it is waged on. There are many good souls here in the celestial who have not gone into a new incarnation. There always are." She smiled. "And they will always be available to assist in both the physical and the spiritual, where I am. Unfortunately, there are always evil souls on this side, as well. The main difference is that those who walk in the light will always respect the gift of free will and allow the individual spirits to make their own choices. But Minotti, as evil as he is, has taken that gift away from those suffering in the flames of their own creation and has chosen to mold their desires into his own. That leaves those who only work for the good," she hesitated as she looked at Jesse, then at the others. "We are left to move in faith and trust."

Samuel stood up, causing Serella to float back a few feet as he began to walk back and forth before the others. "How do we know we will have the support of all the good souls that are able to come to our aide?"

Jesse moved quickly to her side. "Don't worry, Serella. Samuel needs to pace. It's alright."

Serella looked at him and smiled, then turned to Samuel and moved forward only a foot. "We don't, Samuel. It's their choice. They'll neither be punished nor reprimanded in any way, if they decide not to come to our assistance, as you might expect they should. They each are settling their own karmas in their own time and that is the only obligation they have, to perfect their spirits for the Creator. How they interpret that obligation is, again, by their own choosing."

Samuel shook his head and turned around, throwing his arms in the air. "Great."

"Serella," Diana said, leaning forward. "Assuming we go up against Minotti and Audra with a small amount of force to support us, what should we expect to accomplish?"

Serella looking lovingly at Diana and moved to within three feet of her. "Our intent is to restrain Minotti's life energy until it can be moved into a new physical form."

"A child?" Diana asked.

Serella nodded. "Unborn, of course, but in fetal form."

"Then what?"

"Once a soul has entered the physical state it will remain there until its new form, its body, is destroyed or has expired."

"Then what?" Diana asked.

"Then, if the entity has been properly molded, properly nurtured and taught, it will have been given a new direction for its remaining lifetimes," Serella said.

Samuel looked up at her. "And how are we going to help you hold something we can't see? What can we do from this side to help restrain Minotti until a new physical form is found?"

"You aren't going to hold him from this side," Serella said. "This entire battle will be fought on both sides at once."

"What?!" Diana, Samuel, and Christian all echoed the same thought.

"Yes," Jesse said. "That's how Minotti appears to be structuring this battle so that he cannot be defeated here or in the eternal realm."

Christian ran his fingers through his hair. "You've got to be kidding. How are we supposed to fight a battle on both sides when we can't see what's happening up there." He pointed to the sky. "Or whereever," he said, shrugging as if he was lost.

Serella moved toward him and touched his hand with the tip of her finger's aura. "It is the truth, Christian. It is real."

He looked up at her. "Can this battle be won?"

She smiled. "Yes."

"Will it?" Samuel asked.

"I don't know," she answered him.

Diana looked at her and sighed. "What can we do from this side to help? Explain to us what's happening on the two sides, exactly."

Serella floated back to hover beside Jesse. "On this side, you are already seeing what's been happening to Roni. She is Audra's primary weapon against Christian. All she wants to do is make Christian so emotionally distraught that he is out of control, leaving her able to take his distress into herself for even more power." She looked at Christian. "So far, her plan has been working, but she isn't finished. She is also planning to go after Samuel by bruising your friendship and his relationship with Diana." She opened her arms to all of them. "You must all remain in positive mind sets. You must do whatever it takes to remain happy, faithful, and trusting. Do not feed her hunger for power. You must find a positive side to absolutely everything from this moment on."

"But that will only work against Audra," Samuel said. "What about Minotti?"

"Minotti is waiting for Audra's power to reach a particular level of his own choosing, then he plans to absorb her into himself the way she has been absorbing souls from the other side into herself." A sad look suddenly spread across her face and her aura turned dark. "Once that is done, the two strongest, negative souls on this side of existence will be united and it will only serve to make the battle more difficult for all that is good. But if we are able to halt Audra's progress right now, it will buy time, anger Minotti, distract him from his current course of picking up spirits and make him go after her with more intent."

"What good will that do?" Samuel asked. "He'll probably just take her energy into himself earlier than he'd planned."

"Maybe." Serella's darkened light stopped shimmering and froze. "But I'm planning to make Audra turn on him before that happens so that she is already prepared to fight him. That will cause a battle within their own dark side of existence, force Minotti off balance, enable us to surround his energy field and guide it to the child that waits for a soul to be born with."

"What a terrible fate to be given to an unborn child," Diana said. "It doesn't seem fair to start a young life out in such a way."

Serella smiled. "My dear," she lovingly said to Diana. "In truth, everyone starts out in such a way." She hestitated as if waiting for a reaction from Diana, then continued. "Each time a soul returns to earth it does so for its own enlightenment, its own teaching, its own lessons. This time will be no different for the soul that is currently known as Minotti."

"Amazing," Diana said. "And this will all happen at once?"

Serella nodded. "In an instant."

"When do we get started?"

Serella smiled. "Right now, Diana. You must all start right now to find the positive in everything and encourage those around you to find it, also."

Diana nodded.

"There is something else I need for you to do." Serella stared at her, a gentle look in her eyes.

"Me?" Diana asked.

Serella nodded. "There is an uncut amethyst crystal in Roni's purse. It's been there for a few years."

"You want me to go into her purse?"

"Yes. Take the crystal and place it in Roni's hand." Serella gently raised one arm a few inches. "Not right away, though. Not until after she's home from the hospital. You'll know when."

Diana looked at Serella, her head tilted to one side as if she didn't fully understand Serella's directive. "I will?"

Serella smiled, the color returning to her aura in waves. "Trust me, Diana. You'll know."

"What is it for?" Samuel asked.

Serella slowly focused her sight on him. "Everything in existence is nothing more than various forms of energy," Serella said. "Each form of energy is constantly vibrating at its own speed, at its own intensity." She studied each of them before she continued. "Amethyst is a crystal with healing energy embedded in its structure and it is a stone of spirit. And that particular piece of amethyst has interacted with both Chelle and Roni's energy. As a result, it is now a link between them and itself." She looked at each of them, then focused on Diana. "When the time comes it will facilitate the transformation of energy and the protection of those involved with it. Will you remember to do this?"

Diana nodded. "But, why me? Why not Christian?"

Serella moved closer and reached a hand out to Diana. "It's a woman thing," she said in a sweet, melodic voice.

"That figures," Christian said, a slight chuckle in his voice.

Serella moved back to hover near Jesse and looked at each of them. "Thank you all for being so kind."

Christian and Samuel nodded, but Diana smiled at Serella, an expression of respect and awe on her face.

Jesse was pleased to see everyone in agreement. Their willingness to follow her directions filled his heart with joy, but how was he to tell them about Father Larry? Should he? Oh, how he wished it didn't have to come to the passing of his dear friend, of their dear friend, too. But there was no choice but to tell them the truth and he knew it. He took a deep breath, then spoke. "I think you should all be told one thing, however."

They all looked at him and waited.

"There will be events that will come along within the next few weeks that will test your ability to do this. Heartbreaking events, disappointments, and difficult times to deal with." He knew he was stalling, but he couldn't help himself. Just telling them would cause them pain.

"How soon is all this going to happen?" Samuel asked, deflecting the subject for the moment.

"Yes," Christian added. "How long will we have to go on trying to find the positive in everything?"

Serella smiled. "You should all have been living your lives in that way all along. Had you done so, this would be nothing new to any of you." She shook her head. "I don't know how long it will take, but when it starts you will have no doubt that it has begun."

"Is there something, some sign, that will show us that the time has come?" Diana asked.

Serella and Jesse looked at each other. Jesse felt his own dread of having to tell them, then he felt her encouragement pushing him to be honest with the others and he nodded, then looked back at them where they still waited for the answer. "Yes," he said. "There is one way you'll know for sure." He looked at each of them, then let out a huge sigh. "When Father Larry crosses over, you'll know it has begun."

PART III

"I tell you in truth,
no one can see the kingdom of God
unless he is born again."

John 3:3

Chapter 1

May 6 7:00PM

DIANA stared at Christian, her eyes wide, her mouth hanging open. "Roni's sight is gone?" she asked. "When did that happen?"

Christian shook his head and stared out his living room window at the early evening wilderness of spring. Last year at this time he and Roni had already been out shopping for garden plants at dusk and planting by moonlight. The sight of her digging in the darkness, then carefully placing the small shoots in the ground played through his mind as if he could see her out there right now. He looked at the moon glory she'd planted a few days ago when she came home from the hospital. She knew it was still too soon for planting, but she was afraid she wouldn't be able to work in the garden at all this year. . . . or ever. Already, the moon glory was forming buds for the season. New life, new beginnings, but what about Roni? He felt a lump crawl up in his throat as he thought of the pain she felt. "Her sight in not entirely gone," he said, turning to face Diana. "She can't see out of the right side. But the neurologist that Dr.

Reno sent her to just put her on a different medication to try to control that. It's a steroid that is supposed to bring the swelling down. Something about the nerve swelling up and blocking something." He shook his head, then looked away. "Something like that."

Diana glanced down the hall. "Is that what the contraption in the bedroom is for?"

Christian nodded. "It's an IV, Di. Chelle hooked it up earlier and said she'll be back in a few hours to remove it. Roni has to have it for two hours a day, all week. The nerve behind her eye swelled up and that's what caused the blindness. The stuff in the IV drip is supposed to bring the swelling down."

"You said that," Diana reminded him.

Christian looked at her, trying to absorb what she'd just told him. "Did I?"

Samuel stepped forward, his hands clasped lightly behind his back. He looked intently at Christian. "You need to sit down, relax."

"Oh, I can't," Christian said. "So many years, centuries without love and finally, I find her; the perfect life partner." He saw the concern in both their faces and he knew Samuel was right. He had to settle down. "Now this," he finished.

"But what makes it happen at all?" Samuel asked. "What made the nerve swell up in the first place?"

Christian turned to face both of them. "Dr. Reno explained that a virus got into her body and attacked the weakest part of her system. It's one of the things that can happen when a person has this disease. Apparently, her eyes are the weakest part of her, right now." Christian turned back to face the garden. "This is all so strange. It's happening too fast."

Diana stood up and walked over to him. She placed an arm on his back and the other across his stomach. "Stay positive, big brother. Don't let Minotti do this to you. Roni is sleeping right now and she seems to be perfectly comfortable. Be happy for her comfort."

Christian looked down at his sister and kissed the top of her head. "Thank you," he said. "But I'll tell you, it isn't easy trying to be positive." He looked from her to Samuel. "This isn't easy at all. We're vampires. Don't you feel it? This is so far from our nature."

Diana and Samuel nodded together. "Minotti knew that would be a problem," Samuel said, leaning on the arm of the sofa. "He's got us right where he wants us. He and Audra are both feeding off our fears, our negative sides." He crossed his arms across his chest and took a deep breath.

Christian gave him a severe look. "Are you trying?" he asked. "Are you really trying to stay positive, no matter what?"

Samuel nodded. "I'm trying," he said. "Except that now, every time I go to feed it feels evil. Before this, it felt natural. It's making me question myself, my ethics, you know?"

"I know what you mean." Diana went to sit on the sofa and curled her legs beneath her. Immediately, the tabby cat jumped on her lap and Diana curled him up in her arms, stroking under his chin. "You know how huge my appetite is and I've only fed three times this whole week. I feel guilty just thinking about it, but I also realized that guilt is a negative feeling."

"Me, too," Samuel said, reaching over to add a pat to the top of the cat's head. "Eating three times this week, I mean. I feel like I have to sneak around to do it more than ever before. I feel like a bad man, now. I hate it."

"More negative emotions," Diana said. "We have to stay in the positive enough to like ourselves. And we have to accept our true nature, especially at a time like this. If we don't feed, then we'll really turn evil because we'll want to kill everything in sight, including any people who happen to pass by. I know it's a struggle, but if we look at it and be happy we're able to live, able to feed, able to fight Minotti just by liking ourselves, then we'll be in a much better position when the battle finally begins."

"I see what you're saying," Samuel said. "It's just too much of this silly thinking positive that's making me a little crazy, but I'll get through it. That's one thing nice about being a vampire," Samuel said. "We can get through just about anything." He smiled and looked at each of them.

Christian said nothing.

"Well?" Diana asked him.

He looked at her and shrugged.

"You haven't fed at all, have you?" She shook her head. "Christian, you still have to stay strong. It effects your emotions, even as a vampire. You're playing right into this game of theirs. We are vampires. That cannot be changed. But we can change our attitudes and the way we react to things. Don't be stupid. I know you're upset over Roni. We all are. But there isn't even a chance for her recovery if we don't handle this the right way. It's all energy. You've got to remember that."

Christian listened to her, nodding as she spoke. He knew she was right, but part of his appetite loss was because of his concern for Roni. It was all consuming. Worst of all was the helplessness he felt being unable to see, touch, or physically fight the adversary.

"Come on, old man," Samuel said. "Diana and I are going to eat right now. You come with us. We'll dine together. All of us."

Diana stood up and went to take her brother's arm just as the phone began to ring.

Christian reached for the receiver. "Hello."

"Hello, Christian. This is Father O'Manley." He hesitated and Christian felt his insides turn to jello. "Is Roni at home?"

"Yes she is," Christian said.

"How's she feeling?"

Christian took a deep breath and sighed. "Not good, Father. She's sleeping at the moment. You know she has an IV set up here at home because of her right eye. They're trying to bring the swelling down with steroids."

"Yes, I know," Father O'Manley said, sounding sympathetic, but impatient. "When I was in the seminary one of the priests who taught us had the same trouble. Multiple Sclerosis can be an awful thing when it so chooses. It almost has a mind of its own. You can never tell what it will do next or what symptoms might suddenly appear."

Christian nodded to himself thinking how true the priest's words were. "Something else is on your mind, Father?"

Father O'Manley was hesitant. "I suppose I can give you the news since you're her fiance. But please, tell Roni gently."

Christian looked at Diana and Samuel with a deliberate severity in his eyes. He felt his body tense. "Father Larry?"

"Yes," Father O'Manley said. "He had a heart

attack earlier this evening. He was rushed to Norwood Hospital where he died only an hour ago."

Christian heard Father O'Manley's voice crack, then catch in his throat as he spoke the last few words. And Christian felt his own heart break. Father Larry was the first priest he'd ever known, the first priest he'd ever become true friends with, and now he was gone.

"This is not a good time for this to happen with Roni being so ill," Father O'Manley said after clearing his throat a few times. "But I'm sure she'll want to be at the wake."

"She will," Christian said. "When will it be held?"

Once again, Father O'Manley cleared his throat, then sniffled deeply. "It will start tomorrow and continue for three days," he said. "Evening hours will be from seven to nine."

Christian wondered if the priest knew about his nocturnal habits since he only gave Christian the evening hours, but he said nothing about it. "We'll be there," Christian said. "Thank you."

"You're quite welcome," Father O'Manley said. "And please tell Roni how sorry I am. I know he meant so much to her."

Christian gently touched the rosary that hung across the picture frame on the coffee table by the sofa. Father Larry had given Roni the rosary when she was confirmed by him. "You have no idea how much," Christian said. "I'll tell her. Good evening."

Christian hung up the phone and looked around the living room at Diana and Samuel. There was no doubt that both of them already knew what had happened. Something inside him rose up like a bonfire and he suddenly felt as if he were nothing but a wind-up doll wound into full gear. "It's time."

Diana and Samuel both nodded.

"What do we do now?" Samuel asked.

Diana turned to Christian. "Where's Roni's purse?"

"In the bedroom." He nodded, realizing what she meant. "The crystal."

Diana headed for the bedroom.

"Then what?" Samuel asked.

Christian turned to him. "First, I'm going to check Roni's IV." His eyes narrowed, his eyebrows tilted down creasing his forehead. "Then we're going hunting."

* * *

Audra stood at the foot of Roni's bed with an evil, ear-to-ear smile spread across her face as she prepared to strip a little more myelin from around the nerves in Roni's brain. "There's so much damage I can do," she gloated to herself. "What else can I think of?"

"How about considering Minotti's plans for you?"

Audra turned to see an unfamiliar, female entity floating beside her. It was obvious that she was not of the flames where Audra spent her time. This spirit was surrounded by light. An angel? Immediately Audra wanted to absorb this entity into herself. How strong would she be if she were able to take the power of an angel?

"Don't try it," Serella said to her. "You cannot absorb my energy, unless you want to destroy all the strength you've managed to build up for yourself so far. I am the opposite of everything you are. I'm the opposite of all your nasty intentions. But," she hovered away a few inches. "It's up to you what you choose to do."

"What are you doing here, then?" Audra flashed her an angry sneer to try to frighten her, but there was no reaction from the female entity. "Who are you?"

Serella smiled. "I am simply someone who has come to try to prevent a terrible battle on this side of existence. My intentions are only to keep the peace."

Audra hissed, smiling sarcastically to herself, then turned back to face Roni. "What has that to do with me?"

Serella hovered around to the side of the bed where she could see Roni and where Audra would be forced to face her. "At the moment, everything," she said. "Minotti has been leaving you alone to your own desires for some time."

Audra laughed and turned her head aside in a haughty manner. "That's because he knows better than to play games with me."

Serella's eyes appeared sympathetic. "No, Audra. That's because he's been letting you build up your own strength. When he's ready, he plans to absorb you and all your magnificent resources into himself to save time. It will make him instantly terrible, instantly fierce, ultimately evil. And you will be," she waved her hands as if to brush something out of the air. "Just gone."

Audra turned to stare at Serella in disbelief. She looked into her warm eyes and knew she was telling the truth, but she couldn't see how Minotti would ever hope to get away with such a plan. "He wouldn't dare even think to do anything of the sort."

Serella nodded, smiling a loving smile. "He would and he has."

"What makes him think he would get away with such a thing?" Audra asked, laughing.

"Because you have been so preoccuppied with Roni and the effect her illness is having on Christian that you have no idea where Minotti is or what he's been up to." Serella hovered closer to Roni, reaching a hand out to gently wave across Roni's forehead. Then she turned her attention back to Audra. "You haven't even been aware of all the times Minotti has been right behind you, watching you, and laughing at how easily he could have absorbed you. You would never have seen it coming." Serella looked at Audra with concern in her eyes. "You should never underestimate an entity like him, Audra. He cares for no one but himself and plots against everyone. You've been through enough. But if Minotti has his way you are facing more than you could ever have imagined. Keep an eye on him, Audra. Protect yourself. Roni and Christian are in the physical. They're not going anywhere. You can always get back to them later, but for right now, watch your back and put your own safety first."

Audra nodded. Finally, there was someone else who saw things her way. "I'm going to find him right now." She looked at the female spirit. "Why didn't you tell me this before?"

Serella smiled. "I was afraid. It took all this time to raise my courage to come to you."

Audra let out a raucous, evil laugh. "You've done me a favor, little spirit. Don't ever be afraid of me."

Serella nodded.

"I'll be back when things with Minotti are settled."

"I'm sure you will."

Audra left the room with a new plan on her mind. To find Minotti and confront him before he found her.

Chapter 2

May 6 7:30PM

LARRY looked around at the softly, swirling atmosphere, at the pastel shades of blue and pink, at the pale, green mist that moved with his thoughts. The whole experience was more than he could ever have imagined this side of life would be like, but it did hold a vague familiarity for him. Though it was all so new at the moment, he felt that he was where he belonged, as if he'd returned home, and it felt wonderful.

As he moved through the smokey haze, he saw two very distinct forms approach from a distance, beyond the atmosphere that seemed to have a life of its own. They came closer in gentle movements, blending with the surroundings, then standing out clear and strong. The more he watched them approach the more he suspected who they were and it didn't take long before he recognized them. He was elated. His parents looked happy and healthy, the same as when he'd last seen them nearly ten years ago and they were smiling and waving at him as they approached. His mother was cloaked in layers of orange and yellow mist that surrounded her like a ball gown. As she came closer he recognized the peach dress she was buried in, her favorite color. His father wore his favorite khakis and flannel shirt, not the blue suit he'd worn for his viewing at the funeral home. But his father had never been a suit type of man.

Suddenly, Larry remembered the car accident that happened when they were on their way to visit his sister in Connecticut, but for some reason it didn't matter now. Everything was clear and the full understanding of the moment came at him in an instant. He was dead and so were they, but Father Larry was now on this side of existence for a purpose that he fully understood the significance of. Surprisingly, he was very content and at peace in spite of what he knew lay ahead. He looked around at the lights, the beautiful soft colors, swirling fog, and his heart was full of love. He knew what had to be done. He felt that things were going as they were supposed to and he knew he was right in step with the Creator's own plan He smiled and his mother smiled back. He watched as she put her hands out in front of her as if welcoming him.

Larry reached one hand to her and one to his father.

"Come," his mother said, her face glowing with joy. "We've been waiting to take you home."

Larry nodded, walking between them toward a light so brilliant that he couldn't be certain if it was really a light or another form of life, unseen on earth. Heaven was everything he'd heard and more intense than he could ever have dreamed, if it was even heaven he was in.

"You're simply on the other side," his mother said, smiling. "There is no heaven, there is no hell. There is only life everywhere."

"No heaven?" Larry asked, but he wasn't even truly concerned. "Then where is the good? Where is the evil?" At that moment he entered the light with his parents beside him. He felt the love and the warmth that was part of its very nature and he revelled in the magnificence of its existence. With his parents, he emerged on the other side into a dark tunnel that appeared to be speckled with stars. Once again, it felt familiar as they floated through into the starry darkness. He'd been here before. He knew it for certain, this time.

"We all have," his mother told him. "And you may be here again if you should ever choose to go back."

He nodded as they continued through toward the smaller speck of brilliance on the other side of the tunnel. "What is this? I don't remember this part?"

"This is the passage that separates the physical from the real," his father said. "It will all come back to you. Give it time."

Larry saw his father smile, then turned to watch the darkness start to disappear as all the stars combined in to a solid mass of brilliant light that became brighter all around him.

"Do you have to go through here just to come meet me?" he asked.

"Yes," his mother said. "It makes it easier for you to come home if you're comfortable during the transition. That's why it's always best to have loved ones meet you once you have crossed back over from the physical to return here where it all started."

He nodded, then felt an incredible warmth as he watched everything around him fill up with what seemed to be small, sparkling crystals.

"You're home," his father said.

"Welcome home, Larry." The voice was sweet like his mother's, but it was not his mother's.

Larry's vision quickly adjusted to the surroundings and he was struck with beauty like he'd never known. "Is this still heaven?"

"It is the other side."

Larry looked to his right and saw a beautiful woman surrounded by shades of crimson and dusty rose.

"I am Serella," she said, touching her aura to his. "Come with me."

"I came back early for a reason," he said. "I have a mission to do here for God."

Serella smiled. "I know. You and I will be fighting this battle side by side."

"You, too?"

Serella smiled. "Yes. You see, Larry. There are two very evil entities who are on this side, now. One is working to destroy your friends Roni, Christian, Samuel, and Diana. The other you might remember. Gaetano Minotti."

Larry nodded his head.

"He is working to destroy someone very dear to both of us." She turned to face him. "The angel, Jesse."

Suddenly even the beauty around him wasn't as important as the mission at hand. "Can we stop them? Just the two of us?"

Serella shook her head. "No, but with help from those on the other side, your friends, and the help of the Almighty's army on this side we might have a chance." She held out her arm and the atmosphere parted to reveal thousands of entities in white and pastels lined up all around them as far as they could see. "You and I must be at the forefront of this battle, Larry. It's our loved ones who are in the most danger from all of this. But all those you see gathered here will encircle us with their love and their power to keep the evil that is Minotti contained so that you and I can redirect his energy to a place where it can be transformed. His life energy must be given a new physical existence so it can work its way past all the wrong doings it has created. It must be given a new start and sent to a new incarnation"

"To Chelle and Joe's child." Larry nodded. "I understand."

Serella smiled. "Good. For now, let these good souls surround you and replenish your strength." As she spoke, Larry saw the entities in white encircle them along with his mother and father. He felt their energy flow in and around him, and felt the love they sent to heal his spirit. He heard Serella's voice tell him, "When this is finished you will be able to rest, but for now you must be healed. Let yourself be strengthened with love and all things positive. It is the greatest weapon we will have against the adversaries."

"Where is the evil right now?"

"Lurking," Serella said. "Lurking somewhere dark and fiery."

Larry shook his head, but felt the soothing love envelop him. "What is heaven?" He asked. "I asked my mother if this was heaven, but she told me there's no such place. So what is it that I've spent so much of my life believing in?"

"Heaven is a state of mind," Serella said. "As is hell."

"I don't understand," Larry said.

"Yes, you do," Serella reminded him. "You've simply forgotten. All your time on earth did that to you . It does that to everyone." She caressed his aura with her hand before she continued. "All the goodness gathers together here just as all the evil does the same. Heaven is a joyous, fulfilling way to exist, just as hell is a painful, torturous way. It depends on how you lived in the physical, where you just returned from. If you lived a good life over there, then you'll be able to enjoy a good life here, as well. And that goes the same for those who lived an evil life."

"So those two evil entities we discussed earlier are in a separate part of this world?" Larry asked.

"It's not a world," Serella said. "It's simply another plane of existence. It is actually a very real part of the physical, existing side by side with it."

"But in the physical they can't see us."

Serella smiled. "No, they can't. They are vibrating at a much slower pace than we are and so their physical vision is closed from seeing what vibrates faster than their eyes can perceive. But we're still right beside them, none-the-less."

"Where?" Larry asked. "Where are they?"

Serella spread her arms out before her and the next thing Larry knew, he was standing beside Roni's bed, seeing the faces of Christian, Diana, and Samuel and the concern they were all feeling.

"How did you do that?" Larry asked, astonished.

"I didn't," Serella told him. "You did it. All you have to do is think of a person or a place and you will be there in less than a moment. There are no barriers of any kind here where life is real. No restraints of time, no restraints of solid objects. Nothing is solid here. Such things only exist on the other side and they are cumbersome. The ability to move around so quickly here is as natural as the seasons are on the physical plane. That is something you must remember, even as we prepare to go into this battle that is approaching. You may need to move as quickly as a thought."

Larry nodded. "I'll be ready."

Serella smiled. "We all know you will."

* * *

Boiling anger, foaming hatred, and stinging malice. Audra could feel it all around her. This was not the way it felt on this side before she crossed over to push Roni's illness further along. How long was she gone? She couldn't be sure. Time had no meaning on this side and she'd never seen any reason to look at a clock while she was in the physical playing with Roni's health. Whatever had happened in the short time she'd been gone must have been huge and she knew who had caused the catastrophic change. What she saw now, what she felt now was more intense than anything she'd experienced. The power, the fear, the sheer terror was greater than anything she'd ever been able to cause even in her death sprees on earth. This was hell in biblical proportions and Audra knew Minotti was at the heart of this drastic change. The power was frightening, but it was exactly what Audra had expected from him. It was exactly what she had hoped to be able to create herself which was the very reason she had searched for him so intently. Still, maybe that other female entity was right. Maybe it was true that Minotti showed her how to cross over to the physical just to get her out of his way while he prepared the celestial realm for his own comfort. She wouldn't put it past him, but then that meant that he'd been playing at this game all along, right from the moment they'd finally met. Maybe even longer. She decided to confront Minotti as soon as she found him.

The flames danced around her like a hurricane with no direction. It was nothing but hot chaos. In its own right it was glorious, but it would have been so much more enjoyable if Audra had been there to plan it, to create it. The searing heat brushed through her evil aura and gave her a jolt of intense energy that seemed to hold itself in check, waiting for Minotti's command. It frightened her to think that he was even able to control these flames as if they were an army. The power it must take to do such a thing. Power that she still coveted. No, she couldn't let him have it. She had to find a way to absorb him into herself.

First, she had to find him.

She moved through the flames in search of someone who could direct her to him, but there wasn't a soul around that she might ask to see if they knew where she could find him. The entities that were left here when she'd gone to work on Roni had all but vanished, probably taken into Minotti by now. So, it was him against her. Men! But she couldn't blame him. She was preparing to do the same thing to him. The only diffence was that he wouldn't know what to do what all the power he'd aquired, anyway. But Audra would know exactly how to handle it.

Audra pushed on through the scorching inferno. She felt her aura glow with the disgust of Minotti's back stabbing ways. She felt her soul burn with her own anger of betrayal, but she laughed a hideous laugh. Right from the beginning she had hoped and planned to absorb him into herself, getting sidetracked only occasionally. Still, it was originally her idea. Minotti just got the plan underway quicker.

Suddenly, she saw him in the middle of it all, hovering above the peak of flames where the tips broke off and soared higher as if to see which flame could still grow more. And he saw her at the same time. She stopped for a moment, watching him slowly swing his arm in her direction, his finger pointed at her, and she decided to wear an attitude she was sure he wouldn't expect.

"I've been looking for you," she said, beginning to approach him as if nothing had happened. "Where have you been?"

Minotti lowered his arm and cast a puzzled look in her direction. "I've been here preparing the way for us." He opened his arms wide to display his flaming creation. "It is nearly all ours. At least this part of it is finally complete."

Audra nodded. "I see what you've done. Impressive." She looked all around, daring to take her eyes from him. "Very impressive."

Minotti laughed a loud, boisterous laugh. "Come up here with me and survey all of hell." He lowered his arm to her with his hand outstretched. "I think you will be pleased."

Audra took the chance, took his hand, and let him raise her to his level. She looked around at the dancing flames, the broken tips of fire, and smiled. "You've done better than I would have dreamed of doing myself."

"I believe I'll accept that as a compliment."

Audra looked at him and slightly bowed her head. "And you should. But I'll admit that I'm a little hurt. You didn't even leave a single soul for me. How will I be able to work beside you if I have no way of growing to your level of strength?"

Minotti let our a huge round of laughter. "You won't need anymore souls," he said. "I have a feeling you're quite strong enough already."

Unexpectedly, Minotti pushed his hand through her form of energy, and although she felt the pain and the searing heat, she didn't flinch, didn't move.

"I believe I may have underestimated your powers, my dear, Audra."

Audra smiled a coquettish smile and turned away, still feeling the pain of his touch. "You should know better. Never underestimate the power of a woman." She turned back to him. "Never."

Again he laughed. "Stay close to me," he said. "We have more to do to prepare for the carnage I have planned for this side of life. We still have all the good, little souls left to absorb, and I believe that will be quite delicious."

"We?" Audra asked, flirtateously. "Now it's "we". She stared at him, purposely boring her gaze through him. "You've been planning from the beginning to use me," she said. "And now you simply want me out of your way. You're not fooling me. All you have planned is to absorb me and destroy whatever life is left here. You know what will happen to you if you absorb any of the goodness around. It will destroy you. How do you plan to prevent that from happening?"

Minotti laughed his insane laugh. "That it so true," he said. "I did plan to simply take you into myself and be rid of you. But as you said, I underestimated your power. I had no idea you were truly as strong as you've proven yourself to be. I don't think yours is a power I want to be without."

"As part of yourself?" Audra asked him. "Or by your side?

Minotti took her fiery hand in his and Audra felt the maniacal hatred cut through her very existence. "By my side," he said. "Always by my side."

Audra smiled, knowing the entity she stood beside was a danger even to herself. "I feel so much better." She pulled her energy back to escape the torturous grip he'd had on her and did her best to behave as if there was nothing intended by the gesture, but Minotti gave her a suspicious look that made her feel uneasy.

"As for getting rid of any goodness on this side, I believe my fiery creation speaks for itself."

Audra looked around her and knew he might just be right. Maybe that little, female entity was wrong when she said that absorbing any goodness would only destroy her. Maybe she and Minotti were both too powerful now to be destroyed. "I believe it does." She looked at Minotti and saw the same suspicious look still holding in his eyes. She felt a sharp, painful sensation poke right through every part of her being and she was suddenly petrified.

"Maybe it would be best to rule this new kingdom together," he said.

"Instead of what?" Audra deliberately looked at him as if she hadn't a clue what he might be talking about.

"Nothing at all, my dear," Minotti said, still laughing. "Nothing at all."

Chapter 3

May 7 6:00PM

CHRISTIAN handed Roni the glass of water he had just brought from the lounge downstairs. The air in the funeral parlor was still and musty, but the open front doors allowed a cool breeze to enter the old building giving respite to the rooms inside. Christian was heartbroken to see Roni sitting in the wheelchair the church had loaned them in order for her to easily attend the wake. She still had no feeling in her legs, but the treatments for her eye already seemed to be working. She had told him earlier that she could see vague images and few outlines from time to time. Still, Christian was worried about her frame of mind. Between her constant physical pain and now the emotional set back he knew she was feeling over Father Larry's death, he wondered how much more she could handle. It had been difficult to tell her the news, see her reaction, feel her heartache, and keep to himself how much his own heart suffered over the loss of such a good friend, but he had to stay positive even throughout this terrible ordeal. He placed a hand on Roni's shoulder and gently rubbed her skin through her blouse. "Can I get you anything else?" he asked her.

She looked at him briefly, shook her head, then turned to stare at the casket where Father Larry's body lay.

Christian felt a tear trickle from his eye as he looked at his sister who sat by Roni's other side. Diana smiled and shrugged, then leaned closer to Roni. "I can't believe all the flowers," she said to her. "They're so beautiful."

Roni looked at the mass of color that surrounded Father Larry's humble, wooden casket. "He was very popular."

"I can see that," Samuel commented as if he were talking to himself.

"Everybody loved him."

"He was an easy man to love," Diana said.

A single tear flowed over Roni's right cheek as she stared at Father Larry's empty shell.

Diana looked up at Christian and Samuel, leaned back in her chair where Roni couldn't see her, and pointed to the false smile on her face. Both men got the message and nodded. *This isn't easy,* Christian thought to his sister.

I know, Diana said, *But Jesse and Serella said it's important. Let's not let them down.*

Christian nodded.

Where's the crystal? Diana asked.

Christian looked at her for a moment as if he had no idea what she was talking about. Then he glanced down at Roni's purse where it lay by her side on the floor. *It should be in her purse,* he said to Diana.

Diana nodded, then turned to Roni. "Yesterday when I went in your room to check on you I accidentally knocked your purse over. There was a beautiful amethyst crystal that fell out and I put it in your hand. I hope that was alright to do."

Roni slowly turned her head to look at Diana. "I keep forgetting all about that crystal," she said. "Chelle gave it to me for good luck when I was going to close on the house." She looked back at the open casket. "I was supposed to give it back to her, but I forgot."

Diana briefly glanced at Christian before she continued. "Has she ever asked about it?"

Roni shook her head.

"Then I wouldn't worry about it."

Roni nodded, but didn't say anything.

"How are all of you holding up?" Father O'Manley asked as he approached and pulled up a chair to sit near them. He did not give them time to answer before he turned to look at Father Larry. "It's so sad to see him go this soon," he said, shaking his head. "He'd become a good friend and mentor to me."

Christian, Samuel, and Diana exchanged glances that showed they all knew they had to find the positive even in this situation. "He's gone home," Christian said, smiling. "He's quite fortunate."

Diana nodded. "No more aches and pains. No more day to day problems. Now he gets to relax and enjoy his rewards for all the good things he did while he was here."

Father O'Manley nodded. "That's a wonderful way to look at this." He smiled at all of them, then turned toward the entrance. "Oh, another friend of Larry's just came in. I'll be back." He stood up and headed for the opening into the room where people continued to stream in to pay their last respects.

They watched Father O'Manley walk to greet the newcomers and were all surprised to see Jesse standing in the middle of the entrance, surveying the room. He nodded to Christian, Roni, Diana, and Samuel, greeted Father O'Manley, then walked over to where Father Larry's body lay. He appeared serene as he knelt down and prayed for quite some time, then placed a hand over Father Larry's that were folded neatly across the middle of his body, leaned over to kiss him on the forehead, turned, and went to greet the friends who waited for him. He took Roni's hand in his and patted it. "How are you feeling?" He asked her as he looked directly into her eyes. "Any better?"

She shook her head. "No, but it's nice to see you, again."

Jesse smiled. "My sentiments exactly."

Roni stared at him. "You couldn't stop this?"

Jesse shook his head. "I am not God," he said. "I'm simply one of His messengers. Larry is home, Roni, and happier than he could have ever been here." He rubbed her hand. "And you know what a jolly fellow he was."

Roni smiled, obviously in spite of herself. "I'll never forget that Santa Claus smile of his."

"Neither will anyone else." Jesse let his hand drop to the arm of the wheelchair, then turned to Christian. "I see Roni's glass is empty and I could use a little water myself. Would you care to show me where the lounge is?"

Christian nodded. "Sure. I just came from there." He bent down to kiss Roni on the forehead, then glanced at Samuel who stepped foreward as if on que. "I'll be right back, Sweetheart."

Roni nodded and smiled.

When they reached the lounge downstairs there was no one around. Christian refilled Roni's glass, then stepped aside to let Jesse use the water bubbler, but Jesse was already seated. "What now?" Christian asked him.

Jesse glanced up at him and let out a soft chuckle. "Oh, Christian. Will you please relax."

"It's not easy under the circumstances," Samuel said, coming to Christian's defense. "All this trying to be pleasant and positive in the middle of Roni's health problems and Father Larry's death, not to mention the battle that we know is going on, or about to go on, in a place were we can't go to do anything to fight it. I don't like being a blind spectator, Jesse. This just isn't for me."

"I understand," Jesse said. "Believe me, I do. But the actual battle has not begun. There's no way to know when it will. Only Minotti and Audra know what their plan is."

Christian sat in the seat next to Jesse and leaned forward, Roni's glass still in one hand. "Please explain to me what our positive attitudes have to do with any of this."

"Yes," Samuel said. "And explain to me how it is possible that there's no way to know when the fight actually begins. How do you know it hasn't started yet?"

Jesse patted Christian on the back as he smiled at Samuel. "You're both used to fighting what you can see and touch."

"Hit is the operative word here," Samuel interjected. "We're used to being able to hit the enemy where it will do the most damage. And feel ourselves doing so in the process."

Jesse nodded. "Yes, Samuel. But this time it is a battle of faith and will. Those are two intangibles that mean more in life than anything you will ever see or feel. What you ***will*** to happen, if it's done with passion, true and direct, will come to be. There's no question about that. It is one of the laws of the universe. But if there is the slightest bit of doubt, the slightest fear that what you will is impossible, the slightest question in your mind that the ability to will anything is silly, then you have destroyed the possibility to give life to what you desire. No, this time it's best for the battle to be fought on the side of reality where all life begins and rests. Human doubt would only cause its own loss this time."

Christian sat up and turned to face him. "What about all this positive attitude stuff?"

Jesse looked at him and smiled. "Entities such as Minotti and Audra get their energy from negativity. They look for it. They soak it up like a sponge. They're attracted to your anger and your hatred, your disappointment and your fears. They live and feed on it as if it were food for their souls, but it only adds to their evil strengths." Jesse took a deep breath. "Roni is the magnet for Audra which means that whoever is near Roni feeling angry or upset, worried or sad, is feeding Audra the energy she needs to keep causing Roni's illness to get worse."

Samuel stood up and began to pace across the lounge. "Oh, I see. So instead of being upset because Roni is sick, we should be happy." He spun around to face Jesse, anger burning through his reddened eyes. "That's a crock! It would take a sick-minded individual to be happy when someone they care about is going through troubled times."

Jesse shook his head. "I'm not asking you to be happy because Roni is sick. Don't exaggerate, Samuel. Get rid of that negative energy. Sarcasm is a prime target."

Samuel froze. "I can't do anything."

"Yes, you can," Jesse said. "Look at Roni and be happy that she's alive. Be happy that she's coming along so well. Be happy that she and Christian have each other. Let the feeling grow. Be happy you and Diana have each other. Keep looking for things to be happy about without paying any attention to the things that are going wrong. Do you understand?"

Samuel stared at him for a second, then nodded. "Better than I did a few moments ago."

"Good. Then sit down and relax, please."

"Are we going to know when the battle is started?" Christian asked Jesse. "I know what you just said before, but there has to be a way for us to know."

"I imagine you'll sense it simply because you're all sensitive beings, but you have to accept right now that you cannot be a physical part of this one. You've got to get over the frustration of not being able to handle it yourselves because otherwise it will only cause you an immense amount of frustration."

Samuel sighed. "Diana should have been with us to hear all this."

Jesse shook his head. "She doesn't need to be here. She already knows."

Christian and Samuel looked at each other, then at Jesse. "How?" Christian asked.

"I'm sure you don't want to hear this, but the truth is quite simple." He looked from one of them to the other before he continued. "Female energy is already in tune to the truths in the universe." Jesse glanced from one to the other before he continued. "Things of a spiritual nature don't usually require explaining when women are involved." He looked at both men. "Women just know."

"Women's intuition," Samuel said.

SH

"It's very strong," Jesse said. "Female entities all need that kind of intuition in order to raise their young properly, teach and guide those around them, and nurture all who need them. Female energy is very powerful because it is at the core of all life. It has to be."

"Well, I feel like chopped liver right about now," Samuel said.

Christian breathed a huge sigh. "You've got to stop it with the sarcasm, Samuel." He smiled. "Please?"

Jesse laughed, then patted both men on the back. "See. You can even have little spats in a very positive way." He sat up straight. "Look. Do you remember how Serella chose Diana specifically to place the crystal in Roni's hand?"

Both men nodded.

"I didn't understand that at all," Samuel said.

Christian leaned over and patted his friend on the head in a playful manner. "Female energy, my friend."

Samuel brushed Christian's hand away and stood up. "I can't wait until all this positive silliness is over. I like you better when you're being serious."

Christian chuckled. "I'm actually having fun," he teased Samuel.

"Yeah, well,. . ."

Jesse rose to stand beside Samuel. "We should probably be getting back."

"Wait a minute," Samuel said. "I have to know. If women are so important and in tune with everything, then what about us?"

Jesse smiled. "I knew you'd ask." He took in a deep breath, and released it slowly. "Male energy is different. It balances female energy in the physical.

See women are primarily spiritual creatures, whereas men are basically physical beings. It's no coincidence that wars have been fought and run by men with a few women scattered through the structure. Had the roles been reversed, women would not have fought in physical wars. They would have fought as women did in ancient times, with nature's magic, with the strength of the soul and the spirit, with the power of will."

"You're not saying much for yourself," Christian said.

"Both sides do cross over," Jesse said. "Look at some of the enlightened beings, Jesus Christ, Siddhartha Buddha. Both were men, both were very much in tune with the truths. On the other side of the coin, you have Joan of Arc, a woman connected to the spiritual as she should be, but with the physical dealings of a man. Every human being has both male and female energy as part of their being. And every human balances it differently." He sighed. "The last two battles you two have been involved with were of this world where male energy had been used to fight. This time, the battle will be fought on feminine terms, in the spirit."

"But will the good side win?" Samuel asked.

"I don't know the answer to that question any better than I knew the answer to your previous battles," Jesse said. "All I know is that your support is needed in keeping things positive. The first place Minotti and Audra will go for replenishment will be to the grief surrounding Roni because of her poor health and Larry's death. That's where you two have to be strong."

Christian and Samuel looked at each other and nodded.

"Good," Jesse said. "Now let's get back upstairs. I just wanted to take the time to make sure you two were alright with everything. I don't expect to see you until this is all over. Serella knows I'll be joining in the battle on that side with her and Larry."

"What?" Christian rose with a start. "You're going back?"

Jesse stared at him. "Shortly. But not now."

"Wait a minute," Samuel said. "You never told us anything about you leaving. When did this all come about?"

"It's been coming on for some time," Jesse said. "I've been in the physical far too long. I've come to doubt my own abilities and the protection of the One Who Sent Me. That's not a good thing. I have to get back in touch with my own reality."

Christian and Samuel looked suddenly very somber.

"Smile," Jesse said. "Nothing negative. Please. I shouldn't have told you. I wasn't going to, in fact. Now I know I was right. I shouldn't have said a word."

"No," Christian said. "It's just a shock. Everyone we know and . . . love is leaving. I never expected you to leave, too. You were the one I always knew I could depend on."

"I'm not leaving for good, Christian." Jesse looked at him, then turned to Samuel. "I am only taking a rest. I'm no good to anyone as things are going. I'll be back."

"When?" Samuel asked.

"When I'm fully refreshed."

"What do we do in the meantime?"

"Samuel, you're grown men. You know the difference between right and wrong. You don't need me for that." Jesse put a hand on Samuel's shoulder. "You can always pray."

All three men were suddenly silent as the weight of this newest development sank in. Christian felt as if he was falling into a pit, but he knew he had to stop himself from sinking any further for Roni's sake. He didn't want to end up being more fuel to feed Audra or Minotti's energy.

"So, is that why you knew the battle hadn't started, yet?" Samuel asked him. "Are you going to be called back when it starts?"

"Something like that," Jesse said. "But for now, let's just enjoy whatever we can until that becomes necessary."

Samuel sighed as he gave Christian a doubtful look.

"Let's get back upstairs," Christian said. "Stay positive, Samuel. It's a good thing for Jesse to get strong and heal himself. He's our friend. We have to take care of him the same way we've taken care of each other."

"And Roni," Samuel said.

"Exactly." Jesse smiled as he put an arm around Christian and one around Samuel. Together they left the lounge and headed back upstairs to the wake.

Chapter 4

May 9 8:00PM

CHELLE adjusted Roni's IV drip, then sat on the bed beside her, watching her breath slowly to the beat of her own heart. It was the calmest she'd seen her all day. "That should be better," she said, checking the drip one last time. It had been a long day. Father Larry's funeral mass, then the procession to the burial site, followed by the bereavement breakfast for family and friends. Through it all, Chelle had done her best to console Roni as she cried almost non-stop. But Chelle couldn't help her own crying which only added to Roni's sadness. Losing Father Larry had taken a huge toll on everyone, but Roni was showing deeper signs than the rest of them who were still strong enough to hide much of the hurt. It was obvious how weak Roni has become both physically and emotionally.

Chelle had been watching her turn pale and visibly drained of energy as things progressed. She'd hardly eaten for days and her condition was like a roller coaster, good one day, worse the next. Chelle was worried about her, but determined to cheer her up as much as possible.

"I noticed the other day that you were sleeping with a very familiar rock in your right hand," Chelle said, smiling. "I almost forgot about it."

"Oh, Chelle." Roni sat up, gingerly. "I'm so sorry. I keep forgotting all about it. I know I have to give it back to you. In fact, I was going to do it when Diana asked me about it, but. . . . . "

Chelle nodded with an understanding smile on her face. "You forgot, again."

"I'm sorry," Roni said, reaching for her purse. She removed the stone from the side pocket and handed it to Chelle. "Here you go. Thanks for loaning it to me. It must have done me some good because I closed on the house without a problem."

Chelle held the stone in her palm. She put it up to the light and watched the colors glisten all around its outer edges as a single movement brought the stone to life. Then she looked at Roni and lowered her hand with the stone in it. "Here." She placed the crystal back in Roni's hand. "There's a reason you've been forgetting about this for so long." She closed Roni's fingers around the stone. "Hold on to it for awhile longer." She shrugged. "Maybe even for good."

Roni's eyes began to fill with tears once again as she stared at her closed hand.

"Don't, Roni." Chelle rubbed her friends shoulder. "I will find another stone somewhere else. They're all over the place. I really want you to have this one. I think it was meant for you."

Roni nodded, but said nothing.

"Get some rest," Chelle said, her heart breaking for Roni's pain. "I'll be here until the IV is finished tonight. Joe has been running around for the wedding all day and he's working on something with his dad right now, so I'm in no hurry. I'll be here visiting with Diana and the rest of the vampire clan if you need me." Chelle stood up. "Right now, I'm going to make a pot of tea for us. Any preference?"

Roni shook her head, placing her hand over her heart with the amethyst still in it.

"OK. Then I think it will be. . . . "

"Surprise me," Roni said.

Chelle smiled. "You got it. Now just rest. Try to get some sleep, too."

Roni nodded as she closed her eyes.

Chelle left the room, closing the door to within inches of the frame in order to keep the noise out, and went to the kitchen where she put a pot of water on the stove to boil. Then she went in the living room and sat on the sofa, feeling a bit uncomfortable with nothing but vampires all around her. She wondered how Roni did it.

Diana looked at her and smiled. "Is it because we're vampires?"

Chelle remembered their telephathy. She looked at them, shrugged, and shook her head. "No. I guess I just don't really know any of you."

"You know my brother," Diana said, waving a hand at Christian.

"Yes, but that's different," Chelle said. "He's practically married to my best friend." She briefly glanced at Christian, remembering all the small, verbal battles they'd had in their past. "We didn't hit it off too well in the beginning, though."

Diana nodded. "I know. They told me all about it."

"They?"

"Yes. Samuel and Christian." She laid a hand on Chelle's arm. "There's nothing to be afraid of."

Chelle felt the cold touch of her hand and tried not to give away her surprise. She couldn't remember Christian ever touching her skin, so she'd never experienced the sensation for herself, though Roni had mentioned it numerous time. "I guess I really know that, deep down in some part of me."

Diana studied her face in a very obvious manner, watching her expressions as if she were a lab animal. Chelle wondered if she were reading her mind at that moment.

"Yes, I am," Diana said. "And I'm happy to know you're really not afraid of us." She leaned back, adjusting her legs beneath her. "We're not that much different than you. Remember, we were mortal at one time, too."

"I know," Chelle said. "I guess it's just like meeting any new people. You never know if you'll get along until you try."

"Exactly." Diana leaned back a bit and stretched her hand across the back of the couch. "How's Roni?"

"A little better," Chelle said, picking a piece of lint off her jeans. "Calmer. I hope she gets some sleep. She needs that more than anything else, right now. I just can't stand to see her like this. Especially after all the things we've been through together. She's always been so strong. It just isn't right. She seems to be falling apart in every way possible."

"She hasn't slept much at all since Christian gave her the news about Father Larry's death." Diana looked at the two men, then reached over to pick up one of the cats from the floor. "She's probably very tired. She'd have to be after all this."

Chelle nodded. "And with her disease she's more susceptible to picking up any little bug she comes in contact with, now. Sleep is so important for her." She looked across the room and thought of all she'd seen Roni go through in the past few years. She tried to comprehend how quickly the energetic young woman who was so much a part of her life had become nearly void of any kind of life for herself. Maybe all the turmoil was what caused it, but her turmoil began with Christian. She shook the thought off. She didn't want to resent him when her best friend loved him as much as she did. It wouldn't be fair to anyone.

"There's always turmoil," Diana said.

Chelle looked at her, surprised, then shook her head. "I'm not used to hiding my thoughts," she said. "I don't even know how."

"You can't," Diana said, smiling. "But don't worry. There's no offense taken. Turmoil has as many causes as it has remedies. It's very true that much of Roni's turmoil seems to have begun when she met Christian. Let's face it, dating a vampire is a unique situation to find yourself in. But Roni and Christian share a love like few others do. Their natures have no place in a love like theirs, but still they manage to overcome that little barrier as if it were nothing at all." She let the cat crawl up the couch and settle on the back of the seat behind her. "It doesn't matter who Roni would have found herself with, Chelle. There would have been some sort of turmoil because relationships practically invite it just because of the changes they cause those involved to go through. Don't think for one minute that you and Joe won't have your own little turmoils as your lives together move forward. It's inevitable. The only difference with Roni is that she might not be dealing with the kind of illness she's facing right now if it wasn't for her involvement with Christian. But hopefully, we'll be able to take care of that as soon as we get passed this turn of events with Father Larry's death." She quickly looked from Samuel to Christian. "Still, let's look at the good things that are happening, instead."

Chelle gave her a questioning look and wondered how she could possibly expect that from any of them. "That's a little difficult, right now. Don't you think? I mean you guys are all living forever so you probably don't see things the way us mortals do, but I, for one, can't see anything good that's happening, right now."

"Well, for instance, you and Joe are expecting a child." Diana looked at Christian and Samuel once more. "What can you think of?" she asked them.

"You're planning your wedding," Christian said with a nod. "Finally."

"Funny," Chelle said to him, but inside she enjoyed the little joke, for a change.

"Your best friend is alive and doing better because of you," Samuel added.

"But she could be perfectly healthy," Chelle said, feeling her own empathy for Roni's pain. "I can't fix what's wrong with her. No one can. That's the most frustrating thing of all."

"No one is perfectly healthy," Diana said to her.

Chelle stared at her. "You are."

"In my own way," Diana said. "But nothing is perfect. Not even the existence of a vampire. Everything has its drawbacks."

"You mean the blood thing?" Chelle said, a sarcastic edge to her voice.

"The 'blood thing,' as you say, is enough to make Roni choose to stay mortal," Christian reminded her, frowning. "I'd say it's a big enough drawback for some."

Chelle studied each of their faces, surprised at how calm and sincere they appeared. "I guess I'm just looking at things a little negatively because of everything that's been happening. It's so frustrating wanting to fix everything, being trained to fix everything, then finding myself in this position where I can only do so much, but nothing gets fixed at all. It makes me depressed." She started to trace the edge of the couch with her fingers.

Diana leaned forward. "Well, don't let that happen," she said. "Look at the bright side of things. Don't drain your energy by wasting it on things you can't control. Concentrate on what's going good and build yourself up." Diana stared into her eyes. The motherly expression on her face was the last thing Chelle would ever have expected to see. It surprised her and it made her relax at the same time.

"OK," Chelle said. "You're right. I can hear myself telling Roni the same thing."

"Then take your own advice." Diana leaned back and nudged Chelle's elbow. "I believe your water is boiling."

Chelle heard the whistle and stood up. "Thanks for the pep talk," she said to Diana.

"Don't mention it," Diana said, winking at her. "Go make your tea."

Chelle nodded, then turned and hurried to the kitchen.

* * *

Jesse went out on to the porch to prepare his body for the meditation that would take him to the other side for an indefinite amount of time. He didn't know how long the battle would last, didn't know what to expect at all. He only knew that he was needed on that side very badly. He spread the wool blanket he'd brought with him on the bench, then laid down on it. He pulled the other half of the blanket over himself to keep his body warm when his temperature began to drop and folded the end up beneath his head for a cushion. He tried to determine if there was anything else he might need, but quickly decided everything was set. He began to meditate, and continued until he was deep enough to separate himself, his spirit, from his physical body. When that was done, he looked down at himself, sleeping on the porch, then turned away and allowed himself to be carried across the threshold between the two realms. He let himself travel through time and space, willing himself to go straight to meet Serella and Larry. It didn't take him long. He was prepared for this moment and his determination to put this evil to rest once and for all was stronger than he ever remembered it being. He had no trouble meeting up with the circle of spirits who were replenishing Larry's energy, and he quickly located Serella, who wasn't far from Larry, but he was troubled by the turmoil he felt should not have been on this side. He looked around for some indication of where it was originating and saw a line of deep orange in the distance that was approaching even as he watched. Instinctively, he knew the lights were actually the flames that grew around Minotti and followed him where ever he and Audra went. "It's time," he said to no one in particular.

All the other entities turned to face him, then

looked toward where he was looking to see what he saw.

"It's them," Serella said. "They're coming."

"To do what, exactly?" Larry asked.

Jesse turned to him. "To take your life energy into themselves, convert it to evil in an instant, and take control of everything that has ever been created on both sides of life."

"Maybe not," Serella said. "I believe I convinced Audra that it would destroy her to try such a thing with good energy."

Jesse continued to stare at the orange horizon. "And Minotti will quickly tell her how untrue that statement was. But I commend you, Serella. At the very least, you may have saved yourself when you were in her presence." He watched the orange glow grow bigger as he concentrated on pulling in all the rejuvenating energy he felt so as to prepare himself for what needed to be done. "It's now or never." He looked out over the mass of good souls gathered for a single purpose and held his arms out for them in a gesture of unity. "Concentrate and give your souls to the Creator for the eternal love and protection that is always there for us. We will need this more than ever."

As the others bowed their heads in personal communication with the Universe, Jesse closed his eyes and willed himself to stand before God, once more. He felt Him move in and around him, felt the eternal strength that would outlast all that had ever existed. When he truly felt the Father with him he wasted no time stating his request. "Stay with us," he said. "I know I have to ask and so I am asking on behalf of everyone here. Protect us."

Jesse felt the response deep in his spirit. "My greatest protection is with you."

Jesse smiled inwardly. "Thank you, Father."

He felt the Father's joy as he backed away and returned to where he was now needed. He surveyed the crowd and felt their anticipation, love, and trust. "Are you ready?" He could feel the mass reaction of a single spirit and knew the intent and determination was there. "Then let's stay together and go meet the adversaries." He turned toward the advancing flames with Serella and Larry flanking him on either side, and headed into the one battle that should have been fought centuries ago. "Let's put an end to this."

Chapter 5

May 9 9:00PM

"I'D better check on Roni," Chelle said, standing up. "I've been enjoying our conversation so much that I didn't even see the time fly."

"I looked in on her about a half hour ago," Christian said. "She was sleeping."

Chelle nodded. "Good. She needs it." She picked up her tea mug from the coffee table and took it to the kitchen, then went to the room where Roni lay sleeping. Chelle stared at her friend. How strange to see her appearing as if she was perfectly healthy, as if nothing about her had changed. The memories they shared tore at Chelle's heart as she watched her slumber and saw how normal everyting seemed to be, except for the plastic line that fed her body the medicine she needed to finish healing her eye. If only there was something she could do to stop this disease from poisoning her friend. She sighed as she reached up to check the contents of the bag that hung suspended from the metal pole beside the bed. A little less than half full meant there was still another hour to go. She sat on the bed beside Roni and checked the shunt that had been sticking out of Roni's arm for the last four days. When she turned her arm over, the amethyst crystal fell from Roni's hand. It made Chelle smile as she reached over to retrieve it from where it had rolled across the bed. She looked at it, remembering when Roni had given it to her for the first birthday she had after they became friends. She smiled, then placed it back in her friend's palm. "Let it heal you," Chelle said. She looked at the bedroom wall and whispered, "Dear God, let it heal her." Chelle made the sign of the cross on herself, then began to pray. "God, wherever you are, whatever you're doing right now, I'm asking you." She stopped. "And you know I never come to you for anything. Good or bad, I just don't come to you. I haven't prayed much in years." She looked at Roni, sleeping, oblivious to everything Chelle was feeling. "She's important to me, God. So, for all the things I could have come to you for but didn't, I'm asking you now to pay attention to me and hear me." Suddenly, Chelle felt a desparation she hadn't felt in years. "Please, God, find a way to heal her." She stopped, not knowing what else to say, but somehow she knew He was listening. She couldn't explain it, but she knew. She looked at Roni, at the IV, at the hand that held the crystal, but still didn't know what else to say. She made the sign of the cross and mouthed, "Thank you." Then she stood to leave the room.

At that moment Chelle felt a strange uneasiness that she couldn't explain. It was as if something huge had just happened, yet nothing was different. She went into the hall and looked at the three people sitting in the living room. Everything was still the same as it had been when she left the room. She glanced back in the bedroom, but only saw Roni still lying in the same position, breathing the same rhythm as she was only moments ago. Chelle stood in the doorway and shook her head. It must have been the pregnancy playing with her hormones. She grabbed the door knob and felt it, again. What was it? She released the door and looked into the living room once more. What was happening? Something told her not to leave Roni's side, though she had no idea where such a feeling was coming from.

"Is everything OK?" Christian asked her.

Chelle looked at him standing in the middle of living room, smiling as he waited for her to answer. What should she do? She could hear Father Larry's voice telling her to be honest. But she didn't want to alarm anyone. This time she heard Joe's voice in her heart and knew it was better to be safe than sorry.

"Are you alright?" Diana asked.

All three of them had turned to face her. Christian had taken a few steps toward her, a curious, yet concerned expression on his face.

"Not really," Chelle said.

Immediately, all three of them were in the room with her, surrounding the bed and staring at Roni.

"What's wrong?" Christian asked. "She's still sleeping."

"It's not her," Chelle said. "I was just getting ready to leave because she's got another hour left in the drip when something just didn't feel right. Everything seemed wrong, uncomfortable. It wasn't so cozy in here, anymore."

Diana looked from one to the others. *It's begun.*

* * *

Jesse saw two life forms soaring above the advancing field of flames and he knew it was Minotti and Audra. They were the only spirits left on the dark side since Minotti had found and absorbed all the others that were spending time dealing with their incarnate failings. "Serella." He reached his spirit out to her. "I will be leaving you and Father Larry to take care of things on this side without me, if it becomes necessary for me to return."

Serella nodded. "I understand. But, honestly, Jesse. If it comes to that, it may not matter."

Jesse looked at her, admiring the strength of her spirit, but he said nothing.

"We're going to have to surround them," Serella said as she watched the approach of the three spirits. "That means some of us will be immersed in the flames of their wickedness. She turned to the thousands of souls who followed close behind. "Do you all understand what that means?" There was an immense group affirmation that ran through them like a wave.

"Then let's do this." Jesse turned to Larry. "Not what you thought the after life would be like?"

Larry's spirit still carried his heartwarming Santa Claus smile that everyone loved. "Not yet, it isn't," he said to Jesse. "But it will be."

"And if it's not?" Serella asked him.

"Then my spirit was sacrificed for the only purpose it could ever have been sacrificed for." He nodded his head in affirmation, then turned back toward the advancing flames. "For the work of God Himself."

"Well, our determination is there, and the Almighty assured me that we have His greatest protection with us," Jesse said, feeling a tension like he'd never known begin to build. "Let's go."

They moved forward, heading directly for Minotti and Audra while the pure spirits that followed close behind formed a circle that began among the flames and built straight up until they were level with the height where Minotti and Audra hovered. Jesse felt the pain of those who had volunteered to enter the flames of suffering and anguish and he knew it wouldn't take long until their resolve was gone, and they had to stop. "Please let this work, Father," he said as he rose to Minotti's level and faced him with Serella hovering close beside him while Larry concentrated on Audra.

"Don't waste your time," Minotti said. "We've been through all this before and you lost."

"Only the first time," Jesse said.

"You only won in the physical the second time around because I chose to let it happen," Minotti said. "But either way, I still would've been the victor. There is no power like mine. None has ever grown to this strength before. It is greater than anything ever created."

"Except the Creator, Himself," Jesse said, smiling as he noticed the anxious faces of love that surrounded them, determined to do the best they could for the cause.

"Even the Creator never expected this," Audra hissed at Jesse.

"Oh, don't be so sure." Jesse waited, wondering why they were taking so long to make a move. But he soon saw Audra turn to the crowd and reach out with her will. He saw the first spirit pulled from the flames toward her and watched in horror as it easily dissolved into her without a fight.

"Oh, I think I can be sure," Audra said, releasing a maniacal laugh.

Together, she and Minotti began drawing souls into themselves with almost no effort.

"Surround them with your will," Jesse instructed the masses. "Serella and Larry. Block their efforts with love and compassion. It must be the opposite of all the negative intentions they're sending out. We have to drain them and force them to spend more energy. They must be made weaker."

Minotti laughed. "You can try, Jesse. But it will never happen."

Jesse stared at him. "I warned you a long time ago not to make me do this to you. But you've chosen to do it to yourself and ignored my warning. I can't help you, now."

"I don't need your help, Jesse. I only need your life."

* * *

Roni felt herself falling faster and faster through the darkness until her head hurt from the velocity of the rapid decline. She reached out to grab something, anything, that would stop her, but there was nothing. What was happening? Was she dead? Dying, maybe? Then she saw Audra standing before her, surrounded by fire as far as she could see. Roni turned to run, but there was nowhere to go. She was suspended just inches from the peaks of the flames that burned beneath her. She could feel the heat, saw the sparks float around her as they spit and crackled. It didn't seem to be a dream. The vision was too vivid, too intense. Audra was very real as she gave Roni an evil smile, then reached toward her with outstretched arms. Roni felt herself being pulled closer to Audra. She could feel Audra's anticipation, feel her darkness, her hatred. Audra was pulling her right into her own spirit.

"Nooooooooooo," Roni yelled, clutching at the air for something to hold her back.

Audra just laughed as Roni inched closer until she felt the first, burning embrace of Audra's dementia.

"Leave me alone!" Roni yelled, still trying desparately to free herself, but it was no use. Her body ached, her soul was melting into the evil mass of energy that Audra had become. She could feel the anquish of thousands of others surrounding her as she entered the entity that was Audra. At that moment, there was nothing left for her to do and she gave up, letting her soul abandon itself.

* * *

When Roni started to scream, Christian reached for her and held tight, but he couldn't stop her from flailing about in desparation. "What's happening?" he asked Chelle, then turned to Diana. "What's happening?"

"She's dreaming," Chelle said. "I'm afraid she'll pull out the IV if we don't keep her calm."

"I'm more afraid she'll hurt herself." Christian started to shake her. "Wake up, Roni," he said. "It's just a dream." He shook her, again. "Come on, Honey. Wake up." He looked at Chelle. "She won't come out of it."

"I don't understand," Chelle said. "She's not in a coma or anything like that. This doesn't make sense." She leaned forward and took one of Roni's arms. "Come on, Roni. You've got to wake up."

But Roni continued to yell as she reached for something in the air that only she could see.

"All we can do is hold her down until she's relaxed," Chelle said.

It's Audra, Diana thought to Christian and Samuel. *I'm sure of it.*

He looked at Roni, hopelessness and fear was all he felt. Where was Jesse? What was going on? He turned to Chelle. "Where did the crystal go?"

Chelle held Roni's right arm while she searched the bed with the other, then checked the floor. "She must have tossed it when she started swinging her arms around. I don't see it."

"Hold on to her," Diana said. "Samuel, help me find it."

"What's so important about the crystal?" Chelle asked. "It's a piece of amethyst Roni gave me when we first met. I loaned it to her a few years ago, but that's all it is."

Diana looked at her. "I know what it is," she said. "But I don't think you understand the significance of the stone, of any stone. Each one has its own energy, its own vibrational power. Amethysts vibrate with a variety of energies starting with energies that heal, give peace and courage, and the energy of love. That particular stone also has very significant meanings and strength for both of you because of your friendship. For Roni, the stone may help in her ability to get better." She looked at Christian and Samuel. "For the whole situation we're dealing with, it will facilitate peace and give courage to those who are fighting for it. But the energy of love is what will bring it all together through Roni." She turned to Chelle. "Do you understand?"

Chelle gave her a puzzled look. "No, I don't. What does that have to do with what's happening to Roni right now? I don't understand. What situation are you talking about?"

"Stay calm and listen to me." Diana took a deep breath. "There is a large struggle going on in the celestial realm right now. Audra," she hesitated. "You remember her?"

Chelle nodded. "Do I ever!"

"Well, Audra is part of that struggle."

"Audra is dead."

"Exactly."

Chelle looked at Diana, then at Christian. "But Roni is alive."

"Not for long if Audra has anything to say about it."

"Is that what I felt before?" Chelle asked. "Is that what made me uneasy?"

Diana nodded.

"Then you knew this was coming." Chelle's voice was beginning to show signs of anger.

"Yes, we knew."

Chelle looked at each of them. "And no one thought it was important to tell me?"

"You have a child to be concerned with," Diana said. "You didn't need to worry."

"We never thought you'd be around when it all started, either," Christian said, feeling bad that he'd left Chelle out of so much of what had been going on.

"Well, now I have the worry, anyway," Chelle said. "So tell me what to do."

"Alright." Diana looked at her and smiled. "Stay happy and positive. And don't, for even one minute, doubt that it's important. This battle is being fought where we can't see it or participate except from where we are right now."

"And where's that?"

Diana looked around the room. "Exactly, Chelle. We're here in the physical dealing with our own fight on Roni's behalf, but the main battle is being fought on the other side, in Heaven, if you will. This war is happening on both sides of existence at once, and our part in it is small in comparison." She pointed to her chest. "The only weapon we have is in here. Use it."

"How?" Chelle asked. "This doesn't make any sense to me."

"And there's no time, now, to teach it all to you," Diana said. "If you love Roni, then let yourself surround her with those feelings. We all need to will the evil out of this room, out of this realm, out of existence."

"You mean pray?" Chelle asked.

Diana nodded. "If that's what it takes for you to do this, then yes. Pray. Just don't let yourself be afraid, or worried. Have confidence that this will all work out to our advantage and know in your heart and without a doubt that Roni will be alright. She is the battle that's going on in the physical. It's all taking place in her little body while the rest of the war is being fought on the other side between all the good and evil entities."

"Sounds like something out of a horror movie."

Christian gave her a nasty look. "So do vampires, but we're here."

Chelle held up one hand and took a deep breath. "Point taken," she said. "I get the idea."

"Good."

Chelle took Roni's hand while the others watched. "I just want her to get better, if that's at all possible. She's like a sister to me."

"Then stay strong," Diana advised. "Start thinking about all the fun things you guys did together and feel the happiness."

Chelle nodded, then looked at Roni. "I'll do my best."

"That's all we're asking you to do." Diana struggled to smile, then turned to Samuel. "Now help me find the crystal."

Chapter 6

May 9

JESSE looked resolutely at Audra, studying her dark demeanor, feeling her degradation, and wishing so many lives never had to go so far astray. He turned his attention to Minotti and felt the determination in his attempts to destroy everything good. How frustrated both of them were when they were unable to absorb any more of the entities because of the strength of love in the collective will of the good spirits who were amassed against them. But Audra found another way to appease her anger and quickly went right to the source of her hatred. She began to draw Roni's life energy directly from the her physical body and into herself, leaving Roni barely able to breathe, gasping uncontrollably in the physical, and too weak to do anything to save herself. Jesse watched in horror as Roni's very life essence began to slip away from her in front of Christian, Chelle, and all those around her.

"This shouldn't be happening," Serella said. "The stone should be creating a barrier against this evil." She turned briefly to Jesse, looked around as if she were looking for something in particular, then threw her hands up in desparation. "I don't understand what's happening."

"Maybe she dropped it," Larry suggested.

"Maybe she did," Serella said. "But if so, where did it go?" She turned her attention to the bedroom where Roni lay fighting for her life. "I don't see it," she said to Larry and Jesse. "But it's not in her hand, anymore. We've got to find it for them."

"And take our attention away from what's happening on this side?" Larry asked. He looked at Minotti who still fumed angrily in place as he stared at Audra.

"The stone is the only thing to hold it all together on the physical side of life," Serella said. "It has to be found or the entire battle is futile. Without it, Roni will die for sure and Audra will have won her own self-inflicted fight. We can't let that happen. The anguish it would cause for all those around her would be enough to fuel Audra for the remainder of the battle here."

Larry looked from Serella, who stood before him, to Roni who lay dreaming in the physical. He nodded, then took his attention from the eternal side of life over to the physical where he began to search the bedroom, unknown to those who occupied the space where Roni lay.

Jesse nodded while he watched Serella's determination to keep Audra in her line of sight. She was fighting her own internal battle with the memories Minotti had left in her centuries ago and Jesse couldn't help but worry about her. He only hoped she'd be strong enough to fight beside him and Larry long enough to make the difference in their victory. He looked at Minotti and saw the anger that seemed to engulf him when he realized Audra was no longer concentrating on his fight, but had gone off on her own, instead. He watched Minotti's face change from red to burnt gold as he stared at her. "What are you doing?" he roared, waves of hatred rocking everything that could be seen and felt in the universe.

Audra ignored him as she concentrated on her own goals. "I'm taking care of myself as I should have been doing all along." She continued to draw Roni into herself as she spoke. "This is your battle, Minotti. My only fight is with the vampires who turned on me. You fight your own battles."

The air around Minotti turned a deep brownish-green, then went completely black. He grew huge as he sent an arc of energy out from around himself and directed it straight at Audra. It approached from behind her, then grew until it was three times her size, surrounding her so completely that it was obvious no question would be left once it was seen by her. "You should have made a better choice," he roared.

Audra turned to him, an air of wonder surrounded her, but she realized too late what was happening. The look on her face, her gestures, her surprise all told the story of the terror that went through her mind as she saw the mass of energy Minotti had sent to destroy her. It wrapped its fiery arms around her ethereal form and hoisted her into Minotti's angry aura before she could do a thing to defend herself. Jesse watched in horror as Audra literally disappeared into the beast that was Minotti, knowing that if he could do this to Audra, then the rest of them were already finished.

"Alright," Minotti said, smiling. "Who's next?"

* * *

"I see it," Chelle said. "It's tucked in the fold of the comforter by the pillows." She pointed at the bed where the amethyst lay sparkling against the wedgewood blue sheets.

"I've got it!" Diana picked it up and placed it in Roni's right hand, holding her fist closed once the stone was back in place. Roni immediately became quiet and fell back into a peaceful, repose state as if nothing had happened, her breathing fully restored to normal levels of slumber, her body completely relaxed.

"I guess she wanted her woobie," Chelle joked, breathing an audible sigh of relief. She looked at each of them briefly, then shrugged. "What?"

"This isn't funny," Samuel said.

Diana placed a hand on his and gently rubbed his skin. "This is exactly what we need right now," she said. "A little humor might do us all a world of good now that we've got one little crisis behind us." She leered at him, concentration formed strong through her eyes as she continued to smile in the most loving manner. "So smile."

Samuel stared at her for a few seconds, nodded, then forced himself to smile back at her. He raised his eyebrows in question. "Good enough?"

Diana nodded once. "For now." She looked at Roni and saw that she was sleeping quite peacefully. "How's her IV, Chelle?"

Chelle looked at Roni's arm, then up at the bag as it continued to drip in place. "She didn't pull it out," Chelle said, turning back to Diana. "That's a good thing."

Christian released a huge breath, raking his fingers through his dark hair as he did so. "What next?" He looked at Diana. "I hate feeling so helpless."

"No hating allowed," Diana reminded him. "Hang in there. I don't think Audra is a threat, anymore."

"What makes you say that?" Chelle's attention was directed solely at Diana. "It's your telepathy, isn't it?" She shook her head, then looked at Roni's hand to make sure the amethyst was still in place. "Boy, I could use some of that telepathy."

Diana shifted her gaze quickly from Chelle to Christian, then back, again. She smiled. "I can see why Roni enjoys your friendship. You're just one chuckle after another."

"Sometimes," Chelle said. "But tell me. Is Audra really gone?"

Diana nodded. "I'm almost positive something must've happened to her. I can't feel her energy like I could before."

"What do you think happened?" Samuel asked.

Diana shook her head and looked from one of them to the other. "I don't know for sure, but I'll bet Minotti did something to her. They must've had a fight between them. I can't imagine those two being together for any length of time."

"That would make sense," Chelle said.

They all looked at her, surprised.

"Well, when I ran into Audra at the warehouse with Roni that day, we couldn't wait to get rid of her, either," Chelle said. "I imagine this Minotti guy feels the same way. She's annoying as hell. Just her over-inflated opinion of herself would drive any guy nuts. He must really hate her, by now."

Diana couldn't help but smile. "I'm sure he does," she said. "Except that Minotti is a thousand times worse than she ever could have been. He's stonger and more evil than even Audra had ever thought of being."

Chelle stared at Diana, mouth agape. "Oh," was all she said.

"So I suppose we just have to wait, again," Christian said, taking Roni's hand in his.

Diana nodded. "There's no other choice, but this time we're staying right here. If it's just Minotti who's left, then it may be a good thing."

"Or not," Samuel said. "According to what Serella told us on the beach that night, I'll bet Minotti just absorbed the second most evil being that exists into himself. I'd say he probably got his second wind just now and is getting ready to start the real battle. Our fight on this side might have just begun, as far as we know."

Diana nodded. "That's exactly why we're staying put."

* * *

Minotti's aura pulsed and throbbed in rapid succession as he began absorbing one spirit after another. Jesse watched them melt into each other, powerless to keep his will away as one after another disappeared without a fight.

"No more happy vampires," Minotti sneered. "No more morality, Jesse. It's all mine. Every one of you and all of Creation will now be a part of me and I will control every move you make."

"For who?" Serella yelled. "Who will be left to

experience your power? You're pulling it all into yourself. Who will be left for you to impress?"

"Silence!" Minotti glared at her, fire burning in his eyes. "I tried to own you once." He stretched his arms toward her. "Now I do!"

Jesse watched Serella glide right into the energy that surrounded Minotti with fear on her face as the beautiful colors that displayed her big heart were darkened. He felt his soul shiver and a sickness invade his spirit as he watched her turn to him, one arm outstretched as far as she could push it toward him. He knew he was being witness to the one thing that had always been Serella's biggest fear, to be taken by Minotti, again, but with no escape this time. Now it was happening right before his eyes. He watched Serella fade away and disappear into Minotti. She was gone.

"Nooooooooooooooooooo!" Jesse yelled, but before anything could be done Jesse watched as Larry followed Serella into the same demise while Minotti laughed so strong and hideous that all of Creation shook. Though Larry accepted his fate without a fight, it made the whole incident worse, breaking his heart as if it had been created for just that purpose, to break over and over, again. His soul was shaken with the pain of mortal fear and the realization that even he, an angel created by God, could do nothing, now. He opened his arms wide to the universe and looked around as if there should be a physical entity there for Jesse to take out his frustrations on. "Where's the greatest protection of all that you promised?" he asked the Father, shaking his arms to the world around him. "Why have you lied to us?"

SH

"He's never been real," Minotti said, still laughing. "He's been a figment of your imaginations, a daydream. There is no Creator. You were all born of each other's visions and wishful thinking. There's never been one supreme power like you wanted to believe."

Jesse lowered his arms and turned on him. "You're wrong. There was no guesswork when He created me and all the other angels. We never had to wonder where we came from. We were told at the beginning. We always knew what our purpose was."

Minotti looked around as the last of the souls melted into him, his arms outstretched to his sides. "Then where is this all powerful God now that He's at the hour of His own annihalation? Where are all His other angels? I think they turned tail and ran from me. That was the smart thing for them to do. Every angel for themself." Minotti began to laugh his sinister laugh all over, again. "Maybe this time you'll learn."

Jesse knew Minotti was right. It was time to resign himself to the fact that he was also facing the hour of his own destruction, but he'd seen it coming. He stood in place, frozen at the hour of the one battle mankind never expected to see. There was only one thing left to try. "You have nothing to teach me." He raised his arms in front of him and willed all the love he could muster to pour out of him and flow to Minotti, but it was no use. Minotti had soured Jesse's heart by the pain and destruction he'd inflicted on so many souls who had done only good through their existences. The strongest hurt for Jesse was seeing Serella and Larry go down into the depths of Minotti's soul without a fight.

"I win."

Jesse felt the pull begin in the center of his being as he was drawn closer to Minotti. The only pain he felt was the pain of disappointment, of centuries spent believing in a power that turned its back on him, of seeing all those he loved and cared for destroyed. Jesse's soul ached from the memories of all the work he'd done in his centuries spent on earth, in the land of illusions where all that was physical was laid out as nothing more than a proving ground for the souls who needed to boost themselves back up to a level that would allow their reunion with their Creator. Jesse's efforts now proved futile at last as he watched Minotti pull him closer. All the battles he fought, all the advice and life saving efforts he'd handled behind the scenes where no one but God would ever know. All of it flashed before him as he watched the world around him grow darker with every second that passed. Was his existence just a waste of time? What good did any of it do? The anguish, the heartache, the intense darkeness.

Suddenly, with no warning, the darkeness was gone. Life stopped going black as quickly as it had started and Jesse found himself staring into the center of a small blue flame that burned from within the orange and red fire that was everywhere. He watched it quickly grow to proportions that seemed to outweigh the flames of hell in a mere moment. The vision was astounding, as was the feeling of strength and certainty that Jesse felt take hold and start to grow in and around him. He saw a sharp glint as of something metallic and he turned to see a sword began to protrude from the center of the flame, a sword whose sharp point burned in blue fire that was beautiful and cool to see, but Jesse knew it was hot enough to disintegrate whatever came near. He watched as the hand that held the sword moved from within the blue flame until it became an arm, then an entire being and suddenly there were other magnificent entities, the likes of which even Jesse had only been told about, but had never seen. In his heart, he knew what he was just allowed to witness, but even to an angel it seemed an impossibility. Yet, there they were, and most important, most impressive, was the entity with the blue sword of flames. Jesse watched him advance toward Minotti with his shield at his side, and an entourage of other entities all of whom exuded a power so fierce it resonated with every thought, with every movement through time and space, and its total strength was incredible.

"Michael," Jesse whispered, then watched as the archangel himself turned toward Jesse, smiled, then continued on his quest to send the beast away.

Chapter 7

May 9 10:00PM

"DO you feel that?" Chelle looked at Samuel, then at Christian, and finally at Diana. "Do you feel it?" She looked around the room, at the ceiling, placing her arms out to her sides. "What is it?"

Diana shook her head. "I feel it, but I'm not sure what it is. All I know is that it's very powerful and very . . . " She shrugged. "Good."

"Good?" Samuel asked.

"That's how it feels," Diana said. "Concentrate. Whatever it is, let's feed it. Only good thoughts. Lots of love, especially toward Chelle's baby so it has a good start."

Chelle tilted her head to one side as she studied Diana. "That's a beautiful sentiment coming from a vampire," she said. "I'm honestly touched."

Diana sighed. "I still like you, even though you have a strange way with words." She turned to Christian and Samuel. "Let's concentrate." She took Chelle's hand and placed it over the hand in which Roni held the amethyst. "Keep your connection with her. Maybe it will help heal her in some way."

Chelle nodded and took Roni's slightly closed fist in both of her own hands and held tight. "I'll try anything," she said. "I just want her back to normal."

Diana took Samuel's and Christian's hands. "Now concentrate. If this is all we have to offer this time around, then let's do our best."

* * *

"Even you can't stop me," Minotti said, watching his opponent advance. "All of you combined don't have the power to destroy me. What you're working with is nothing more than simple stories told to give false hope to those who know deep inside themselves that there is truly no hope left, anywhere."

The archangels flanked Minotti on all sides, the energy of their colors showing themselves in brilliant shades of every color in the rainbow and many in between. They began to close in with Michael in the lead.

"It won't work," Minotti said. "Nothing you do will work against me."

They moved in closer, until they stood shoulder to shoulder, three deep, with Michael in the middle, his sword raised to strike. "Go now," Michael said to Minotti, his vision boring into Minotti's spirit. "This is the only time you will be asked."

Minotti released his demented laugh and shook his head. "Don't waste your time." He raised his arms. His nearly black aura that pulsated with the life forces of all the souls he'd absorbed, grew around him until it began to cover the archangel, but Michael continued to move within it, undaunted. "Wait a minute," Minotti said. "Stop right where you are and enter my soul." But Michael advanced until he was an arm's length from Minotti, his flaming, blue sword poised and ready. "No, this isn't possible," Minotti shouted. "This can't be."

"It is all possible with the Almighty," Michael said as he allowed his sword to pierce Minotti straight through the heart. "There is no room for you," he said, cutting into Minotti's aura so deep that a thousand spirits, good and bad, were released simultaneaously. "They will all be set free to return to where you found them." With his sword of blue flame, Michael held the gaping hole in Minotti's aura wide open, releasing spirits in every direction while Minotti looked down at the opening in the center of his being, unable to do anything to stop what the Archangel Michael had begun.

Jesse watched in total awe as even those who where paying for their transgressions amidst their own fire were set free and allowed to rush to the safety of their personal hell, passing before him in a mass of multiple colors. It was truly a beautiful sight and one that lifted his spirit as he watched it all unfold around him. He looked at Michael and saw that the archangel was smiling at him. Jesse tilted his head, not sure if he understood.

"Be his guide into the child," Michael said in a deep, soft voice that flowed with the energy around them. "We have this under control."

Jesse nodded, astonished that Michael was aware of the plan to put an end to Minotti's terror. He raised his head once more just as the spirits of Serella and Larry were released to settle beside him.

"Go with him," Michael said to them, his armor glowing in the light of his own aura. "He needs you, now."

They nodded.

"One more thing," Michael said as he tore open Minotti's aura even further. "Never doubt the Father." He glanced at Minotti, watching as his energy began to fade and his form started to shrink. "Never."

Jesse nodded, then smiled, as he felt himself being pulled down to hover just above the bed where Christian, Diana, Samuel, and Chelle were all gathered around Roni, watching to see if she would show them any signs of what was happening in the battle on the other side. Serella and Larry were still hovering by Jesse's side.

"That was him?" Larry asked. "I've only been on this side for a few hours and already I've seen Saint Michael? That's incredible."

His huge, smile filled Jesse's heart. "It was also my first time," he said. "I'm so grateful it was shared with you two." He looked at each of them, then heard Michael's voice. "Stay strong and guide this angry spirit where he has to go."

Jesse felt Michael's power blow by him and knew Minotti's spirit was coming next. "Same as before," he said to Serella and Larry. "We must encircle him with love and compassion, thankfulness and joy, and don't stop until we know without a doubt that he is where he is supposed to be."

All together they directed their energy into a circle like a hurricane that swirled and rotated among the three of them creating a tube of pink and blue light, the colors of love and spirit. As the colors moved in and around each other, bands of lavendar formed, the color of the spirit, of healing. It was an incredible sight to see and even more astounding to be in the center of it.

"This is beautiful," Larry said, gazing at the hues of light around them.

"This is how your thoughts and feelings appear on this side," Serella said. "It can be magnificent or it can be terrifying. But this is the most beautiful thing I've ever seen. You can't hide your true feelings because they form in colors that are real. You may say you're happy, but your colors will show the truth. Nothing can be hidden here. The truth is safe on this side, no matter what that truth is."

Larry nodded as he was encircled with lavendars and blues. "I see that."

Just then a cloud of gray began to desend through the center of the emotional tunnel.

"Minotti?" Larry asked, staring at Jesse.

Jesse nodded. "Stay strong, happy, and full of everything good. We are well protected."

They watched as Minotti's spirit, now smaller, but elongated, continued through the spiralling tunnel. They saw his arms flailing out as if to try to stop his decent into a new life and heard his voice cry out in anguish.

"Where is he going?" Larry asked.

"First, through the amethyst crystal," Serella said. "Amethyst is full of vibrations that welcome love. It will be the first step in settling his anger and neutralizing the evil he became before he enters the child where his life energy will be reshaped into that which is only good. Then it will be up to Chelle and Joe to make things right with his spirit." She ran a gentle hand around Chelle's head. "They are both good souls." She smiled. "They will do well."

"What about Roni?" Larry asked.

"Amethyst is also the crystal of healing," Serella said, her colors of crimson and rose showing all around the room. "Minotti started Roni's illness. Now it's time for him to take it back." She looked from them to Roni's closed fist and smiled. "As he passes through the stone, all the evil he has done to Roni will be reattached to him and it will have to be part of the purification process as he continues through the amethyst. As long as Roni holds the crystal, all that Minotti caused for her will be removed."

"Do they know that?" Larry asked, indicating the three friends who sat by Roni on the bed.

Jesse smiled. "They know the crystal is important, but none of them really know why, exactly."

Serella looked at him and smiled.

"Well, maybe Diana has a good idea," he said to Larry who nodded, then went back to concentrating on Minotti's spirit as it continued through the auric barrier.

"Because she's a vampire?" Father Larry asked.

"No," Serella said. "Because she's a woman."

* * *

Chelle suddenly doubled over in pain, hyperventilating, and moaning as she moved to clutch at her stomach.

Diana grabbed for her. "I know it hurts, Honey, but whatever you do, don't let go of Roni's hand."

"Something's wrong with the baby," Chelle said. "It's too young. This can't be happening."

Diana pulled her closer to Roni, then placed her hands around the crystal in Roni's hand. "You've got to trust me, Chelle. I know it's hard, but you have to. You've been through this sort of thing before and you know it will turn out alright if you have faith and believe."

Chelle bobbed up and down, back and forth as she held on to Roni's arm with one hand and tried to steady her stomach with the other. Her breaths were shallow as she gasped for air, then quickly exhaled as if she was only allowed to retain a limited amount in her lungs.

Diana stroked her back and gave her as much support as was needed. "Hang in there, Chelle," she said. "It won't be much longer, now."

Chelle nodded and in seconds her breathing slowed to normal. She turned to Diana and allowed herself the luxury of one huge breath before she finally spoke. "Did you know about that, too?"

Diana shrugged. "Sort of."

Chelle shook her head and looked away. "Just tell me I'm not sacrificing my child. That's all I want to hear." She looked at Christian. "I want your word."

Christian nodded. "You've got my word. You aren't doing any harm to your child and you're saving Roni at the same time."

Chelle let out a few deep breaths as she listened. "You'd better be right. Here it comes, again." She doubled over, again, crunching herself up and holding her breath, but she did not let go of Roni's hand this time. "How long is this going to continue?"

"I don't know," Diana said.

Chelle looked at each of them.

"None of us know," Samuel added, a sympathetic, sheepish look on his face.

"Can you at least tell me what's causing the pain?"

They looked at each other. *It might frighten her,* Diana thought to them. *We can't.*

They nodded, their attention on Chelle. "Just stay strong," Samuel said, as Chelle began to double over for a third time.

* * *

"His energy mass is beginning to lighten up." Larry said. "He's not fighting as hard, either."

"We're almost there," Jesse said. "Just keep those good thoughts around him."

Larry nodded. "What about Audra? Shouldn't she be channeled into a new life, too?"

Serella looked at them. "She's in Limbo where she should have been in the beginning. That's how it's supposed to be because that's all she really needed." She glanced at the others in the bedroom. "Chelle is in quite a bit of pain. We've got to try to hurry this up. I don't know how much more of this she can take. Minotti still has a little fight left in him. He's not happy."

"He'll have the next nine months to settle down," Jesse said. "Once we're through here, he'll be stuck. And he'll be a handful as a child, but so was Chelle. She's strong enough to handle it, and the love between her and Joe is perfect to reshape Minotti's soul."

"I think that's it," Larry said. "The energy field is empty. Can you feel it? It's not a struggle anymore. He's not fighting back. I really think we did it."

"Keep it going until we're certain," Jesse said. "I've learned not to underestimate that one." Just as he spoke those words, Minotti's head appeared inside the circling barrier, but Michael's arms quickly followed, pushing him down into the barrier and Minotti was gone, once again.

"Now," Michael's voice was heard so calm and soothing. "Close the tunnel."

Jesse moved back, his ethereal form relaxing in an obvious manner. Serella and Larry followed his lead and did the same. They hovered about the bed and looked at each other, then watched Chelle who was just straightening up after another pain had wracked her insides. She still held Roni's hand.

"It's done," Jesse said. He looked up. "Thank you," he whispered to no one in particular, yet to everyone who could hear him.

All three of them heard a beautiful murmur of voices speak the soft words, "You're welcome." Then the voices faded away and became nothing more than the subtle sound of wind blowing gently in the distance. Jesse knew the greatest protection was gone, but it had served its purpose well.

* * *

Diana looked at Chelle, her hand on her shoulder as she studied her face. "How do you feel?" Chelle sat up and looked at Roni, then let go of her friend's hand. "I feel like it's over, whatever it was."

Christian nodded, sitting back and releasing a large sigh. "It is." His smile reflected his feelings of gratitude and relief. "Thank you."

"For what?" Chelle asked.

"If everything went the way it was supposed to have gone, thank you for your part in Roni's recovery."

"Ah," Chelle said, waving an arm at him. "What are friends for?"

Diana shook her head in amused disbelief and laughed. "Still, Roni is very lucky to have you."

"I know," Chelle said, shaking her head. "I tell her that all the time." She stood up and began to undo the IV drip, then looked at everyone who still sat on the bed. "Two hours is up. If I really did have anything to do with curing her disease, I'd hate to end up killing her because I was too busy celebrating to remove the bag that's about to fill her veins with air." She stared at them with an eager expression that told them she wasn't kidding. "I'm a nurse. Remember?" Still they didn't move, so Chelle undid the rest of the IV drip, then removed the shunt, since it was the last treatment Roni would need to have. Then she cleaned Roni's arm, discarded the debris in the proper container, and packed up the items that had to be returned to the hospital. When she was done the other three still sat on the bed watching her as Chelle stood up and looked at them. "Now what?"

Together Diana, Samuel, and Christian got off the bed and headed for the door without saying a word.

"What?" Chelle said. "Doesn't anyone want to help get this stuff out of here?" She turned to Roni and brushed the hair from her friend's forehead. "I hope you're really better," she told her, then turned to pick up the equiment she'd be able to carry, but to her surprise, it was already gone. She went to the door and saw that all of the medical equipment was piled in the hallway. She turned off the light in the bedroom to let Roni rest and closed the door part way behind her. "Vampires," she mumbled under her breath, then chuckled as she went to join them in the living room.

Chapter 8

June 4 Dusk

RONI and Chelle sat in the waiting room at the back of St. Joseph's cathedral and prepared themselves for the sound of the organ that would let them know it was time for the ceremony to begin. Chelle straightened the blue topaz necklace, turning the clasp to the back of her neck. "Something borrowed, something blue," Roni said. "I've had it for a long time, but it had to be around your neck today. It covers two of the traditional wedding day categories."

Chelle nodded, fingering the large blue stone that hung around her neck. "It's perfect. Thanks for loaning it to me." She touched the stone that hung around Roni's neck, briefly, and smiled. "Maybe I'll hang on to it for awhile, if you don't mind."

Roni smiled, running a finger along the necklace she wore. "The feeling is mutual," she said. "You just keep it for as long as you like."

Chelle laughed, then turned toward the mirror. "We never do anything in a small way," she said, adjusting her veil. "Even when we spied on Audra when she was still a vampire, we couldn't do it without getting caught."

"And nearly killed," Roni reminded her. She gave herself the luxury of one last look in the hallway mirror and freshened her pale lipstick, straightening a spot that appeared a bit jagged.

Chelle nodded, her face suddenly taking on a sentimental expression as she watched her friend prepare for the huge step they were both about to take.

"What?" Roni glanced back at the mirror once more. "Did I get something on my face?"

"No," Chelle said. "I just can't believe this day is here, and you look so beautiful."

Roni smiled, reaching a hand toward her friend while she touched the amethyst crystal that hung around her neck with the other. "Don't start crying, yet. You spent all kinds of time on your make-up to look just perfect and this wedding is only going to happen now, at this point in time. Don't ruin it for yourself. You can cry all you want when you and Joe are pronounced man and wife, but until then you've got to hold yourself together."

Chelle nodded, then touched the topaz around her neck with one hand and the amethyst around Roni's neck with the other. "Thank you."

Roni did the same thing, placing her hands over the hands of her friend. "You're very welcome," she said, then reached over to hug her. "Now pull yourself together. I hear the organ and I believe that's our cue."

* * *

Christian sat in the pew with Roni's family, waiting for the wedding procession to begin. He looked at

Joe who stood before the altar facing the back of the church with his brother beside him as best man. Suddenly, the crowd rose to their feet in response to the bridal introduction the organist had just begun to play.

Christian was surprised to find he actually felt nervous. This was really going to happen. Roni was going to be his wife before the hour was over. After the years they'd known each other, after the terrifying things they'd been through together, they were finally going to give themselves to each other for the rest of Roni's life and the rest of Christian's eternity.

"Any minute, now," Diana whispered to him.

Christian didn't say anything. He was full of anticipation when he saw her standing in the back of the church, and his heart jumped inside his chest. She wore a gown made of georgette in a color that mimicked the Jackmanii clematis that grew along the trellis in the back garden, or the delphinium she'd planted just last year that grew so tall it seemed to meet the sky when they lay on the deck together at dusk. It was the color of the crystal that healed her body, the very crystal that hung around her neck and sparkled as she walked toward him. He thanked God for the gift that allowed him to watch her walk down the aisle, knowing there was no sign of the disease that had left as quickly as it had grown inside her. He saw her smile at him, and he let himself melt inside as he returned the smile. When she reached the pew, she stopped, kissed him, then proceeded to the altar to wait for Chelle to follow. All eyes in the church were on the bride, but Christian's remained on Roni.

* * *

Chelle stood at the back of the church and watched Roni walk down the aisle before her. She felt her heart fill with gratitude for the friendship she cherished and the turn of events that restored Roni's health. She didn't fully understand all of what happened, but she didn't have to. She was so overwhelmed by what was about to happen in her own life that nothing else mattered at this moment. She took her first step toward the altar knowing her dreams were coming into focus, becoming real. Joe was the man who completed her soul and she carried his child with her as she walked down the aisle to begin their new life together. It was more than she ever imagined she'd have, but she was aware of the price and the responsiblity that went with it. No one told her, but she knew she also carried Minotti's spirit. Her intuition opened that door and made it clear to her the minute the battle was ended, but everyone stayed in the room to watch her care for Roni's IV. She knew it then, and she felt honored that she'd been entrusted with such a huge charge. With Joe as the father, their child had the perfect guidance to carry him through his life. Chelle was determined that nothing would cause them to disappoint the Almighty.

She looked at Joe as she approached the altar. Her father lifted her veil, kissed her, then handed her to the man of her dreams. Mr. Gambert and Joe shook hands, and Chelle was left with her husband-to-be as they faced the altar and each other in the eyes of God.

* * *

Roni felt as if she were floating through a dream as she stood before the altar, facing Father O'Manley with Christian by her side. She was especially moved when Joe accompanied Chelle to stand at Roni's other side as her witness in full bridal regalia, knowing an angel stood beside her husband-to-be. She felt Jesse's angelic presence, though his physical self stood before her, and she knew that life was perfect on both sides.

She heard the words Father O'Manley spoke, heard Christian's vows, but she was more aware of the feelings that coursed through her, the love, the gratitude, the awe of the moment. She felt the gold ring go on to her finger, looked into Christian's eyes, and melted. Everything in life was as it was meant to be since the day she and Christian first met. Everything they'd been through, all the trials and tribulations, all the heartaches and close calls, finally came together, settled, and made the moment what it was always meant to be. Perfect.

* * *

Larry was filled with love as he watched all the people whose lives he'd been a part of witness the ceremony he had put together with Father O'Manley. He was especially proud of Chelle for her conscious decision to raise her child by the laws of goodness in spite of what she knew instinctively to be true. He only wished he could have been there in the physical with everyone else, able to unite Roni and Christian. But he'd made his decision and he knew more than ever that it was the right one. Now, as he watched this beautiful union of people so in love, he saw just how right it was and he was pleased with himself for taking the chance to insure that Roni and Christian's marriage took place in the church as Roni wanted. He saw the reactions of the family and the tears of joy that made him feel as much a part of the event as if he'd been on the altar beside Father O'Manley. When Chelle and Joe exchanged their vows, their rings, and were pronounced man and wife, he felt a sense of pride soar through him like he'd never expected to feel. He watched with anticipation as Father O'Manley motioned for Roni and Christian to step forward to exchange their vows, knowing that he was finally able to see, for the first time, the total consumation of love in both the physical and spiritual world.

Larry watched the entire ceremony. He heard Father O'Manley read every word of Father Larry's prepared speech for the beginning of Roni and Christian's exchange of vows. Especially his favorite quote by a sixteenth century bishop whose name he could never remember that was read to them as a blessing. "Marriage has less beauty and more safety in a single life. It's full of sorrows and full of joys. It lies under more burdens, but it is supported by all the strengths of love and those burdens are delightful." How appropriate those words were for them. He could only guess at how appropriate they would become for Chelle and Joe as they began raising the child Chelle carried and the soul within that child. A huge burden that he prayed would become one of delight for them and for itself. Yes, things were finally made right.

* * * *

Everything about her was as angelic as the man who stood by his side. Christian glanced at Jesse, nodded, then turned his attention back to his bride. It was Roni's turn and he listened to her every word, watched every movement of her eyes, her lips, her hands. The ring went over his cold finger and turned his soul warmer than he ever thought possible. She was his for all eternity, and he belonged to her. There was nothing more he could have hoped for, nothing more he wanted. When they turned back toward the priest, and Chelle returned to her rightful place at the core of the proceedings, he stayed beside his wife, with his best friend by his side feeling more human than he'd felt in centuries. He turned to Jesse. *Thank you.*

* * * *

Jesse nodded, smiled, and sighed, when Christian thanked him. The hardest part of the ceremony for him was knowing there was more to be accomplished now that these four people had finally reached their destinations in life. There was more Jesse needed to take care of for himself, but he was an angel. He had all the time he needed to make things right in his existence.

He turned to watch Chelle and Joe walk back down the aisle once the ceremony had reached its end, followed by Roni and Christian. He stood to the side, but Christian reached for him and pulled him in line beside himself. Jesse was pleased to make this last trip down the aisle of St. Joseph's beside his best friend. But what now? He'd already told them what to expect, but he'd been able to quelch their concern and upheaval because of the battle they'd had to get through first. Nothing had been discussed since that first time, but Jesse felt it as sure as he felt his very existence. It was time to go home. But first, there was much celebrating to do and a wedding reception to enjoy. The rest would have to wait.

Chapter 9

June 11 11:30PM

CHRISTIAN walked along the sandy beach in front of Jesse's house, listening to the June bugs run their small bodies into each other, and feeling the evening coolness that had settled along the shore. There was no one around and it made Christian feel a bit uncomfortable, as if he was trespassing in an old cemetery that no one had been near for years. It struck him as odd, since he'd been to Jesse's so many times in the past few years and he'd always felt a warm welcome the minute he stepped on the ground. He looked around and took a deep breath. Something wasn't right. He walked up the front porch stairs, saw the front door wide open with only the screened door closed before it, and he waited for Jesse's footsteps to come greet him, but there was no movement anywhere around. He stood motionless, listening for a tell-tale sign that would show him what was going on, but he heard nothing. He reached for the screened door handle, hesitated a moment before he opened it, then jumped when he heard Jesse's voice from the side of the house.

"I'm glad you could make it," Jesse said, approaching as if from thin air. "I was beginning to get a little worried about you." He walked up the stairs slowly, then looked up at Christian. "Were you planning to go inside or is it alright to sit out here?"

Christian let go of the door handle, then turned around and took a seat on the railing of the porch. "What's going on?" he asked. He felt even more uncomfortable than he had so far. There was something about Jesse's demeanor that was different, as if he belonged somewhere else and had just come to visit. "You asked me to stop in."

Jesse nodded to him, but didn't say anything.

"Well, I'm here."

Jesse took a few steps back and motioned for Christian to do the same. "Would you like to walk with me for a bit?" He stood waiting until Christian stepped off the porch railing and walked down the stairs.

"Are you feeling alright?" Christian asked him as they started to walk along the water's edge. "I must tell you, Jesse, something doesn't feel quite right this evening."

Jesse held out his hand to Christian. "Take this," he said.

Christian placed his hand out, palm up, and received the keys Jesse dropped in it. "What's this?"

"Keys," Jesse said. "To the house."

Christian stopped walking and looked at him, studied the worry lines around his eyes, saw his partial smile, and he knew. "You're leaving," he stated more than asked. "You're going home, aren't you?"

Jesse nodded. "It's time." He looked out over the water. "It's been time for quite a while now, but I just couldn't make myself do it." He turned to Christian.

"This last battle gave me many reasons to turn to the Father directly. And I was able to see how easy it has always been for me to make that journey whenever I needed to." He started to walk again, taking in the atmosphere as if for the first time before he spoke. "Now, I've let so much time pass that I need to experience a lot of healing before I'm ready to come back and pick up where I left off." He looked sideways at Christian and smiled. "Do you think you'll still be here when I'm ready to come back?"

Christian shrugged, unable to believe the time had actually come for them to say good-bye. It just didn't seem possible. "First Father Larry, now you." He shook his head. "I'd like to say I'll still be here," he said, trying to keep his feelings under control. "But what if something happens along the way to cause me to leave this world? Who can ever say, Jesse?" His stomach was folding over into knots as he rolled the keys around in his hand. The keys to Jesse's house. "Why did you give me these keys?" he asked.

Jesse smiled. "The house is yours," he said. "I'd like to think it will still be here when it comes time for me to return, someday."

"This isn't the first house you've ever had," Christian said. "It can't mean that much to you."

Jesse smiled and nodded. "Oh, but it does," he said. "Not because of the house as much as the memories that have taken place here that never took place anywhere else I've ever lived on this side."

"You really are tied to us," Christian said, smiling. "An angel who can't let go of his temporary home." He shook his head and looked at Jesse with a serious expression on his face. "That's not a good thing, you know."

Jesse nodded. "And now you know why I have to go home." He looked out across the water in silence for some time before he spoke. "There's a part in the bible I'm sure you'll remember. 'The first shall be last and the last shall be first.'"

"I'm familiar with it," Christian said. "Though I must admit, it never made much sense to me. What makes you bring it up now?"

"Do you have any idea what it's really about?" Jesse asked him.

Christian shrugged. "In all honesty, no. I can't say that I really do, unless you're simply referring to the obvious."

Jesse smiled, then nodded as he drew in a deep breath. "And that's what has caused so much confusion in most of those beautiful sayings that flow throughout the entire text." He looked at Christian. "That passage holds so much meaning. It refers to the soul's journey through its learning times."

Christian looked at him, dumbfounded. What the heck was he talking about?

"Have I baffled you? I didn't mean to. But I do want to share this with you before I go." Jesse shifted slightly where he sat, then leaned against the porch rail and looked up at the evening moon. "You see, when you take the time to really think about it, so much comes to light. When a soul is here in the physical, that soul is going through so many lessons as we all do. Sometimes we each have the tendency to reach a point where we think we've learned all we need to learn. We get cocky and become know-it-alls regardless of the subject. But we have to always remember that unless we realize and accept the truth that we're always at the bottom, in last place, of our own development, then we'll never be able to proceed further and continue to learn. But when we stay humble, accepting our own ignorance for what it is, then we will always be able to keep moving forward, keep improving ourselves. Thus, by accepting our last place status, it automatically allows us to keep heading for first place in our soul's existence. It's a journey toward the truest wisdom, Christian. And even I don't know it all, yet."

"Ok," Christian said. "But I still don't think I understand what that has to do with you deciding to leave."

Jesse looked at the ground and appeared to be thinking before he explained himself. "I've put myself in last place by my closeness to this physical existence," he said. "I've stunted my own growth by not allowing my humility to keep pushing me forward. Even angels never stop learning, never stop growing. But I've allowed myself to do both." He looked up at Christian. "That's why I have to go back for awhile. I have to reach for the next level of wisdom that's been waiting for me to be ready. And I need to settle my own soul."

"I understand," Christian said, but he felt the anger and betrayal begin to grow inside as he allowed himself to feel abandoned. They looked at each other, swatting a few mosquitos out of the way and taking in the gravity of what was happening to their friendship, to their lives. "What am I going to do with your house?" Christian asked. "Roni and I have a house of our own."

Jesse shook his head and shrugged, then looked around at the oceanside landscaping that had been his front yard. "Whatever you decide to do," he said. "Use it as a summer home. Do whatever you see fit."

He turned to face Christian. "Just keep it close by so that it's still here."

Christian picked up a flat rock and skipped it across the water so that it bounced four times before it was done moving. "You might not even want it when you come back," Christian said. "Did you ever think of that?"

"I did."

"And?"

The late, spring breeze kicked up making the warm air feel a bit more cool as Christian stared at Jesse, waiting for an answer. Jesse smiled. "Just do this one thing for me," he said. "I'm not asking you for anything else."

Christian looked at his friend and nodded. "What about everyone else? Don't you want to say good-bye to them, too?" He put the keys in his pocket, patted his pants leg, then stood in place, waiting.

"I thought of it," Jesse said. "But everything that caused me to be a part of your life started on a ship headed for the states centuries ago." He looked toward the house for a few seconds, then turned around. "We were friends long before I came to know anyone else. It all started with just us, so I'm saying good-bye to you. You can give my sentiments to everyone else and explain to them why I didn't call them all over, if you'd like." He turned to face Christian directly, staring into his eyes, a tear nestled at the corner of his own right one. "But the truth is, Christian, that it started with us. It only seems right that it should end with us." He put his hands on Christian's shoulders and stared long and hard at him. "For now."

Christian felt himself begin to tear and he knew he had to keep himself in one piece. He and Jesse had been together since 1410 AD, and had shared everything that had happened to both of them since that time. He always thought Jesse would be in his life through all that life would throw at either of them. A friendship as old as theirs never wore the scars that would eventually cause it to end as so many others did. Yet, here they were, struggling to say goodbye to each other until a time that neither of them could know.

"It's just for now," Jesse said again, and Christian nodded. They walked back toward the house in silence, thinking about their past, their memories, the things they might have experienced, but won't be able to now. Not for quite some time, at least. But neither of them said a word. Only Christian struggled with his emotions and wondered what Jesse was going through, but he never asked.

"It's time," Jesse said. "We could stand here talking all night long, but the exact time for me to leave would have to arrive, eventually. Let's get this over with." His eyes held Christian's gaze for what seemed to be an eternity until he put his arms out. Christian walked into his embrace like a child and began to cry. "I'm sorry," Jesse said, to him as he sniffled behind his words. "I have to do this."

Christian nodded and pushed himself away. "I know." He brushed the tears from his face, nodding as he spoke. "Go on." He reached in his pants pocket and removed a handkerchief. "Go before I do everything in my power to stop you."

Jesse motioned toward him, but Christian's face flared up, his fangs showing clear as the stars above and glistening in the moonlight. "You wouldn't," Jesse said to him. "After all that we've been through, something like this would go through your mind?"

He shook his head as he looked away and lowered his arms.

"Go," Christian said, leering, his eyes glowing pink.

Jesse took one last look at his house, then turned to Christian. "I understand," he said to him. "You have always been a true friend." With that he turned and began to walk along the shoreline. In seconds, he was gone.

Christian watched until he couldn't see Jesse anymore before he sat down on the empty front stairs and cried until there was nothing left in him. It must have been an hour or more before Christian finally stood up, exhausted, and walked up the stairs into the house. It felt empty just like he felt inside. There was no sign of life anywhere. Even the herbal smell of jasmine and sage that Christian had always associated with being at Jesse's seemed to have disappeared. It simply smelled like any old house. Christian sat at the kitchen table and looked out over the water, watched the small waves fold over each other onto the sand. He could still see Jesse's footprints out there along the sand, but they were disappearing quickly as the ocean played its nightly roll with the tides. It didn't seem possible, but just looking around the house told him how true this really was. What were they all going to do, now, without Jesse to turn to, to bail them out when they were in the deepest trouble they could ever find? Who would he turn to with the major questions of life? Would there be someone else to guide them through their challenges? He shook his head unable to believe that God who had cared so much for all of them would suddenly leave them stranded like this. But maybe this was the final test for them. Maybe this was to be the true test of all they'd learned from Jesse over the centuries. Maybe this was the time for them to put it all to the test and decide how to spend their lives.

Christian stood up and gave himself a quick tour of the house. The beds in both bedrooms were made. There were no clothes to be found anywhere and nothing was left in the bathroom. It was as if no one had ever lived here. What had Jesse done with everything he'd owned? Did it all just disappear? Christian shook his head as he walked through the living room to the front door. He took one last look around, then shut the doors, locking the main wooden one until he might find the time to come back with Roni.

He stood on the front porch for a few minutes and let the memories of the past few years circle through his mind. All the talks that took place right here between all of them, sometimes just between him and Jesse. He remembered the time he introduced Roni to him and how Diana had met him just a few years ago. Now it was nothing but memories and he sighed, knowing it was time to go on with the next phase of his life. The life he'd begun with Roni and now had a second chance at, thanks to Jesse, Serella, and Father Larry. Christian caught a lump in his throat at the thought of Father Larry. His first friend in the catholic church and he was gone, too.

Christian walked by the last of the footprints in the sand and looked up at the stars, smelled the midnight air, and felt the damp world around him. He sighed. Roni. Again she was on his mind. He touched the keys in his pocket and nodded to the

SH

house as if he was nodding to an old friend. Then he rose into the air and headed home to Roni, to the life he had chosen, to live as Jesse would have told him to. If nothing else, that's how he would keep his friend close by forever.

Epilogue

September

THE old house was empty except for the furniture that was left behind. The cupboards, the refrigerator, the cabinets, the closets; all were empty. It was the perfect situation to find when getting ready to move into a new home, but that was not the intent. Then again, maybe it was exactly what needed to be done. Autumn was just around the corner, and a break away from the celestial life in a secluded area might be the perfect place to go for a little while. She ran her hands along the sheet that lay over the wing-back chair, then pulled it away by the corner to reveal the lush, brown cloth that covered the entire piece of furniture. It was beautiful. She sat down and looked at everything she would have around her in her days of reclusivity, during the Autumn and Winter, if she chose to let her time away go on that long. It would be comfortable to live here, in Jesse's house where he'd spent so much of his time on earth. It might even be nice to try spending time in the physical for a while, to watch the seasons change, and feel the difference in the air when the time came for the temperature to drop and the snow to fall. She liked the way that felt.

She walked out to the porch and surveyed the landscaping. There wasn't much to do. The front yard was a beach, and all the plants Jesse had let go in the Spring had already begun to overgrow. All she had to do was relax as she enjoyed her time away.

The sand felt cool beneath her feet as she walked to the edge of the water and let herself be dazzled by the brilliance of the sun's reflection off the waves. Such beauty. Such sparkle. She thought about how different Jesse was, how much she'd wanted him to come home for all the centuries she waited, avoiding the physical, avoiding him. Now he was in the celestial, he was healing, he was staying by himself. It wasn't at all what she'd expected. He was an angel, but while he was here she never saw all he went through and how it was effecting his spirit. She only saw the physical part of him because she was obsessed with it, with getting as far away from it as she could. What could she have expected from an angel? He came home to heal and that was exactly what he was doing.

The late afternoon breeze brushed by her as she headed further along the beach, stopping every now and then to pick a flower, or watch the last of the dragonflies play with each other. Not like the other side, but still quite beautiful. Besides, she was still ethereal if she decided to go back every now and then. She just needed a place to go so she wouldn't drift past him while he was being treated, wanting to interrupt him, wanting to see him, and knowing how much damage it would do if she had anything to do with him, right now. It was for his own good that she took some time to herself. It would keep her away from him and give her time alone, with his things, but without him. That would do for now. Maybe she would be so comfortable in this house, she would end up living here for good. She knew Christian had keys, but she also knew he hadn't been here even one time since Jesse left. She nodded to herself as she turned around and headed back the way she'd come. When she reached the water's edge, she looked at her brief reflection in the water and smiled. Serella was still beautiful. It was the first time she'd seen herself in many centuries, yet it seemed like it was just yesterday when she'd last seen her reflection. It was her choice to live on this side for the time being and she decided to enjoy whatever it brought her. With Minotti gone for good, there was nothing left to fear. Now it was her time, and she was finally looking forward to life.

Printed in the United States
6784

9 781401 016005